Danai had just fallen asleep when she heard someone arguing with her father. It was a woman. Her mother was at work, so it couldn't be her. Her parents seldom argued. When one was mad at the other, if they couldn't discuss it civilly they would give one another a timeout to calm themselves down. It was the same way they treated Danai when she did something that truly irritated her parents. She was told to go to her room while her parents discussed how to handle the infraction.

Danai heard bits and pieces of a one-sided conversation.

"… coward."

"… saw the attack."

"… didn't have the balls to act."

"… call the police."

"… turned away."

Spineless."

I0631005

Her father remained silent. Then the woman stopped talking. Danai heard a growl. She tiptoed out of her room and hid behind a wall that led to the living room. She saw her father. Saw a huge cat, black as tar. The cat jumped onto her father's back and bit him in the back of his head. He fell to the ground.

The cat then changed into a woman. She was naked. Danai tried to get a good look at her face but it appeared shrouded by fog.

he woman spotted Danai. Their eyes met. The woman's eyes were reddish-yellow. Danai backed away, fearful of what this woman would do to her. Several minutes later, Danai heard the front door open, then close. She waited in her room for an hour. The woman … the big cat might be waiting for her. She finally came out of her room. The woman was gone. Her father was on the floor, a pool of blood surrounding his head.

She held onto her father's hand. Didn't let go until her mother returned hours later and called the police. "I'll get her for you, Daddy," she said aloud as her mother pulled her away and sent her to her room.

SILENT SCREAM

BY BARY HOFFMAN

GORDIAN KNOT BOOKS

PROLOGUE

(Oklahoma Territory / Cherokee Nation: Winter 1878)

She silently made her way out of the *daub house*. She shivered, her teeth chattering as the wind pelted her. It had been cold in the home It was brutally frigid outside.

Her family and a dozen others had made this barren land their home for the winter. In the distance was a forest. The night before, a jaguar had been killed by one of the tribe's braves. Jaguars seldom traveled this far north making the kill all the more sweet. Its pelt now hung on two wooden poles. She had heard it call to her. Or maybe it had been the unrelenting wind that chilled her to the bone.

She made her way to the jaguar, removed her meager clothes, and snuggled within the animal's skin, warmed by its fur. She slept. Before dawn she awakened, dressed, and made her way back to her family's home.

In the morning she tended to her chores. She made a fire. She and three other girls from the tribe cooked small portions of food. At sixteen, she was the oldest of the four. The others complained of the biting cold that sapped their energy. She gave them a cold stare that spoke volumes. It was frigid for everyone. *Do your chores and remain silent.* She didn't have to say a word.

For the next two nights the jaguar called to her. She slept within its cocoon, its warmth comforting her, energizing her for the brutal day to come. The chill of the wind had sapped her of what little strength she possessed. With so little food, she was rail thin. She often imagined a gust of wind tossing her in the air. She'd plunge to earth with every bone in her body splintered. But the warmth inside the jaguar's skin invigorated her. By the third day she was doing the chores of the other girls without complaint.

On the third night a storm assaulted the village. Rain pelted, sparing no one except her—the skin of the jaguar protecting her from the elements. A bolt of lightning struck the jaguar. It seemed to come to life, yanking itself from the poles that held it and wrapped itself around her like a second skin.

She and the jaguar became one. She padded off towards the forest, hunger gnawing at her. It was time to search for prey.

She would never return to her village.

CHAPTER ONE

**Philadelphia, PA
(1962)**

Bly padded past the Southwark Projects at 4th and Washington Streets. Charcoal black, she couldn't be seen by any of the residents in the three towers on this moonless night. The few street lights put in to make the projects safer at night had been broken by teens throwing rocks at them. The bulbs were replaced every three or four months, only to be smashed within a day.

Bly crossed the street oblivious to her surroundings. Instinctively she knew she would be giving birth before the night was over. Where could she go without being disturbed? A thought crossed her mind. Yes, the church would do. She crossed the street, retracing her steps.

She didn't see the car approach. Its headlights were off. She was hit by a glancing blow. She was stunned for a moment. The car swerved around her and sped away. No one was of any value in the projects, she knew. Whether she was dead or badly injured meant little to the driver.

She knew one of her legs was broken. There was further damage, but she was able to limp away towards the church.

The Emanuel Evangelical Lutheran Church had once been the pride of the community. Its three massive bells could be heard for miles. Its steeple was a beacon for ships sailing up the Delaware River. A dwindling congregation and lack of funds had taken its toll in recent years. The church had the feel of an old man at death's door.

Bly entered and transformed herself into a statuesque ebony woman. With her injuries, her transformation was incredibly painful, but she could only deliver her child in her human form. Her shattered leg had been too serious for her to heal when she transformed.

As had been done for generations before her, she had taken a mate when she was sixteen—a stranger whose name she never knew. It had been a biological imperative that she be impregnated at sixteen, akin to turtles born on land instinctively aware the sea was their home. She had hoped to raise her daughter, but she knew her injuries would deprive her of that desire.

An hour later she held her daughter in her hands. With her own blood she scrawled the name she had chosen for her on the child's stomach—Aiyana … Eternal Blossom, her tribe's translation. She placed the child in a box she found at the back of the church, covered her with a ragtag blanket she had also found discarded. She placed the box on the pulpit in the church. She kissed Aiyana on the forehead, then changed back to a jaguar. She limped out of the church. She would find somewhere to die far from the church, her mission in life fulfilled.

BOOK ONE

CHAPTER TWO

(Philadelphia; 1978)
Aiyana

Aiyana stood naked in front of a mirror. Today was her six-teenth birthday. She would lose her virginity tonight and would become impregnated, fulfilling her biological imperative.

She stared at herself and smiled. She didn't smile often, but her best friend Kneisha—her only real friend, actually—said it was infectious.

"Infections?" Aiyana had replied. "You sayin' my smile makes others sick?" She knew what her friend had said. She was forever jerking Kneisha's chain. Her friend was a bit gull-ible and took everything way too seriously.

"I didn't say—" she'd begun.

"I know what you said, girl," Aiyana had interrupted. "Just playing with you. Do I really have an ... *infectious* smile?" Aiyana would be the first to admit she was more than a little insecure.

"It's radiant," Kneisha had said. "You should smile more often."

"You're one to talk," Aiyana had snapped back. "Last few months you seem to have left your smile under your pillow."

Kneisha had changed the subject. Aiyana hadn't pried. She knew her friend must be dealing with some awful shit. Kneisha had acted similarly when she was thirteen—sullen, brooding, and moody. She would confide in Aiyana when she was ready.

Looking into the mirror, Aiyana saw a young woman with a tawny complexion. Her nose was a bit too wide and she had a zit she longed to pop on its bridge. She knew she drew stares from the boys at school. She had high cheekbones and what others, except for Kneisha, said were penetrating brown eyes. Kneisha, who could see past the superficial, had called her eyes predatory. Aiyana couldn't argue the point—didn't even try with her friend.

She had long, straight, lustrous black hair that made its way down to her pert behind. She was thin without being scrawny. Her legs, in particular, were muscular. While not into team sports, she excelled in track. She enjoyed the solitude of running alone, not relying or being dependent on teammates. She could take full credit for victories and blame for losses. Her coach had unsuccessfully tried to convince her to be part of the school's relay team. Aiyana had declined.

A month earlier she had confided to Kneisha that she would lose her virginity on her sixteenth birthday. She didn't explain why. Some things had to be kept from her best friend.

The two had been window shopping on Walnut Street in Center City, Philadelphia. Being dirt poor, it was all they could afford. In the window of Janine's, a far too expensive women's boutique, Kneisha had pointed to a sheer see-through blouse selling for $80.

"That's bitchin', Aiyana," Kneisha said. "Wear that on your sixteenth birthday and you'll have your choice of guys."

"Like I could afford it," Aiyana had said glumly. She did like the look.

"With no bra," Kneisha responded, as if she hadn't heard Aiyana.

"Wouldn't that be a bit much?" Aiyana had asked.

"It's see-through, but the pattern would—"

"Leave little to the imagination," Aiyana had interrupted.

Two weeks later, Kneisha dragged Aiyana back to the store. Janine's was having a going out of business sale. *Everything Must Go!* a sign screamed.

"I've been coming by every day since I heard the store was closing. Last week the top was $60," she said pointing to it in the front window. "Four days ago it was $30. Today it's—"

"Eighteen dollars," Aiyana said indifferently. Still way too much for her to afford.

Kneisha took a ten-dollar bill from her jeans. She had told Aiyana to bring what little money she had been able to save from babysitting jobs. "You know my sixth sense. Someone's going to buy the top today. Might as well be you."

Aiyana had nine singles. Kneisha gave her the ten-dollar bill. The top was hers.

Now Aiyana put the blouse on and looked at herself in the mirror. "Leaves little to the imagination," she said aloud. She could clearly see her breasts and dark brown nipples. She took off the blouse and put on a bra, then put the garment on again. She shook her head. With a bra, the blouse was a tease and nothing more. It was all or nothing, she decided, and removed her bra. A pair of tight black jeans left her midriff slightly exposed. She knew she exuded sexuality. She smiled at the thought.

CHAPTER THREE

Up through the age of ten, Aiyana had lived the typical life of a girl growing up in the projects of Philadelphia. She knew she had been adopted by Marcus and Selina Jackson when she was an infant. She had no idea who her birth mother was.

Not yet an adolescent, she hadn't been harassed by the gang that ruled the projects. She hadn't yet experimented with drugs. Hadn't been groped by teens when she rode the elevator. She had intentionally worn baggy t-shirts that hid her breasts, which were beginning to grow. She was a *kid*, she had heard more than one teen say. That was a good thing when living in the Southwark Towers. When she was twelve or thirteen, she knew she would begin to be viewed as a sexual object by these same teens. It would mean constant harassment that no girl welcomed.

There had been more than a few drive-by shootings that she knew of, with half a dozen fatalities. It was to be expected. She noticed that most of the shootings hadn't been reported on the news. Both of her parents worked two menial jobs to make ends meet. Like most of those her age, she didn't think she would live past the age of twenty. If she did, she would end up a single mother with three or more rugrats, all with different fathers.

She had her first period the day she turned eleven, and her life irrevocably changed. When she went to sleep that night, she was assaulted by dreams that revealed her heritage and provided guidance for all that followed.

She dreamed of a sixteen-year-old Indian girl who hid from the winter cold by sleeping within the pelt of a just-killed jaguar. Saw lightning strike the animal. Saw it appear to come to life, wrap itself around the adolescent, and make its way into the forest.

Then, like the trailer for a movie that didn't linger on any one scene too long, she saw the jaguar transform itself back into the same girl. She then saw her having sex with a stranger. This woman hadn't even asked the man his name. Saw her pregnant and then delivering a daughter who could also shape-shift into a jaguar.

The scene repeated itself numerous times—a different woman bedded by a stranger, then giving birth to a child who could morph into a jaguar after she began menstruating. One image lingered. Only once was a male child born to one of these women. After giving birth, the mother became a jaguar who then devoured the newborn child. The next image showed the same woman holding her newborn female child.

Aiyana felt like a dry sponge dropped in a puddle. She absorbed not only the images, but the knowledge passed down from woman to woman.

The final sequence was the longest. A jaguar passing by the projects, being hit by a car then transforming into a woman, giving birth in what appeared to be a church. Aiyana realized it was her mother when she wrote the baby's name on its belly. Her mother then limped out of the church. Aiyana could sense she was mortally wounded.

Aiyana awoke, having transformed into a jaguar. She padded over to a mirror and peered at herself—the reddish-yellow eyes in the mirror meeting her own. Still looking into the mirror, she morphed back to her human form.

Aiyana sifted through her new memories. She had a biological imperative to continue her family line. At sixteen she would be impregnated and give birth to a female child. The father would be a stranger. She would name her daughter Nita, which meant *Bear* in its Cherokee origins.

The revelations in her dream empowered Aiyana. She wasn't just another black girl from the projects who would either die young from drugs or violence or lead a mundane life like Kneisha and other female acquaintances. She wasn't sure if she was a girl with a jaguar within or a jaguar who hid behind the facade of a human. Regardless, she was a power to be reckoned with and had a purpose to her life. She would persevere to continue her family line and, with luck, raise her daughter.

Her life didn't change dramatically with her new revelations. Every once in a while she would take a bus to the art museum as darkness enveloped the city and enter the woods of Fairmount Park. She'd transform into a jaguar and practice stealth. More than once she would come upon teenagers making out on a blanket. A part of her wanted to pounce and kill, yet she held her ground. The jaguar she had become didn't wantonly kill. Jaguars killed solely for sustenance and self-protection. These teens were innocents. They would be spared. But cross her ... her mouth watered at the thought.

When she transformed back to her human form she noticed a strong musky odor that would repulse other humans and draw unwanted attention to her. A thorough shower was required, although personally, she loved her animal odor.

CHAPTER FOUR

Aiyana kept mainly to herself after she had learned about her heritage. She chatted with other girls in her class but made no close friends. Isolation, she knew, would lead to unwanted scrutiny and possible confrontations. She had to blend in with her peers without drawing undue attention to herself. A part of her wondered—even feared—if the jaguar within her would be unleashed if she became embroiled in a fight with one of her classmates. So far she had been in control of the jaguar within but she still worried it might emerge if it felt threatened.

She was surprised when she came to the aid of Kneisha Gaines, a new girl who had arrived at school two months prior to Aiyana's eleventh birthday. Kneisha's father had perished in an automobile accident. She and her mother had moved into the projects, sharing an apartment with Kneisha's uncle. Aiyana paid no attention to the new girl until after she had shapeshifted into a jaguar on her birthday. She didn't know why, but Kneisha had begun to intrigue her.

The two couldn't have been more different in appearance. Kneisha was dark-skinned and had tight, short curly hair. Unlike Aiyana, who was toned from running track, Kneisha had yet to lose her baby fat. She wasn't fat, but she referred to herself as "chunky." She had a broad nose, wide lips, and brown eyes that, unlike Aiyana's, expressed no outward emotion. Her major assets were her breasts, which had begun to sprout before her other female classmates' and had caught the eyes of the boys in her class. She wasn't into athletics, unlike Aiyana. She was in choir. Later, when Aiyana went to Kneisha's church, she saw that her friend had been given a number of solos. She had a sultry, soulful voice that brought others to their feet. Only then, Aiyana saw, did Kneisha's eyes light up. When singing, she was an altogether different person. Aiyana wondered if that was part of her attraction to Kneisha. The Kneisha who sang at church was like an emerging presence deep within that was unleashed with song.

The popular girls at school often picked on Kneisha. She had entered school mid-year and was part of no clique. Sometimes she wore the same clothes two days in a row. Aiyana would later learn Kneisha just didn't have that many changes of clothing. Aiyana's family, while poor, was able to afford a bit more of a diverse wardrobe for their adopted daughter. Aiyana would have gladly let Kneisha borrow her clothing but she was far leaner than her friend. Kneisha was a walking invitation to be bullied.

The major clique in Aiyana's class nicknamed Kneisha "D-Cup", referring to her far larger breasts than her classmates'. It was a name that stuck and even other loners referred to her by her nickname. Aiyana felt the barbs were due to jealousy. At eleven, even the popular girls were flat-chested.

Things came to a head one day at recess. Four of the popular girls had surrounded Kneisha. Aiyana didn't know why they were bullying the girl that day, but four against one rubbed her the wrong way. Since the jaguar in her had emerged, she found that in her human form she was stronger and faster than before. Jaguars, she learned from books at the library, were solitary creatures. They hunted alone, never in packs. These girls gained confidence in numbers rather than approach Kneisha one on one.

Without thinking, Aiyana got into Brenda's face. Brenda was tall and big-boned with a mouth that spewed insults and profanity. She was the leader of the pack. Put Brenda in her place, she knew, and the others would retreat.

"Leave Kneisha alone," Aiyana told Brenda.

"What's it to you, bitch?" Brenda snapped back.

"She's a friend," Aiyana replied. The word just came out. In fact she had never spoken to Kneisha.

"You should dress her," Brenda responded. "Tell her to do

something with that nappy hair of hers."

Aiyana noted that Brenda was talking as much to her friends as to Aiyana. And Brenda had lost some of her swagger with Aiyana standing up for Kneisha. The Aiyana standing up to Brenda was an unknown, she knew. Brenda wasn't quite sure what to make of her.

"Her hand-me-downs are all ratty," Brenda went on at the urging of her friends. "She's got a personality to match."

"You don't want to fuck with me, Brenda," Aiyana shot back, her eyes locking with Brenda's. Aiyana noticed a small bit of urine snake down her leg. She could smell the jaguar within her.

Brenda backed up. There was a frightened look in her eyes. "She's yours, bitch," she said, her voice quivering slightly. She led the other three girls away.

"Why help me?" Kneisha asked. "You were outnumbered and I mean nothing to you."

"They're cowards," Aiyana answered. "Coming at you four against one. You saw Brenda back down when I confronted her one on one. A fucking bully who refuses to act alone. She needs her harem to intimidate others."

"Would you have fought Brenda?" Kneisha asked. "She's bigger than you."

"I would have knocked her on her fat ass," Aiyana replied.

Kneisha laughed. "You're odd—" she began.

"Then steer clear of me," Aiyana snapped.

"Odd in a *good* way," Kneisha quickly clarified. "I didn't mean to offend you. I apologize."

"Don't apologize," Aiyana said. "It shows weakness." She paused. "Look at the way you carry yourself, staring down at your shoes even when confronted. You avert your eyes when others look at you. It makes you a target. I could ..." she started, then shrugged.

"Teach me how to stand up for myself?" Kneisha asked.

"Why the hell not?" Aiyana said, with the hint of a smile.

The two quickly became friends, much to Aiyana's surprise. She found the two had more in common than she expected. Both were introverted at school. For Aiyana it had become her nature after she was given a peek at her heritage. Once chatty and friendly, she had adapted to the solitary nature of the jaguar. She might have become the target of bullies, but once word of her confrontation with Brenda spread, she was left alone. Kneisha, for her part, was new at school. Making friends midyear was no easy chore. The two found they could chat for hours about classmates, their fondness for R&B music, and the TV programs they began to watch together.

Kneisha would cheer Aiyana on at track meets. Aiyana somewhat reluctantly went to Kneisha's church to hear her sing. She tuned out the minister's words, which initially disappointed her friend.

"What did you think of the reverend's sermon?" Kneisha asked the first time Aiyana had attended her church.

"Interesting, I guess," Aiyana replied.

"What was his message?" Kneisha asked, with the hint of a smile.

"God is good?" Aiyana asked in return.

"No, he advocated pre-marital sex," Kneisha said.

"He did?"

"No, silly, you weren't listening."

"I came to hear you sing, not to listen to a reverend's blabber," Aiyana said. "I could name every song you sang," she quickly added. "Your voice gave me goosebumps. I didn't know it, but I was on my feet clapping when you sang."

"Yeah, right," Kneisha replied.

"There you go again with your insecurity," Aiyana shot back. "You've got a bit of Gladys Knight mixed with Aretha Franklin, but you also hit the high notes like Dionne Warwick. And there's something ... something indefinable. It makes you unique."

"You're not shitting me?" Kneisha said. "Being a good friend?"

"Do you see the congregation when you sing?" Aiyana asked.

"I-I'm in a world of my own. *Honestly,*" she said. "I sing to God. Sometimes I think he hears me."

"Girl, the congregation was on its feet, clapping and stomping their feet," Aiyana said. "I never heard so many Amens in my life. Like in that song *Shaft*, you're a bad motherfucker."

Neither girl was into boys for different reasons. Kneisha, being religious, was reluctant to date. She wanted to save herself for marriage. For Aiyana, males were a means to procreate when she turned sixteen—nothing more.

And they both shared a bit of a wild streak.

When they were both twelve, Kneisha came over to Aiyana's apartment after school. Kneisha had been unusually subdued and wore an oversized, moth-eaten sweater. As usual, Aiyana wasn't subtle.

"Why are you hiding your boobs?" Aiyana asked.

"Can't a girl wear a sweater?" Kneisha replied.

"It's more like a tent. And I still say you're hiding your tits," Aiyana countered.

"My bra won't fit anymore the way my tits are growing. Blouses I have are already popping their buttons. My mother doesn't have the money to buy me new clothes. She says to wait until my birthday. Tell that to my boobs."

"That's four months off. No way you can wear a sweater for the next four months," Aiyana said, shaking her head. "Let's go shopping."

"With what money?" Kneisha asked. "You come into an inheritance?"

"Got a buck-forty-two to my name," Aiyana said.

"How—"

"Who said we were going to *pay* for new clothes?" Aiyana cut her off. She told her friend of her plan.

"Shoplifting? What if we get caught?" Kneisha asked.

"We run like hell," Aiyana responded. "Seriously, we won't get caught."

They walked to Center City and past a number of stores until they found one that was crowded. They each picked out two outfits. Kneisha also picked two bras—one that would fit her now and another one size larger. They went into the changing room and put one of the outfits on and their clothes they had worn over it. They returned one of the outfits and left the store.

Two blocks away Kneisha began to laugh uncontrollably. "I-I almost peed in my panties, I was so scared."

"Aren't you also ... exhilarated, I guess is the word. No, *jazzed*," Aiyana corrected herself.

"Kinda," Kneisha answered. "And if we *had* gotten caught?" she asked.

"We're twelve. They're going to tell us to stay the hell away from their store. We won't go back there again, anyway," Aiyana added.

"We're going to do this again?" Kneisha asked.

"Hell yes. Your tits aren't going to stop growing, girlfriend," Aiyana said. "You could use some jewelry to go with your new threads."

"I've created a monster," Kneisha said.

They shoplifted once every two weeks or so. Sometimes it was just candy at a convenience store. At a store that carried all kinds of odds and ends with just one cashier, Aiyana told the teen who was eyeing her the moment she walked in that she had to pee.

"We ain't got no bathroom for customers," the tall light-skinned boy told her.

"You want me to pee in my panties? Leave piss on the floor you'll have to clean up?" Aiyana hopped from one foot to the other.

"Give me a look at your tits and you can use the employee's bathroom," he said.

"You're shitting me," Aiyana said

"Just how bad do you have to go?" he countered.

"Not here," Aiyana said. "At the bathroom before I go in."

He led her to the back of the store. At the bathroom door Aiyana lifted her top. She wasn't wearing a bra. She was no tease. She gave the cashier a good long look. She saw he had an erection.

He reached out to touch her. She swatted his hand away. "If I gotta take a shit you can cop a feel. Eyes only to pee."

When Aiyana came out Kneisha had left the store.

"Don't be a stranger," the boy said as Aiyana headed for the door.

Aiyana smiled.

At an alley two blocks away she met Kneisha. "I got all kinds of shit," she told Aiyana. "Stuff I don't need. Don't want. I was nervous he would catch me so I just grabbed all I could."

"We can sell what we don't want to Carl Bivens," Aiyana said. "You should see what he has in the trunk of his car. We won't get a lot but cash is always good. Oh, I had to give him a look at my tits to use the bathroom," she added.

"You *didn't*," Kneisha said.

"Why the fuck not?" Aiyana shot back. "What's the harm in giving him a peek? God didn't give us tits to keep them under wraps. You use what you got."

"You're too much," Kneisha said.

"If I gotta take a shit I gotta let him touch them," she said.

"We're going back there again?" Kneisha asked.

Aiyana thought for a moment. "It's easy pickings, but no."

"You don't want him to touch you," Kneisha said.

"Like I care. Look, touch, no big deal. But we agreed to never hit the same store twice. It would be just our luck his boss notices all the shit you took is missing and next time we go there it's our ass. We've been successful because we've stuck to our plan—no store twice."

All was good between them until just after Kneisha's thirteenth birthday. Over a three week period Aiyana noticed subtle changes in her friend. At lunch she'd pick at her food. A "B" student, she began to flunk quizzes and didn't turn in homework assignments. Her eyes were often bloodshot. Aiyana knew she had been crying. And she insisted on coming over to Aiyana's house every day after school. Often Aiyana's mother would invite her to stay for dinner. She never refused.

Aiyana had held her curiosity in check but after a third week she was worried for her friend.

"You going to tell me what's bothering you?" Aiyana asked. "And don't give me that shit about you being fine. You're not. Haven't been since your birthday."

"You swear you'll keep it to yourself?" Kneisha asked. "No telling your parents or the fool school counselor?"

"My parents don't want to get mixed up in your business.

And I don't trust *any* adult at school. What you tell me stays in this room."

"My uncle … he-he began raping me the night of my birthday," she began. "He says he puts a roof over my head and food on the table. Now that I'm a woman—those are the words the bastard used—it was time I began to pay him back for his generosity."

"So you let him—"

"Shit, no," Kneisha cut Aiyana off. "I told him fuck no, but he wouldn't take no for an answer. Dragged me into his room and …" She couldn't go on.

"How often?" Aiyana asked, her voice cold.

"He works nights. That's why I've been coming over every day after school. Still, at least half a dozen times."

"Does your mother know?"

"I haven't told her," Kneisha said. "We got no place to go. My moms hardly makes any money working at 7-Eleven. I just gotta deal with it. No one ever said life was fair."

Aiyana tried to console her friend. Let her cry. When she was cried out, Aiyana told her to get some rest. Soon her friend was asleep.

Aiyana left the house knowing what had to be done.

At Kneisha's apartment her uncle Lester opened the door. "You looking for Kneisha? She ain't here. Spends her time at some bitch's house."

"My apartment, and I'm not looking for Kneisha," Aiyana said, then entered. She closed the door behind her. Kneisha had told her that her mother would be at work. It was just the two of them. She wore a top that she had outgrown. With no bra, Lester would see the contours of her breasts and nipples. He was staring at them now. Had an erection. She removed her top. "I hear you like to fuck young teens," she said. She slipped out of her jeans and panties.

"I like my women to have some meat on them," Lester said, his eyes on her naked body.

"I got a pussy. Figure that is enough for someone like you," Aiyana said. "You can have me if you leave Kneisha alone for a week."

"And then?" Lester asked.

"You can have me again. A willing partner," Aiyana added. "Let's go to your room."

"Why give yourself in place of Kneisha?" Lester asked.

"Do you want to talk or fuck me?" Aiyana answered with a question of her own.

Lester turned and led the way to his bedroom. Aiyana morphed into a jaguar. She had learned that when she transformed her clothing was torn to shreds. When she ventured to Fairmount Park now she either removed her clothes before the change or brought a second pair of jeans and a top which she kept in a canvas bag she hid behind a tree. She had taken off her clothes in front of Lester both to seduce him and make sure she had something to wear when her task was complete.

Before Lester could turn around, Aiyana jumped on his back. Her powerful jaws tore into the back of his head and into his brain. He was dead before he hit the floor. Her *first* kill.

She shifted back to her human form, dressed, then left the apartment. When she returned to her room Kneisha was still asleep in her bed.

Aiyana showered. She could smell the stench on her. It was the odor that permeated her skin when she transformed back to her human form. Much as she enjoyed the smell, it wouldn't do for Kneisha to notice it when she awakened. Lying next to her friend, Aiyana replayed her first kill. It had been exhilarating. She felt ... invulnerable. And she felt no regret, no remorse.

Aiyana didn't see her friend for the following two days. When Kneisha finally returned to school, Aiyana saw she had a bounce to her step that had been missing since her birthday. She sat next to Aiyana and smiled. Aiyana wouldn't say Kneisha was carefree, but a great burden had been lifted from her shoulders.

At lunch Kneisha explained her absence. "My uncle was killed," she began. "*Don't* say you're sorry," she quickly added. "I'm not. My life has been a nightmare since I turned thirteen. You won't see me grieving."

"How did he die?" Aiyana asked. It would have seemed odd if she didn't ask.

"The back of his head was bashed in ... no, more than that.

There was a hole in the back of his head. The police have no idea how it occurred. One cop joked that it looked like an animal attack." She paused. "A black man killed in the projects. There won't be much of an investigation."

Kneisha had been right. No neighbors had seen or heard anything. Lester had a good number of friends he went drinking with, but no enemies. Three days later Kneisha's mother received a call from a detective. The case had been closed. There were no leads to follow.

CHAPTER FIVE

Aiyana put on a denim jacket to hide her see-through blouse from her parents. It was mid-May and still warm outside even though it was evening.

Outside she removed the jacket. She urinated a bit, felt the warm liquid slide down her thigh. Just as with jaguars in the wild, the scent of her pee would draw a mate. In her dreams since she was eleven—which recurred regularly but in far more vivid detail as she got older—her ancestors mated … aggressively, was how she would describe it. Sometimes even violently. Love or any form of affection had nothing to do with it. Sex was solely to procreate. She would follow suit.

She hadn't taken more than a dozen steps from the entrance of the tower she lived in when a boy strolled up to her. He was maybe a year or two older than her. He was a head taller than her, light-skinned with short-cropped curly hair. He wore a red bandana, a t-shirt with holes in it, and baggy jeans. She could see a scar on his left shoulder.

"Where you going, sweet thing?" he asked.

She ignored him.

"Ain't you got no manners?" he asked her. He was now walking next to her. "Just making conversation."

"While staring at my tits," Aiyana shot back.

"You hardly got them covered. They jiggle when you walk," he said and laughed. He put his arm around her shoulder then grabbed her left breast.

"Get your filthy hands off of me," Aiyana said.

He put two fingers on either side of her nipple and squeezed. "I don't think so," he said and squeezed harder. "You know you want me."

Aiyana slapped him in the face.

"You shouldn't have done that, bitch," he said. "We coulda had a nice time. Now I'm just gonna take what you're offering."

He pushed her against a four-foot high planter. Someone from the city put plants in the planter in March or April but teens like this one tore them to shreds within a day. Now only dirt remained. He ripped her blouse and began to massage her breasts. She screamed, telling him to stop. He unbuttoned the top of her jeans and pulled them down. She tried to slap him again but he grabbed her arm. With his other hand he slapped her in the face, drawing blood. He took out a knife—a switchblade, she knew—and held it against her neck.

"Raise your hand to me again and I'll slit your throat." He ran the blade against her cheek. Blood dripped into her mouth and onto the ground. He pulled her panties down, then the zipper of his jeans. He entered her and thrust himself in and out of her until he ejaculated.

As he assaulted her, Aiyana looked at the three towers that made up the Southwark Projects. Her screams had drawn the towers' residents to their windows. First just a few, but by the time he entered her several dozen people were peering down at the scene. Some looked horrified. Others just curious. A few turned away after a minute. Most continued to watch, transfixed. Not one came to her aid. And she heard no police siren in the distance. No one had the balls to even make an anonymous call for help.

As his semen entered her, Aiyana scratched his hand. He would barely notice it, but she had left her mark on him. Retribution would follow.

Done with her, he pushed her to the ground and zipped up his jeans. "Was it good for you?" he asked and laughed.

Aiyana remained silent. She had gotten what she desired. She didn't want to antagonize him further. She could have transformed and torn him to shreds but there were all those eyes peering at her from the towers. Cowards one and all. She had disdain for them. As for her rapist, well … her scent had attracted him. It hadn't driven him into a sexual frenzy. He had violated her of his own free will, but she had invited the attack.

Like her ancestors, she knew she had been impregnated. So she remained silent. Bored with her, he sauntered off.

Yes, it had been good for her, she thought to herself.

CHAPTER SIX

Estefan Morales and Russ McGowan were parked four blocks from the Southwark Projects. Morales was a rookie beat officer, three months out of the academy. His partner had been on the job for two years. They had been paired two months earlier.

Morales wouldn't say they were friends. He'd never had McGowan over to his home for dinner and had never been invited to his partner's house. Morales got the sense that McGowan resented him from the day they were partnered. Estefan had made attempts at small talk. McGowan responded with a shrug or a grunt. Sometimes he just ignored Estefan completely.

They eventually formed a decent working relationship. They began to talk about the job, steering clear of intimacies most partners shared. From his actions and the gossip Morales heard from other officers, he knew McGowan had no fondness for minorities. The department, according to McGowan, was forced to promote blacks and Hispanics over more qualified Caucasians to meet quotas mandated by the mayor. He was even more hostile towards women. They should be meter maids or traffic cops, he insisted, but political pressure forced the advancement of clearly inferior women to positions they weren't qualified for. Morales had been told that one of McGowan's favorite jokes was what would be considered the ultimate hire for the department—a black female lesbian so three quotas could be met in one fell swoop.

Tonight they sat in their patrol car in silence. It was just shy of 11p.m. Their shift ended in an hour. Morales looked at his partner. Russ McGowan was twenty years old, tall and solidly built with a full head of wavy brown hair. He was handsome, but he had cold blue eyes. He had a commanding presence about him which would draw others to him. Morales, on the other hand, while the same height as his partner, was lean, his face pockmarked from the ravages of acne. McGowan had been in his uniform for their entire eight hour shift but he looked like he had just reported for duty. Estefan looked like he had slept in his uniform the night before.

They made an odd couple, in many ways the polar opposite of one another.

McGowan looked at Morales. "You got ambitions, Estefan?" he asked. "You don't want to spend your life on patrol, do you?" he added.

He speaks, was Estefan's first thought. McGowan had never asked him a personal question. He couldn't recall him ever using his first name. This was no casual discussion, Morales sensed. McGowan had an ulterior motive.

"I'd like to be a detective ... *homicide* detective," he added. "I know it sounds cliche but I enjoy the pulse of the street, the thrill of the chase, the hunt for elusive clues. I fully understand that few homicides provide a challenge ... Russ... but a homicide detective told me there was no greater rush than pursuing a killer who made the hunt difficult."

"That's it?" McGowan asked. "Don't you want to climb the ladder? Become Philly's first Hispanic Chief of Police?"

Morales thought the last statement contained more than a little hostility. Did McGowan see him as a threat to his own advancement? "And get further away from the action?" he responded. He paused a moment. "One day maybe I'll make sergeant. With two kids and more to follow, if my wife has anything to say about it, financial considerations may get me off the street. But as a sarge, I'd still be close to the action. I have no desire for further upward mobility. I want to steer clear of the politics of the department."

"You a team player, Estefan?" McGowan asked, as if he had ignored his last statement.

"In what sense?" Morales asked. He wondered why the twenty questions after two months of general disinterest.

"Doing what's in the best interest of the squad," McGowan responded. "You mentioned the homicide unit. Say you caught a case that I had interest in pursuing. Would you give it up to me, no questions asked? I'd owe you a favor."

"Depends on the case," Morales said after a moment's thought. He knew he was hedging, but it was as far as he would go without knowing the particulars of the homicide. "I'm not looking to bank favors. Just do the job. Like I said, the politics of the department I can do without."

Morales knew McGowan, unlike him, was a political animal when it came to his own advancement. Whenever detectives arrived on the scene they had responded to, McGowan made it a point to make small talk with them. When detectives no longer needed them, McGowan often brought them a cup of coffee before he and Morales left. A small thing, but he wanted to be known by his superiors. Wanted to ingratiate himself to them.

"Ignore the politics of the department at your own peril," McGowan replied. "You're Hispanic, Estefan. There's lots of pressure on the department to promote minorities and women, even if they're not qualified and haven't paid their dues. You got a leg up on me being Hispanic. If a promotion is between you and me, you'd get it, everything else being equal. I'm a dying breed—a white man trying to advance against the tide of special interest groups with political clout."

"A cynical view, but I can't dispute your point," Morales said. "You'd level the playing field, wouldn't you?" he asked.

"Damn right," McGowan said. "Kiss ass of the brass if I got to. Collect those favors you think so little of. Steal a high-profile case from you if it will help me."

"So you have no moral compass. Just looking out for number one," Morales said.

"Not so, my friend," McGowan responded. "I'm the ultimate team player. Those who are loyal to me go along for the ride when I'm promoted. I take them with me and make sure they get treated fairly. Say I'm a lieutenant. I don't leave behind those who had my back. If a sergeant's position opens up, one of my guys gets it. The others end up working with him rather than some stranger. They know I'm in their corner."

"But you'd step on those who got in your way, wouldn't you?" Morales said.

"The law of the jungle, my man," McGowan said. "If you're not with me, you're against me. I'd squash you like a bug."

"You saying I should watch my back?" Morales asked. This had gone beyond playful banter between partners, he knew. McGowan meant every word he said.

"We're buds, Estefan," McGowan replied. "We're talking hypotheticals a long way in the future. But you scratch my back, I'll return the favor, is what I'm getting at. I'm looking for team players, not lone wolves. You and me working together could wield a lot of power."

Morales didn't believe him for a moment. McGowan was glib, but Morales had the feeling the two would eventually clash. Before he could reply their radio barked.

"Unit 611. Southwark Projects. Fourth and Washington. Priority 1. Sexual assault."

"Shit," McGowan said. "No way we'll get off by midnight."

CHAPTER SEVEN

Morales saw a young woman slumped against a planter when they arrived at the scene. He could see her top had been ripped off, exposing her breasts. He grabbed his jacket from the back seat. McGowan followed him, seemingly more than willing to allow Morales to take the lead. A girl attacked in the projects was not the kind of case where he could collect favors.

Morales bent down next to the tawny black girl. A teenager, fifteen, maybe sixteen. He placed his coat to cover her bare breasts and genitals. He saw now that her jeans and panties had been pulled down to her knees.

"I'm Officer Morales," he told the girl. "You can call me Estefan. I'm not going to ask you about your attack. Detectives will be here soon. You'll be telling your story to them ... more times than you want to. Do you live in the Southwark Projects?" he asked.

The girl nodded.

"Then just two questions. Can you tell me your name and what apartment you live in? You'll be taken to the hospital. Your parents will want to meet you there."

The girl stared at him. He saw a gash on her cheek but was reluctant to touch her. With her jeans and panties pulled down to her knees it didn't take a rocket scientist to infer she had been raped. She was traumatized and possibly in shock. The last thing she wanted was to be touched by a male, even a cop. McGowan had called for paramedics when they got to the scene and ascertained the call wasn't a hoax. All Morales wanted to do was comfort the girl until the paramedics arrived.

"Aiyana ... Aiyana Jackson. Apartment 12C," she said. "The

center tower." She paused. "Dozens saw what happened. Not *one* came to my aide." She fell silent.

Morales passed along the information to McGowan. Told him to speak to Aiyana's parents and then canvas apartments for witnesses.

"You know they'll all deny seeing anything," McGowan said. "These people only care about themselves."

Morales knew McGowan would utter the same words if they had been outside a predominantly Hispanic tenement, but said nothing. "Then stand here, and when the detectives come, they may have something worse for you to do. Canvass for witnesses and … well, out of sight, out of mind."

"Good thinking," McGowan said. Morales thought he sounded surprised at his partner's foresight.

When McGowan was gone Morales sat down next to Aiyana. "You can lean against me if you want," he said.

He saw Aiyana scrutinize him. She was hesitant, suspicious. Cops, after all, did little more than harass those in the projects. She finally put her head on his shoulder.

"I'm not going to tell you everything is going to be all right," Morales said. "But I'll do everything in my power to see you through this."

"You got kids, Officer—"

"Estefan," he corrected her. "A boy and a girl with another on the way. My oldest, Angelica, is only three."

"A pretty name," Aiyana said. "Bet you're a good father."

"How would you know that?" he asked.

"How you treated me," Aiyana replied. "Your partner … he wanted nothing to do with me. You didn't hesitate. You know, putting your jacket around me. Comforting me."

An unmarked car and an ambulance arrived simultaneously. A twenty-something, squat, dark-skinned black female paramedic came over to them. Her partner remained at the ambulance. They must have been told this was a sexual assault call. The women looked at him.

"Morales," he said, anticipating her question.

"Let me take over now, Officer Morales," she said, not unkindly.

"Please don't go," Aiyana said, her eyes meeting his.

The woman bent down. "My name is Heather, sweetheart. I need to take a look at that cut on your face. Then we'll take you to the hospital. Officer Morales has to report to the two detectives coming over," she said and turned her head towards two advancing figures. "I'll make sure they leave you be until you get to the hospital. Not everyone's as considerate as Officer Morales."

Aiyana looked at Morales and smiled. "Thank you, Estefan."

Two detectives greeted Morales when he stood up. A woman dressed in a suit, complete with a tie, was clearly in charge.

"Detective Georgia Pines," she told Morales after he identified himself. "This is my partner Paul Abernathy. Where's your partner?" she asked. Pines was a good head shorter than Morales, but stood ramrod straight to make herself look taller, he thought. She wasn't attractive, appearing even more dour since she wore no makeup. She had blonde spiky hair. He couldn't tell if she had a decent body with the suit she wore. She was big-boned but didn't appear fat. She looked to be in her late thirties. Her partner, Abernathy, was a short, squat man, a good fifteen pounds overweight with thinning brown hair. He was a good ten years or more older than his partner. His off-the-rack suit had seen better days. He looked bored, completely deferring to his partner.

"McGowan ... Russ McGowan is informing the girl's parents, then canvassing for witnesses."

"What did the girl tell you?" Pines asked.

"Her name is Aiyana Jackson," Morales said, taking an instant dislike to this woman. "She lives in apartment 12C in the middle tower."

"And about the attack?" Pines asked. She had scribbled the information Morales had provided her in a small notepad.

"I didn't ask her," Morales said.

"That what they teach you at the academy, Officer?" Pines asked. "To do *nothing*? Let the detectives do all of the work?"

"She needed comforting, not an interrogation," Morales said, trying to rein in his temper.

Pines shook her head. "Go and help your partner canvass. I'm done with you."

Aiyana began to scream as Pines finished her sentence. "I don't want to go to the hospital alone. I want Officer Morales."

Morales heard Heather trying to comfort her but Aiyana was insistent. Heather came over to them. She seemed aware she had to report to Pines. "Look, Detective ... the victim may be in shock. Can Officer Morales accompany her in the ambulance?"

"So victims dictate what you do?" Pines asked, hostility clearly evident in her voice.

"The girl's in shock, Detective," Heather said again, meeting Pine's stare. "She's been raped. Her cheek has been cut with a knife. It'll leave a scar. Is it too much to ask to honor her request?"

Pines remained silent.

"Do you really want her to continue making a scene?" Heather asked. "Want someone calling a TV station saying we're abusing the victim of a rape?"

Pines looked at Morales. "Go with her but let her know in no uncertain terms that I'll be questioning her at the hospital. I'm not all that certain she's a victim."

"What's that supposed to mean?" Morales asked. "Her blouse was ripped off. Her jeans and panties were pulled down to her knees."

"Yet you didn't ask her if she had been raped," Pines countered. "Go with her but make sure she understands I'm the one in charge."

"Yes, Detective," Morales said, then walked towards the ambulance.

CHAPTER EIGHT

At Jefferson Hospital, Aiyana was taken to the ICU. Pines and Abernathy showed up several minutes later.

"She tell you anything?" Pines asked Morales.

"The paramedics were administering to her," Morales said.

"What the hell are you good for?" Pines replied. "Find someone to take you back to the projects. Canvass for witnesses with your partner. I don't want to see you back here. Understand?"

Morales nodded and left.

On returning to the projects, Morales met McGowan at the entrance of the center tower. "Any luck?" he asked.

"Yep … all bad," McGowan answered. "These people don't look out for one another. Makes me want to puke. *No one* saw anything, so they say. A damn waste of time. Let's get back to—"

"Our orders are to continue to canvass," Morales interrupted. "From a detective with a stick up her ass," he added.

"She must be a real bitch to get a rise out of you, Estefan," McGowan said. "I've never heard such language from you."

"Stuff it, Russ," Morales said. "The female detective didn't give a damn about the victim. Questioned whether she had been raped. I want to find someone to confirm she was assaulted."

"This detective have a name?" McGowan asked.

"Pines. Georgia Pines," Morales said.

"I've heard of her," McGowan replied and nodded. "A real piece of work, I'm told. Still, one of the rare female cops with a set of balls. Victims don't need to be mollycoddled. Most of the time their stories contain lies. Pines gets to the truth." He paused. "You, Estefan, go soft on the victim. Believe everything each one spouts. But you want corroboration this girl was raped, so I guess we canvass."

Morales spoke to the first two apartments' occupants from outside their closed doors. "We ain't seen nothing," he was told both times. At the third apartment, a husband and wife greeted him, introducing themselves as William and Susan Townes. This time, he was invited inside.

"Please don't make too much noise," the woman whispered to Morales. "Our daughter, Danai, is asleep. She's five and I don't want her upset."

"So you saw the attack that took place tonight," Morales replied, when they were seated.

"Don't matter what we seen or didn't," William answered. "Ain't no way we're going to testify."

"We can provide protection for you and—"

"Bullshit," William interrupted. "You're a wide-eyed kid thinking you can make a difference here. How long you been police?" he asked.

"Not long," Morales answered. "But—"

"But *nothing*," William continued. "There is no police presence at Southwark. The projects are ruled by gangs, drug dealers, and thugs. We come forward, we're the next victims. We gotta live here. We got a five-year-old to protect."

"Ten years from now it might be … Danai, right? … Danai who could be assaulted," Morales said.

"We gotta worry about the here and now, not some distant future," Susan chimed in.

"Why did you let me in, then?" Morales asked.

"To educate you to life in the projects," William responded. "It's a shame what happened to that child tonight," he said, "but she's not the first and won't be the last. We'll pray for the girl but that's all you'll get from us."

Morales left and was about to knock on another door when his police radio beckoned.

"Get your ass back to the hospital … *now*." It was Pines.

"I thought—"

"You're not paid to think," Pines barked. "Do what you're told."

Morales told McGowan he'd been summoned.

"I'll drop you off," McGowan replied. "I'm canvassed-out. Not one fucking person admitted to seeing anything. These people don't protect their own. Animals," he added.

Morales was going to tell his partner what William Townes had told him but he remained silent. McGowan was set in his ways. His opinions were carved in stone. Trying to convince him otherwise would be like talking to a brick wall.

At the hospital Morales went to the ICU. Pines glared at him. "Your *friend* won't let me interview her. She'll only talk to you."

"I'll talk to her, then," Morales said.

"How long you been out of the academy?" Pines asked.

"Three months."

"God protect me," Pines said. "No way you're going to question her. You're not qualified," Pines shot back.

"What do you want me to do?" Morales asked.

"Be all Officer Friendly and convince the girl to cooperate, then get the hell out of my investigation," Pines spat back.

Morales went into Aiyana's room. She lay in her bed silent, her eyes following his every move.

"You and Detective Pines got into a pissing contest, didn't you," Morales said. "You must be feeling better."

Aiyana gave him a weak smile. "She looks at me like I'm a skank. *I'm* the victim. I'll only talk to you."

Morales sat on the edge of the bed. "Look, Aiyana, I've been a cop for all of a minute. Pines is trained in investigating sexual assaults. Give her a chance. You'll see she's on your side."

"You don't believe that shit for a second ... Estefan," Aiyana replied. "Tell her to go fuck herself. I talk to you. No one else."

Morales smiled. "You're not making life easy for me. She's going to want to eat me and spit me out..." he began but didn't finish.

"Out your ass," Aiyana said, her smile widening a bit. "I'd say I'm sorry but I'd be lying. I won't talk to that woman. Shit, she's already condemned me."

Morales raised his hands in surrender. "If I convince her, will you be straight with me?" he asked. "No bullshitting me," he added using her salty language.

"Cross my heart," Aiyana said.

"I'll give it a shot," Morales said and rose.

In the hallway Morales told Pines that Aiyana was adamant.

"That little bitch won't dictate who speaks to her," Pines said. She pushed past Morales.

"Take a breath, Georgia." It was Abernathy—the first words he had uttered in Morales's presence. "Hear Officer Morales out."

Pines turned to Morales. "Why should I give in to her?"

"I've built a rapport with her," Morales began. "She's looking to regain control—what her rapist took away from her. Give her what she wants. She promised to be forthcoming with me."

Pines was silent for several moments. She wore a perpetual scowl. "Fuck it," she finally said. "I'll feed you questions through an earpiece. Do as you're told, Officer."

Twenty minutes later an earpiece was delivered by another young officer.

"Go off script, Morales," Pines said, "and I'll have your ass."

CHAPTER NINE

Morales went back into the ICU. "Aiyana, Detective Pines has agreed that I interview you. You must be completely honest with me. She doesn't have a lot of faith in my ability."

"What do you want to know?" she asked.

"Why was she out at 10 p.m.?" Pines prompted him through the earpiece.

"Why were you out so late?" Morales asked. "You know the projects are dangerous, especially at night."

"It's my sixteenth birthday," Aiyana said. "I was going to meet my friend Kneisha at a club to celebrate."

"She had fake IDs for both of you?"

Aiyana nodded. "Got them from a friend to celebrate my birthday."

"Why celebrate your birthday at a club with strangers?" Morales asked.

"We just wanted to get away from it all," Aiyana responded.

"From what?"

"Southwark—the projects," she answered. "I've seen boys— one ten years old—killed in a drive-by shooting. Been offered drugs dozens of times. I always refused," she added quickly. "Since I began developing ... you know ... breasts, I've been groped almost daily. The projects are ruled by gangs ... *animals*. It's depressing. So my friend suggested we get away from it all for one night."

"Talk about the alleged assault," Pines instructed.

"So you left your apartment around ten, right?"

Aiyana nodded.

"What happened?"

"This boy came out of nowhere. He pushed me against the planter, ripped off my blouse, pulled down my jeans and panties and … and raped me," Aiyana said in one breath.

"Did she fight back?" Pines again.

"Did you try to run or push him away?" Morales asked.

"I screamed for help," Aiyana said. "Told him no, told him to get off of me, like they taught us in school. He was stronger than I was. And he had a knife. Said he'd cut my throat if I didn't stop screaming." She paused, as if in thought. "I did scratch him. I'm not sure where."

"Why did he cut your face?"

"Because he could. Because no one came to help me," Aiyana said, her voice rising. "I looked up at the towers. There were dozens of people who heard me scream. I saw them looking out of their windows. All they did was look. Fucking cowards. No one called the police until the boy left." Tears streamed down her cheeks. "They just stared."

"Have her describe him."

"Can you tell me what he looked like?" Morales asked.

"I never got a good look at him," Aiyana said. "Didn't recognize him from the projects. He was black, but not dark-skinned. I never saw his face."

"What about his clothes?" Morales continued.

"Baggy jeans and a t-shirt."

"Was there a picture or a logo on the shirt?"

Aiyana shook her head.

"His voice?"

"What do you mean?" she asked.

"Did he have an accent?" Morales said. "You said he was a light-skinned black, but he could have been Hispanic."

Aiyana shook her head. "Definitely not Hispanic."

"Any scars or tattoos?"

"He was on top of me so fast I never got a good look at him," Aiyana said. "And like I told you, I was looking at the bastards staring down at us from the towers."

"Get her to talk about her sexual history."

"Sorry, but I have to ask, are you a virgin?"

"You mean do I sleep around?" Aiyana said. "I was a virgin

until tonight. There was blood on my thighs. I'm not a slut."

"Then why was she dressed like one? A see-through blouse."

"That blouse of yours—"

"What about it? It was my birthday," Aiyana snapped. "I wanted to feel sexy, but that doesn't mean I was asking to be raped. White girls in safe neighborhoods dress sexy. Here, if you have a vagina you're prey. And police are never around unless there's a dead body." She paused. "I'm tired. All talked out. There's nothing more to tell."

"Ask *her about her sexual history,*" Pines told him again. *"Oral sex."*

Jesus Christ, Morales thought. Pines had gone too far. "Get some sleep now, Aiyana," Morales said. "I'm here for you if you need me."

Morales left the room.

Pines was in his face when he got to the hallway. "I told you to stick to the script. You didn't. She may have been a virgin but we need to know her sexual history. You too squeamish to ask?"

"It's irrelevant," Morales said. "She was raped by a stranger. Do you disregard a prostitute who is raped? Do you demand to know *her* sexual history as part of your investigation?"

"Nothing is irrelevant," Pines barked. "This girl—"

"Aiyana," Morales said. "She has a name."

Pines glared at him. *"Aiyana* was going to a bar to celebrate her birthday. Gimme a break. This blouse," she said holding up a plastic evidence bag to show Morales. "See-through and she wore no bra. Her tits were there for anyone to see. So, tell me she wasn't going out to get fucked on her birthday. I wanted you to explore that, as well."

"Are you saying she wasn't raped?" Morales asked, trying to rein in his anger.

"I'm withholding judgment," Pines said. "You learned virtually nothing because you don't have the balls to ask the tough questions. Get the hell out of here. Don't return. She can ask for you all she wants. You're off the case."

CHAPTER TEN

Georgia Pines knew she had a chip on her shoulder. She knew that, because she was born with a vagina instead of a penis, she was at a disadvantage in the police department. She had developed a tough exterior early on and had clawed her way up all her life.

Her mother was Irish, from the squalor of South Philly. Her father? Her damn mother told her he could have been one of several men she had slept with. She'd slept with each of them once and didn't even recall their names. And she hadn't seen any of them again.

From an early age, Georgia was aware of a steady parade of strangers who passed through their small apartment. There had been one bedroom she and her mother shared. When Georgia outgrew a hand-me-down crib, she slept on a mattress on the far side of the small bedroom. Her mother would bed a stranger with Georgia in the room. She learned about sex from observing. At first when her mother groaned and screamed she thought she was being hurt. She was tempted to jump on the bed and with her small fists pummel the stranger. But, after the stranger was … done with her mother, she would laugh and chat with the man. Why if she was being hurt would she laugh? Georgia wondered to herself.

To her credit, Georgia would grudgingly admit, her mother never let her so-called lovers touch her. More than a few expressed interest when Georgia was six or seven. Some suggested a threesome when Georgia was ten. More than a few offered money. Corrine Pines was adamant: Steer clear of her daughter.

The family, if you could call it that, lived on welfare. Corrine had a few menial jobs, but she was hotheaded and often lost her temper with her employers when she was accused of thievery. The fact was, Corrine *did* steal from wherever she worked. Yet she felt she deserved the benefit of the doubt. Irrational, yes, but that was Corrine Pines in a nutshell. She'd tell Georgia she had been fired unjustly and then place money she had stolen on the table. She wasn't a prostitute, but if her lover of the moment—usually a one-night stand—offered to pay for some rough or kinky sex, she never said no.

When Georgia was ten, her mother sat her on the bed for a sex talk. "You know the birds and the bees shit," her mother told her. "So that's not what I'm going to talk to you about. We're the inferior sex, Georgia. You'll learn it soon enough. Teachers think boys are smarter than girls. There are a lot of jobs women can't get because they don't have a cock. And we get paid less than men for doing the same job."

"Why, Mommy?"

"Don't ask me why, Georgia, because I ain't got no answer. It's just a fact of life. *But*, our pussies and our tits are the great equalizers. You want a job bad enough, you let the boss fuck you to get it. Want a raise or promotion, you spread your legs. God may have created man as the top dog, but he didn't leave us defenseless. Most men think with their cocks, not their brains. Never underestimate the power of the pussy."

Georgia didn't know if she loved her mother—didn't really know what love was. But she had put her mother's practical advice to good use. She lost her virginity in the ninth grade. She agreed to let Jimmy Stefani fuck her if he dropped out of the race for junior high school president. In the eleventh grade she let her biology teacher screw her for an "A". She never could make heads or tails of what was taught in biology and needed an edge. And she had slept with her sergeant half a dozen times to become a detective in his squad.

She was short, but muscular from working out. She had to be tough as nails—physically the equal of most men. As a patrol officer, she intentionally instigated fights with fellow cops at the bars they frequented. Male cops wouldn't fight a woman. It was a no-win situation. Win and you earned no props; lose and you're the butt of jokes. Still, she forced fights with profanity-laced tirades. She could have beaten most of the men she fought, but she always let her combatant prevail. She made sure to leave him bruised, though. She knew by putting up a good fight she would earn the respect of her fellow officers, where she would have gained an enemy if she was triumphant. She often became drinking buddies with those she fought. She held no grudge against them. They were a means to an end.

She often bedded those she fought. While no beauty, she had large breasts that seemed to mesmerize her follow officers. She didn't particularly enjoy sex. She faked orgasms—didn't know if she'd ever had a genuine orgasm. But letting a cop she fought fuck her made a friend out of a potential rival, just as her mother had taught her.

She drew a line at having sex with her partners. She got her way by sheer force of will. She would gain nothing from bedding her partner and it could cause an irreparable rift down the line.

Now thirty-three, she had made detective, but she wasn't particular ambitious. The homicide unit was her goal. She had no desire to be a sergeant or lieutenant—a supervisor of others. She was hot-tempered like her mother and knew she would be unable to tolerate the mistakes of detectives in her squad. They would be aware of the scorn she held for them. No, she was not meant to supervise others.

Her partner for the past year, Paul Abernathy, was pretty much burned out. He had put in eighteen years and talked about putting in his papers after two more years. He was more than willing to let Georgia take the lead in cases. He was an ideal partner for Georgia—never challenging her authority or how she worked a case. If she needed the so-called "good cop" to question a victim, parents, or a suspect, she turned to Paul, who willingly obliged.

This rookie cop, Morales, had tested her severely, along with the victim of the alleged rape. No one dictated terms to her. Yet against her better judgment, she had allowed Morales to interview the victim. A mistake, she now knew. But her partner had been right when he suggested she not question Aiyana Jackson until the morning.

"Let her sleep," Paul told her. "Make her think she's in control. Start fresh tomorrow. Tell her *your* boss pulled Morales off the case even though you requested that he remain. Then you're not the bad guy."

She was going to tell her partner to keep his opinions to himself, but reconsidered. Abernathy was a pussy but every once in a while he offered her a pearl of wisdom. She merely nodded. The two left, leaving a patrolman at Aiyana's door.

"You wanna go and get a drink?" Abernathy asked Pines in the lobby of the hospital. "Things got hot between you and that rookie patrol cop. You could vent at me."

Pines looked at her partner. They had *never* gone out for a drink in the time they had been working together. *What was his motivation?* she wondered. "You think I'm going to let you fuck me?" Pines said. "Think I'm vulnerable because I let that bitch victim throw me off of my game? You know I don't fuck—"

"Partners," Abernathy finished for her. "Your pussy's so tight, Georgia, I wouldn't be able to get my cock out. Then you'd never be rid of me." He paused. "I have no desire to fuck you, Georgia," he added.

Pines laughed. "You have a way with words, Paul. Don't you find me attractive—fuckable?" she asked.

"You don't fuck your partners," Abernathy repeated her words.

"I could always make an exception," she said.

"I may be a burned out detective, but I'm no fool, Georgia," he said. "There's no upside in bedding me. You'd only screw me if I had something you wanted. So, a drink or two and we chew the fat. Maybe come up with a strategy for tomorrow. Nothing more."

"As tempting as your offer is, I'll pass," Pines responded. "You … handled me well today, Paul. It's appreciated. But I need to be with myself to formulate my next move," she added. *I work best alone,* she was tempted to add, but held her tongue. She didn't want to collaborate with her partner. Didn't want to talk work over drinks. Didn't want to talk about herself, which she knew Abernathy desired. Her mama hadn't raised no fool.

CHAPTER ELEVEN

Pines walked into Aiyana's room at seven the next morning. She knew Aiyana was being released from the hospital at ten.

"I have some questions for you," Pines said. There would be no pleasantries, no "How are you feeling?" Pines wanted to immediately establish that she was in control and wasn't going to take any shit from this teenager.

"I only want to speak to Officer Morales," Aiyana said.

"You're out of luck," Pines shot back. "My boss took your buddy off the case. He's a rookie beat cop. Green as grass. My boss chewed me out for letting him speak to you in the first place, so I'm not in any mood for one of your tantrums. Morales refused to ask you tough questions. I still question whether you were raped."

"You're shitting me," Aiyana said.

"You didn't talk to Morales that way," Pines said. "Got a mouth on you just like everyone else from the projects. You had Morales wrapped around your little finger. You softened him up. With me, I get the real you. I've been dealing with sexual assaults for two years. I'll know if you're shitting me."

"So you think I made it all up," Aiyana said. "There were plenty of witnesses in the towers watching me be raped."

"None who have come forth," Pines shot back. "Maybe you twisted the facts. You had sex last night. The question is, were you raped or were you putting on a show with your boyfriend for those in the towers? If so, that's lewd and lascivious behavior, not to mention perjury and it's *you* who will be going to prison."

"I didn't know the boy," Aiyana said. "He *raped* me."

"I'm going to speak to your friend Kneisha. Speak to your classmates and teachers. Check out every detail you give me. So be straight with me. Now, how many boys have you had sex with?"

"I told Officer Morales I was a virgin. Telling you the same thing."

"Your buddy Morales didn't press you," Pines continued. "Being a virgin doesn't mean you didn't engage in sexual activity. You live in the projects. You're an attractive girl with a nice rack. Tell me you haven't been hit on."

"I've been harassed," Aiyana said. "I began developing at eleven. Going downstairs in the elevator was always a trial. The stairs would have been worse."

"Harassed how?" Pines asked.

"There were times three or four gang members would get on the elevator. They'd play with my tits. Sometimes … sometimes finger me."

"They wanted more," Pines said. "A handjob. A blowjob."

"I got slapped in the face and punched in the stomach, but I didn't go down on anyone. I don't give a fuck if you believe me."

"How many boyfriends you got?" Pines pressed.

"None. My friend Kneisha is real religious. She's saving herself for marriage."

"And you got religion?" Pines said, her voice dripping with sarcasm.

"Ain't religious, but with boys I follow her lead," Aiyana said. "Ask my classmates."

"You into girls? You and Kneisha … the two of you?"

"I'm not a lesbian," Aiyana said. "You gots your mind in the gutter."

"Okay, then why the provocative top? You wore no bra. You could see your breasts through it. It was like a neon sign—come and fuck me," Pines said.

"Not *rape* me," Aiyana snapped. "It was my sixteenth birthday. I wanted to feel sexy."

"You wanted attention," Pines said. It wasn't a question.

"Damn straight. Wanted all the guys at the club we were

going to to be looking at *me*. Wanting *me*. I wasn't planning on losing my virginity," Aiyana explained.

"But it would have been a damn fine birthday present."

"My blouse wasn't an invitation for rape," Aiyana repeated.

"Girl, you're either incredibly naïve or full of shit," Pine attacked. "Boys your age and older think with their dicks, not their brains. You come in flashing your tits and they want to get into your pants. You weren't going there for stimulating conversation."

"I never made it to the club," Aiyana said. "To be honest I don't know what I would have done if I got hit on at the club. But it would have been *my* choice."

"Why invite danger with your see-through blouse?"

"We're going in circles," Aiyana said. "Condemn me if you want for what I wore, but don't tell me I asked to be raped."

"You're holding something back. I can feel it in my bones," Pines said. "Like I told you before, I'm going to talk to everyone in your life. Everyone in the towers, too. Not about your so-called rape, but your reputation. You're lying ... by omission. When I'm done with you, I'll know what you're hiding."

"Knock yourself out," Aiyana said. "While you're at it, find out why nobody from the towers watching me get attacked came to my aid or called the cops. It's them I have contempt for."

Pines continued to pepper her with variations of the same questions she had already asked, but got nowhere. After an hour she made eye contact with Aiyana. "We'll be talking again when I punch holes in your story. A day or a week from now, I'll learn the truth. Count on it."

Aiyana gave Pines the finger.

Pines shook her head. "Classy," she said and left.

CHAPTER TWELVE

Aiyana seethed after Pines left, then cursed herself. She'd given the detective the reaction Pines desired instead of confirming she was a victim. Pines had played her. Aiyana hadn't told Pines the truth, but there was no one to contradict her. Most of what she said had been accurate. That she'd gone out that night to mate was something Pines would never learn. Still, the detective could make life miserable for her—poking around and talking to classmates, teachers, and residents of the towers. Aiyana wanted to remain under the radar. She knew she was pregnant. She also wanted revenge against those who hadn't come to her aid and hadn't called the police. She couldn't do anything with Pines poking around.

She decided to contact Morales. He might be a rookie beat cop, but he had treated her like a human being. With kids of his own, he wouldn't allow Pines to bully her. Pines had been right—she had played Morales. He would be a sympathetic ear.

She sighed. Maybe she was deluding herself. Morales *was* a rookie. He might get nowhere with Pines. She might have to take on the detective herself. She smiled at the thought.

CHAPTER THIRTEEN

Aiyana had acted like a typical rape victim when she returned home from the hospital, but it was all an act. She didn't go to school. She wore the same PJs while she stayed at home. She didn't shower, showed little appetite, and spent most of her time in her room. Her mother had to change the bandage on her cheek to avoid infection. She refused to see Kneisha, who came by daily. That was her only regret.

Within the confines of her room, Aiyana could be herself. In a manner of speaking, she had summoned her rapist, urinating slightly to attract a mate. Her see-through blouse was also worn to arouse. Even in her human form, she could have defended herself more forcefully. But the path she had seen in her dreams had driven her. Aggressive, even violent sex would end with her impregnated. Even after only three days, she knew she was with child.

Wearing the same PJs and not showering allowed Aiyana to breathe in her animal aroma. Repulsive to most, her stench exhilarated her.

After another day or two, she would slowly climb out of the funk she had manufactured. She would make sure her parents were aware the worst was over. She had no desire to go to—and lie to—a therapist the family couldn't afford. And when she was certain she was pregnant, she would tell her parents it was a blessing and not a reminder of her rape.

Three days after her rape, Aiyana answered a knock on her door at 4 p.m. "Who is it?" she asked, as she would not open the door to strangers.

"Officer Morales."

Aiyana opened the door and smiled at the officer. She had decided not to call him, as he was no match for Pines, a seasoned detective. But she was glad he had come on his own. She invited him in and pointed to a frayed couch which dominated the small living room.

Morales instead went over to a mantle holding dozens of photos in inexpensive frames. He picked each one up several showing Aiyana and her parents when she was seven or eight. "You have a radiant smile," he told her.

He then looked at the photos taken after Aiyana had turned eleven. "Not so much in these," he said, looking at her. "Why the change?"

She wanted to ask why he was visiting, but she reined in her impatience. "Life happened, Officer."

"Estefan," he corrected her with a smile.

"The projects stole my innocence ... Estefan," she went on. "I began ... developing ... you know ... breasts. I was groped in elevators. I became familiar with death. A week after my eleventh birthday, a boy I knew was shot in the head in a fight not far from the planter where I was raped. I was playing double-dutch not far away. The first of far too many deaths of those not much older than I was. There's not much to smile about living in the towers."

"How are you doing?" Morales asked.

She was aware he was appraising her. Knew he could smell the rancid odor of her body. Could see her disheveled appearance. She hadn't brushed her long black hair since her return from the hospital. She looked a mess—intentionally. He had given her an opening, however.

"I'd be doing a lot better if that bitch detective wasn't forever hassling me," she replied. "Sorry about the profanity," she hastily added.

"Pines?" he asked.

She nodded. "She came over the day I was released and had me rehash my rape for an hour. She was trying to trap me in a lie. She asked her questions in different ways, you know, but I knew what she was up to. She spoke to my parents. Made them feel like they neglected me. She had my blouse with her and kept asking them how they could let me out of the house all but topless. She brought over mug books another day and had me go through them a page at a time, asking which looked most like my rapist. I kept telling her I didn't get a good look at him, but she ignored me." She began to tear up.

"I'd give you a hug," Morales said, "but I'm sure you don't want to be touched." He paused. "I have some good and bad news, I guess."

"Start with the bad," she said. "This way you can end on a high note."

"The investigation into your rape is officially closed," he said. "Detectives can't spend more than a few days on most cases. New cases pile up. Pines and Abernathy went back on the wheel today. That means they grabbed a new case. Without a description of your attacker, and with the residents of the towers refusing to cooperate, there was little they could do. I'm sorry."

"Don't be," Aiyana said. "I blame those who didn't come to my aid more than the boy who raped me." She paused. "What's the good news?"

"Well from what you told me, you won't be harassed by Pines anymore."

"When was the case closed?" Aiyana asked.

"Abernathy called me yesterday afternoon," Morales said. "He may not be much of a detective, but he's a decent guy."

"Then why was Pines questioning me this morning?" Aiyana asked. "She also spoke to my teachers today. Kneisha told me."

"I-I have no idea why," Morales said. "Like I told you, the case is closed."

"Not for Pines," Aiyana said. "Look, Offi ... Estefan. I was a fool to go out at night with that see-through blouse. I had a jacket when I left the apartment so my parents couldn't see what I was wearing. But it was humid outside so I took it off. Pines thinks the boy who attacked me may have been my boyfriend. If she could prove it, she told me, she would charge me. When she questioned Kneisha, she wanted to know all the boys I was friends with. Kneisha set her straight. I don't hang with boys. I don't flirt at school. Kneisha is my only close friend. She all but called Kneisha a liar. She asked the same questions when she spoke to my teachers."

"She's out of line," Morales said. "The case is closed."

"Then can I tell her to go fuck herself if she returns?" Aiyana asked. Tears streamed down her cheek. "I'm sorry for the vulgarity. It's not me. She's just been hassling me. I hardly get any sleep at night." She paused. "Not because I'm thinking of the rape. I'm wondering what Pines will do next."

"You might want to use different language, but yes, you don't have to speak to her again. Your parents can file a complaint with her sergeant if she doesn't back off."

"I'm pregnant," Aiyana said. She smiled.

"You couldn't know after just four days," Morales said. "I told you my wife was pregnant. She noticed some changes in her body something like three weeks after she … conceived. She went for a blood test for confirmation. But after just four days—"

"I just know," Aiyana said.

"Let's say you are," Morales said. "Will you have an abortion?"

"Hell, no."

"You want the child of your rapist?" he asked.

"If she looks like me, I'll adore her," Aiyana said. "If not, I might give her up for adoption."

"Will you finish school?" Morales asked.

Aiyana smiled. "There are precious few jobs for those who graduate high school from the projects. I'm a C student. No way was I going to college. And you don't need a high school diploma to work at McDonald's or be a maid to rich white people."

"You're selling yourself short, Aiyana," Morales said.

"You're sweet … Estefan, but you hardly know me. No more talk about school."

"Do you want me to look for your rapist?" he asked. "I can put in an hour or two a few nights a week after my shift."

"I appreciate the offer, but you have a family who needs you. And you ain't gonna find the bastard. If he stared me in the face right now I couldn't identify him. I'm moving on. I'll be a lot better when I'm sure I'm pregnant. I know how I must look to you. How I smell. I'll get over myself."

"Can I come by again to see how you're doing?" Morales asked.

"Six months from now," Aiyana said. "When I'm showing."

Morales smiled. He gave Aiyana his card. "If Pines comes back after you tell her you know the case is closed, call me. My partner told me to begin collecting favors. It's not my thing, but maybe he's right. I won't let her harass you."

"You're a good man, Estefan," Aiyana said. "Come back in six months and we'll celebrate my child."

CHAPTER FOURTEEN

(TWO MONTHS LATER)

"My parents have been so cool since I told them I was pregnant," Aiyana said. She and Kneisha were in her room. Kneisha seemed to be in a world of her own, which had been the case for a good two weeks. "I began showing. I could have worn a sweater, like you did but I blurted it out at dinner," she went on.

Kneisha remained silent.

"So, I got an abortion today," Aiyana said. "Had the little bugger yanked right out of me."

"Uh-huh," Kneisha said then looked at her friend. "You did *what*?"

"I didn't have an abortion," Aiyana said. "You disappeared again. I-I had to get through to you. What's wrong?"

"What did your parents say when you told them you were pregnant?" Kneisha asked, not answering Aiyana's question. "I was kinda listening," she added and gave Aiyana a weak smile.

"We had a long talk," Aiyana continued. She wasn't going to let Kneisha off the hook, but her question could wait. "I told them I wanted to have the baby. If it looked like me, I'd cherish it— cherish *her*, actually. I'm sure it's a girl. If it didn't, I said I would probably put her up for adoption, but that's not gonna happen. She's *my* baby and I'm going to keep her—raise her to be strong."

"What about school?"

"By the time eleventh grade begins I'll really be showing," Aiyana said. "I've looked into it. I can be home schooled at no cost."

"And when she's born?

"I have lots of aunts and uncles, most right here in Southwark. When I'm in school, Nita—that's the name I've chosen for her—will be taken care of by family. She's my responsibility when I get home."

"So, no social life," Kneisha said.

"Don't have one now," Aiyana replied. "Got you though ... *Aunt* Kneisha."

Kneisha took a deep breath. "Not so much. With all that's happened I didn't know how to tell you."

"Tell me what?"

"My moms and I are moving down south ... like in four days."

"Why?"

"With Lester dead, we're having trouble making ends meet," Kneisha said. "Mom is behind in the rent. She would sit at the table deciding which bills to pay and which could wait another month. And she worries about the towers. Lester was killed. You got raped. It could be me next. She says it's too dangerous here. I couldn't argue with her about Southwark being dangerous, but I told her I'd get a job after school. Or drop out and get a full-time job if it meant staying here. She said no daughter of hers was going to drop out of school. Even if I did, all I'd get was a minimum-wage job and she still wouldn't be able to pay the bills. So, we're moving to North Carolina where she has relatives. I have no say in the matter."

"If Lester hadn't been killed, you wouldn't be moving," Aiyana said, aware of the irony. She'd killed Lester to help Kneisha, and now she was going to lose her friend as a result.

"Don't go there, Aiyana," Kneisha replied. "You know what he was doing to me. I had been contemplating suicide. *Seriously.*" She paused. "I know you killed him."

"What are you talking about?" Aiyana said.

"That night when I stayed over after I told you what he had done to me. You killed him. Saved my sanity. Maybe my life."

"How do you know?" Aiyana asked.

"I was awake when you returned. You smelled of his cologne," Kneisha said. "Some cheap shit that made me nauseous. The next day, when I learned he had been killed, it all came together."

"Do you hate me?" Aiyana asked. "I mean, I didn't ask you if that's what you wanted. You were threatened. I acted impulsively. Maybe there was another way..." she said and trailed off.

"Fuck no to both. You're my hero. No one has ever looked out for me like you have. There was no other alternative. *I wanted him dead.* No one will ever know. Promise."

The two embraced. "I don't want to lose you," Aiyana said.

"We'll write. I'll call you one week, you'll call me the next. I'll convince my moms to let me visit, especially after the baby is born. And you can bring her down south for Christmas, spring break, and during the summer. Friends forever," Kneisha said, tears dripping down her cheeks.

Aiyana hugged her again. It was all wishful thinking. For a while they'd write and call. Kneisha might even visit once after Nita was born. But a long-distance friendship? Aiyana knew that wasn't in the cards.

BOOK TWO

CHAPTER FIFTEEN

Danai
(1995)

Sergeant Estefan Morales sat at his desk in his cramped office. Danai Townes, a beat cop, had asked to speak with him. The name sounded familiar. Morales couldn't quite place it, though. It was within his grasp when there was a knock on his door.

Morales appraised the woman who walked in. She was short, no more than five-foot four, a lean light-skinned black woman with shoulder-length hair. Even in the fluorescent light Morales could see tinges of red in her unruly brown curls. She had high cheekbones and an almost gaunt face lit by expressive dark eyes. Like all beat cops, she wore a police uniform which all but obscured her body.

"What can I do for you, Officer Townes?" Morales asked. It was only 10 a.m., but he had already taken off his suit jacket, loosened his tie, and unfastened the top button on his dress shirt. No matter what the temperature outside, his office felt stifling. It was as if the thermostat was permanently set at eighty degrees whether it was summer or winter.

"I want to report a murder—possibly several," Danai said.

"You've got my attention," Morales said. "A possible serial killer. Who is the victim ... or should I say, victims?"

"My father," Danai said. "He was murdered when I was six, seventeen years ago."

"Was there a police investigation at the time?" Morales asked.

"A cursory one," Danai replied. "We lived ... *still* live in the

Southwark Projects. A black man killed is a weekly occurrence. Most are blamed on gang violence. No one was arrested." Danai said. "The case was closed in less than a week. Like I said, there was no arrest."

Morales suddenly recalled why Danai's name was familiar. "I spoke to your parents seventeen years ago after the rape of Aiyana Jackson. Their five-year-old daughter Danai was asleep. That would be you."

Danai nodded. "I turned six two months later," she said. "They said I was asleep, but I wasn't. I was in the hallway when they let you in. You … you weren't like cops I had seen at the projects. They only came when there was a body. They were loud and angry. One even threatened me if I didn't tell him who had shot this boy. You and my parents had a … a civil conversation. I only heard bits and pieces, but you left without harassing them."

"Your parents saw Aiyana's rape but refused to cooperate with me," Morales said.

"Can you blame them?" Danai asked. "The towers—"

"I remember what your father told me—almost word for word—and I can't disagree with him not wanting to testify. Still, when he saw Aiyana being raped he could have made an anonymous 9-1-1 call."

"I was told no one called 9-1-1 until after the rapist fled," Danai said. "My father was wrong. Call him a coward if you want, but he didn't deserve to be murdered."

"You have a suspect in mind," Morales said. It wasn't a question.

"Aiyana Jackson," Danai replied.

"And she's waited seventeen years to kill again?" Morales said. "Why now?"

"Her daughter, Nita, was gang raped six months ago," Danai said. "She's pregnant. I think an investigation would uncover other victims besides my father who were murdered in the past seventeen years. As a beat officer I don't have access to files you would."

"Are you aware I have a history with Aiyana Jackson?"
Danai nodded.
"That I'm sympathetic towards her?"

"That's the reason I came to you," Danai replied. "If I've jumped to an erroneous conclusion, you'll rein me in. But I've done my homework. You're good police. You're not just out for yourself. You're not corrupt. I'm counting on you to do the right thing if we prove Aiyana killed my father."

"*We?*" Morales asked. "I'm a sergeant, not a detective. You've piqued my interest, but I would normally turn the case over to my detectives." He paused and typed into his desktop computer then frowned. "Detective Chompsky was assigned the most recent case. That's the one anyone would focus on initially— not a seventeen-year-old cold case. And, I'll tell you for a fact that Chompsky's boss won't be happy if I try to poach a case his detective says is closed."

"That's why *we* investigate," Danai said, leaning forward in her chair. She ran her hand through her unruly hair. "You and me ... off the books."

Morales held up his hand. "What's the name of the most recent victim?" he asked.

"Shawn Hawkins," Danai replied.

Morales typed on his computer. He was sweating. He wiped his forehead with his shirt sleeve. He read the medical examiner's report, then looked at Danai. Several tangled curls had fallen to her forehead, almost obscuring her eyes. She pushed the hair off her forehead with her hand. She'd done it before and would surely do so again.

"A fatal bite to the back of the head," Morales read.

"Just like my father," Danai replied. "One of the detectives who investigated my father's death jokingly said it looked like an animal attack. Not a dog. A *big* animal."

"You're holding something back from me," Morales said. "Not the way to start a ... collaboration."

"I-I have a theory, but before I share it we should determine just how many other similar attacks there were and if they connect—"

"To Aiyana," Morales finished for her. "And there's the *we* again." Morales scrutinized the young woman sitting across from him. She met his stare. "Your father's death has defined you. Seventeen years. It's why you became a cop, right?"

Danai nodded. "You're my only hope. Say no and I'll have to wait until I'm a detective myself, which will take years. But I won't be denied even if it takes another seventeen years. Meanwhile Aiyana will kill again … if I'm right." Danai wiped a tear that had made its way down her cheek.

"We do it my way or we don't do it at all," Morales said after several moments of silence. "I'll get you a temporary transfer, but we keep a low profile. We focus on your father's death so Chompsky's boss doesn't try to shut us down. Go off the reservation just once and we're done. Agreed?"

Danai nodded.

"You interview Shawn Hawkins's family and also those who witnessed but didn't report Nita's rape. Knowing the projects I'm assuming there were witnesses who didn't want to become involved. They turned a blind eye to what they had seen. You're from Southwark. They just might confide in you even if it's off the record."

"And you?" Danai asked.

"I'll speak with the coroner," Morales replied. "See if there are other deaths that are similar. And I want to talk to the detective who investigated your father's death. We see where it leads us and then determine where to go from there. Work for you?"

Danai nodded.

"At some point you'll have to tell me what you're omitting, especially if there were other victims. Agreed?"

Danai nodded.

"Going all silent on me all of a sudden," Morales said.

"I-I thought you'd blow me off—a rookie beat cop with a preposterous theory."

"I remember your father," Morales said. "He should have called for help, but he was a good man. He was conflicted. And, I think, remorseful that he didn't act. He and your mother were the only residents of the towers who spoke to me other than to tell me to get the hell away."

As Danai left, Morales thought of Georgia Pines for the first time in years. She had dismissed him as a rookie too green to work a rape case. He wasn't Pines. He'd give Danai the opportunity to prove her case.

CHAPTER SIXTEEN

After Danai left, Morales pondered the implications of Danai's accusation. He couldn't imagine Aiyana killing Danai's father in the violent manner she described. She hadn't appeared physically strong enough to take on a man of Danai's father's size. William Townes was close to six feet tall and a good one hundred pounds heavier than Aiyana.

(1979)

Morales had visited Aiyana six months after her attack as he had promised—rather, as Aiyana had instructed. He had called at 11 a.m. expecting Aiyana's mother to answer the phone. He was surprised Aiyana was home. She told him to come over.

Morales's eyes were immediately drawn to Aiyana's midsection after she answered the door.

She laughed. "Told you I wasn't getting an abortion."

Morales saw that she hadn't gained a lot of weight as many pregnant women do. His wife, for example, referred to herself as a blimp with each of her pregnancies. Aiyana's face was still lean, as were her arms and legs. If she didn't live in the projects, he would have assumed she had joined a gym. She wore a sleeveless dress that exposed her slim legs.

"Why aren't you in school?" Morales asked.

"I dropped out," Aiyana said. "I was offered a tutor, but I'm learning about life by living it. My classmates looked at me oddly at school when I began showing. Talked behind my back. They knew the baby's father was my rapist. They never confronted me, but I overhead them at times. Why didn't I get an abortion? Carry my rapist's child? *Gross.* I don't go out much even here at the towers. Those same cowards who watched as I was raped without coming to my aid had the same questions. Kneisha—remember I told you about her?" Aiyana asked but went on before Morales could respond. "Her mother moved her down south. Southwark was too dangerous."

"So you have no one," Morales said.

Aiyana patted her belly. "Got my little one."

"Did you go for therapy?" he asked, knowing the answer.

"You know my parents couldn't afford it and my school counselor was no better than my classmates. I talked to her once. She was judgmental rather than supportive." She paused. "I've come to terms with my rape. He left me with something precious."

After a bit more small talk, Morales left. He wanted to return after Aiyana's baby was born, but he didn't want to be intrusive. From his own children he knew how difficult the first months of parenthood could be. Aiyana was probably getting little sleep. There could also be mood swings. His wife had suffered from those after the birth of their second child. And Aiyana had isolated herself. She had no support system. There was no Kneisha to be her confidant.

Around six months after Morales guessed Aiyana had given birth, he received a call from her. "Hey stranger, want to come and visit? See my daughter?"

He immediately recognized her voice even though she didn't identify herself. He was on the 4 p.m. to midnight shift. He was at Aiyana's apartment twenty minutes after his shift ended.

"The spitting image of you," Morales said, as he held Aiyana's daughter. "Are you happy?"

"Ecstatic," she said. "To be honest I was worried she might look like ... like *him.* But she looks like me, for better or worse," she said and laughed. She then stifled a yawn.

"Not getting much sleep, are you?" he asked.

"Nita's my responsibility. I'm not about to pawn her off on my parents. She sleeps in my room. Sometimes she sleeps through the night. Other times she's ... I guess you could say restless and wakes up two or three times."

"Are you going to return to school?" he asked.

"To what end?" Aiyana asked. She went on before Morales could respond. "I'm a full-time mother. I can live with that."

"Don't you have any dreams? Something you aspire to?" he clarified.

"Any dreams I had died with my attack," she replied. "Even then I was just muddling through school."

"You still harbor no bitterness toward your rapist?" Morales asked. He remembered what she had said at the hospital.

"I have my baby girl," Aiyana said. "I try not to dwell on the past."

"Try?"

"When I take Nita outside I see some of the same people from the towers who watched me get raped without lifting a finger. The faces of those looking down at me are ... etched, is the word ... etched into my mind. They stare at me now. I meet their eyes. They turn away. Cowards then. Cowards now."

"So you haven't completely moved on," Morales said.

"Are you volunteering to be my therapist?" she asked with a smile. Before he could answer she continued. "I've gotten better. A month after the rape, I was so mad at them I went door to door and confronted them. I cursed them out. Asked them *why* they did nothing. Some refused to let me in so I screamed at them through their doors. I accomplished nothing. One or two threatened to call the police," she said, and laughed. "That's *irony* for you. Learned the word at school. They refused to call the police when I was being raped, but when I called them out, calling the cops was their first thought."

"Idle threats, right?" Morales asked.

Aiyana nodded. "They had no desire to be seen speaking to the police. Anyway, now I just silently meet their stares when I'm outside with Nita. They know what I'm thinking. In a way I prevailed. And each day their guilt is compounded. Some rush back into the towers when I come outside. I silently laugh. Others turn away. Guilt festers, Estefan. My presence with Nita reminds them of their cowardice. I can live with that."

(1995)

Now, Morales wondered if Aiyana had done more than just verbally confront her neighbors. She clearly had far more antipathy
for those in the towers than towards her rapist. Was it possible
she couldn't live with just shaming them? It was still difficult to
entertain the thought of Aiyana killing Danai's father. He was
bigger. He was stronger. What had Danai held back from him?
At lunch he'd visit the medical examiner. Maybe Danai had
exaggerated her father's wounds.

CHAPTER SEVENTEEN

Danai couldn't believe Morales had agreed to investigate her father's murder. She had rehearsed what she would tell him dozens of times in front of a mirror. When she had walked into his office, though, she had been tongue-tied. To her surprise, Morales hadn't dismissed her out of hand. When he'd probed, she had found herself trying to convince him that Aiyana Jackson had killed her father. That there had been another similar death recently had piqued his interest. He had been skeptical. Just how well had he known Aiyana? *Is Aiyana a spider who ensnared Morales in her web?* she wondered.

She had one more card to play if he decided Aiyana was innocent. The question was, would he believe her or consider her certifiable? She sometimes questioned what she had seen herself.

For now, she would follow the sergeant's lead. Morales was unaware there had been two other murders identical to her father's—one two years later and another three years after the second. She knew the families. They still resided at Southwark. She would interview them. With three murders plus the more recent one, Morales would have to take her seriously. Someone had killed three people in the same manner within a few years after Aiyana's rape, without anyone tying the three together. Now another had been murdered under similar circumstances.

Danai couldn't say she'd had an idyllic childhood even before her father's murder. She had lived in the projects, after all, where despair was an all-enveloping fog.

Being light-skinned at an all-black school was a challenge. Danai was teased mercilessly. Sharon, one of her tormenters, was black as tar, but skin tone didn't make her any more black than Danai. At least that's what Danai's parents had told her. *Both* were light-skinned blacks.

"Which one of your parents is black?" Sharon asked Danai once.

"Both," Danai replied, wondering why this girl hated her so much just because she was light-skinned.

"You're lying, bitch," Sharon shot back.

Danai wanted to knock Sharon on her ass, but her father had told her time and again—before he was killed—that violence would only be playing into the hand of bullies. "Expose your weakness," he'd told her, "and it's like a target on your back. Rein in your temper and they'll find someone else to harass."

Danai channeled her frustrations into sports. In fifth grade she was on both the soccer and basketball teams. Her mother had played basketball in high school and taught her the game. Her mother would have gotten a scholarship for college if it weren't for disciplinary problems. She was hot-tempered and her many fights got her suspended far too often. She had mellowed with marriage and a child and taught Danai to be a point guard. Danai often had to rein in her own temper. Girls on other teams taunted her about her light skin color—called her Oreo and even questioned whether she was black. Playing team sports allowed her to be aggressive and channeled her rage. She gave hard fouls that were uncalled for. Several times a girl from another team got in her face and shoved her. She controlled herself and backed off. More than a few times the other girl was tossed from the game.

"At your height, Danai, point guard is all you can play," her mother told her. "But it's the most important position on a basketball team. You be da boss."

Her mother taught her skills, but also the psychology of the position. "As a point guard you can't have an ego. You make everyone look better with your passing. You won't have gaudy stats but your teammates will adore you."

Her father's murder left a gaping hole within the family. Her mother no longer smiled. To pay the rent she took on a menial job. When she'd get home she would drink until she passed out. Teaching Danai how to play basketball seemed to be their only connection.

Danai initially became an introvert at school. Each night she relived what she had seen—what she hadn't told the police and later withheld from Morales. She didn't apply herself at school, settling for a C average when with a little more effort she would have been a B or A student.

She could have excelled at basketball at school, but she often became distracted. She ended up on the bench her junior year of high school, then quit the team.

She also became rebellious in high school, though nothing held her attention for very long. She led a demonstration to include abortion and the use of condoms in a sex education class. As the group's leader she was suspended from school for a week.

She later led a sit-in to demand the inclusion of Malcolm X and the Black Panthers in her history class where Rosa Parks and Martin Luther King were the only civil rights leaders in their history text books.

She was suspended again. She saw her principal so often some might have thought they were having an affair. She dropped out of the protest group because they were so fragmented. Some advocated violence. Others just as vociferously were opposed. The two groups clashed more with one another than they would with members of the KKK.

She wore piercings well before they were fashionable— her way of rebelling. She had a nose ring, a tongue piercing, three rings over her right eyebrow and four studs in each of her ears. She added nipple and naval piercings her senior year but couldn't bring herself to add one to her clitoris.

Somewhat sadly, she had removed the various studs and rings when she applied for the police academy.

She had a single tattoo over her left breast. It could be seen when she wore a top that exposed a lot of cleavage or a blouse with two buttons unfastened. The tattoo was of a jaguar.

CHAPTER EIGHTEEN

At lunchtime Morales went to see the chief medical examiner. Ed Cawley appeared to be a solemn man with no sense of humor. Get to know him, though, and he exposed a wry wit and engaging smile. He was 6 feet 7 inches, a splinter of a man Morales could envision working at a funeral home. He wore a black suit to work each day. *Does he have just one*, Morales wondered, *or a closet full of them?* He was sixty-two but looked far older. He had a full head of white hair and horn-rimmed glasses. The last time Morales had spoken with him, he could see a slight tremor in his right hand. Had he been working on the living, he would have been forced to retire. As it was, he had broached retirement to Morales three years earlier and then again the year before. Cawley was a widower with two grown children but no grandchildren, and Morales wondered if one day he would have to be carried out of the morgue. He didn't see Cawley retiring of his own volition any time soon.

The M.E.'s most distinguishing features were his long, delicate fingers—those of a surgeon who worked on the living. He had a crusty exterior to most who demanded quick answers that he often couldn't provide. The dead spoke to him but withheld many secrets.

Morales had always treated Cawley with respect when he was a homicide detective. When he was promoted, one of the first things he did as sergeant was to instruct his detectives to do the same.

"Cawley is invaluable," he'd told them. "Get on his good side and he'll go the extra mile for you. He'll jump you ahead of those who consider him to be no more than a technician."

He now entered the morgue and walked up to Cawley. "How's it going, Ed?" Morales greeted him.

"What are you doing down here, kid? You're a sergeant," he replied. Cawley referred to those he liked as "kid" regardless of their age. Behind the back of those who irritated him, the term "asshole" was often heard.

"Don't rub it in, Ed," he said, and smiled. "I miss our chats." Without family obligations, Morales would have gladly remained a homicide detective. He had no desire to be a supervisor of others and sit on the sidelines during investigations. But the extra pay was a necessity. In several years he might be forced to move further up the ladder to lieutenant—but also further from the action he so missed. Maybe that was one reason he had been so easily persuaded to investigate Danai's father's murder. He felt more alive in the morgue now than he had at any time since his promotion.

"Got a question for you about an old case—a cold case that might be linked to another a few months ago."

"Something *unusual*?" Cawley asked with a glimmer in his eyes.

"Challenging ... and possibly unusual," Morales answered.

"Do tell," Cawley said.

Morales told him about Danai's father. "It was seventeen years ago," he repeated when he had finished.

"When you said cold case, you weren't exaggerating," Cawley responded. He stroked the goatee on his chin. "It wouldn't be in the computer," he said. Morales thought he was speaking as much to himself as to his guest. "They input the most recent data first. There's not enough staff to make a dent in the older cases." He paused a moment. "I'm told computers make things easier, but I like to look at a physical file. Reading what a coroner has to say, you get a sense of both the ME and the victim that you can't find in a computer. Notes in the margin, scraps of paper sometimes, with random thoughts to be explored later, for instance. For William Townes, I'll have to dig up the file—no easy chore."

"If it's asking too much—"

Cawley waved his hand to silence Morales. "If you have a

mystery for me I'd do it in a heartbeat," he said. "Most autopsies I perform aren't even required. A bullet to the head is pretty self-explanatory, for instance. Let me find the file and compare it to the more recent homicide. Come back at 6 a.m. tomorrow."

"That early?"

"You gotta work on my timetable, Estefan," he said. "I do have a day job with detectives down my throat for autopsy results. If I find something juicy we need the time to go over it and I don't want to be disturbed by assholes who have no patience whatsoever."

Morales was about to leave but hesitated. "Since you'll be going through actual files, let me put this in context so you're not flying blind. Townes' death may be—I stress *may* be—related to the rape of Aiyana Jackson. Both are cold cases which weren't solved."

"Thanks for the clarification," Cawley said. "Not sure if it will help but the more information I have the better."

Before Morales left he put a box of Whoppers—chocolate covered malt balls—on Cawley's desk. He wouldn't see it until later. Cawley loved Whoppers, and Morales always left a box when he visited the ME. He had told his detectives they'd be smart to do the same.

CHAPTER NINETEEN

It wasn't until several years after her father's death that Danai was certain she was a lesbian. Her attraction to women wasn't something she could speak to her mother about. Until Rain entered her life, she knew no one who was gay. She wasn't about to walk into a bookstore and ask if there were any books on homosexuality. She feared her school counselor would be judgmental rather than helpful and supportive. And she feared her counselor might contact her mother.

At school, in the ninth grade, she found herself looking at the breasts of a young substitute teacher. They weren't particularly large, but the woman didn't wear a bra. Danai stared at the nipples whose contours she could clearly see under the tight top her teacher wore. That night she dreamed of touching her teacher's breasts. She also found herself, when she was in tenth grade, eyeing female classmates who were more developed than she was. She was careful not to allow her stare to linger.

Fearful of the repercussions of being outed, she dated a few boys. She even lost her virginity to a basketball player on the boy's team in the tenth grade. She hadn't enjoyed the experience at all, but she avoided suspicions that she might arouse if she didn't date.

Rain was a shooting guard on the girls' basketball team. Her dark brown skin was flawless. Her hair was permed straight and she had blonde highlights. Danai thought she was beautiful. She had a gorgeous smile and an infectious laugh. Her body was toned from playing basketball. She had large breasts that often distracted Danai on the basketball court. Danai would watch them jiggle beneath her uniform as she ran back on defense after a missed shot.

Like Danai, Rain lived in the Southwark Towers. They would often walk home together after practice.

One day in the eleventh grade, after basketball practice, Rain asked Danai if she wanted to sit on a bench outside of the towers when they reached home. It was mid-September. A warm mist fell that both enjoyed. Because of the rain, they were the only ones outside.

"Tell me if I'm out of line and this conversation never occurred," Rain said. She had a husky voice Danai thought was sexy. "I've seen you looking at me," Rain said.

"Looking at you?" Danai replied. She wanted to run into the towers. Rain knew she was a lesbian. Would tell everyone on the team—

"Like I look at you," Rain said, cutting Danai's thoughts off. "I-I'm into girls. Well, make that … *shit*," Rain said. She took a deep breath. "This is so fucking awkward." She paused again. "Look, I've *never* been with a girl, you know, like having sex. I don't have a girlfriend. But I look at you on the basketball court and I've caught you eyeing me, too. Am I way off base or—"

"I *have* been looking at you," Danai said, saying it in a rush before fear silenced her. "I just wasn't aware you were interested in me." She paused. "You are hitting on me, aren't you?"

"Bet your ass," Rain said.

Danai blushed. *What now?* she wondered.

"Why haven't you come out?" Rain asked.

"I could ask you the same," Danai responded.

"I asked first," Rain said with a broad smile.

Danai laughed, then sobered. "My father was murdered when I was six. Ever since his death I wanted to be a cop. His killer was never captured. When I first became attracted to girls there were some—not a lot, but enough—articles about the obstacles lesbians faced in certain professions. A lesbian cop would be ostracized. I mean, it's difficult enough for straight women to become a cop and be accepted by male officers. For a gay woman it would be impossible." She paused. "And you?"

"I'm more cowardly than you," Rain said. "I like being the

center of attention at school because I'm the team's star player. I don't want to be bullied. I'll come out when it's time—maybe in college, if I can get a scholarship."

The two became inseparable. As they were teammates, no one thought it odd that they hung together—not even after Danai quit the team. She still came to games to cheer her former teammates on. She actually came to see Rain play, but she applauded the other girls as well when they scored a basket or stole the ball. There was no hand-holding or other overt expressions that might betray them. A lot of girls hung out with other girls in high school.

Three weeks after their chat, they made love—or was it just sex?—for the first time in Danai's apartment. Her mother was at work. It was more a relief for both of them than a pleasurable experience. Both fumbled and stumbled and had no idea what to do. There was no manual when Danai was in high school for how to make out with another woman. With practice, however, they both became adept at giving the other pleasure.

"It's a shame we can't come out," Danai told her lover as they lay next to one another, each staring at the other's body.

"Where did that come from?" Rain asked.

"I want to show you off," Danai said. "Tell others this gorgeous girl is my lover. I sometimes feel like a fraud. We both go to school dances and stay on the opposite sides of the room. I dance with boys who put their hands on my ass when we slow drag."

"I've noticed," Rain said with a smile.

"I want to tell them that my ass belongs to you."

"All of you belongs to me," Rain corrected, then gave a gentle pinch to one of Danai's nipples.

"When school's out we should take a bus to Atlantic City. Lie on the beach and make out under a blanket," Danai said.

"And risk being seen by someone from school?" Rain countered.

"A girl can dream, can't she?" Danai said.

They remained lovers until the end of the summer after both graduated. Rain had a basketball scholarship at the University of Maryland. Danai had been accepted into the police academy.

They saw each other only when Rain had no school and returned home. In her freshman year Rain came out and quickly had a girlfriend who was on the basketball team. She and Danai remained friends but drifted apart.

Danai was careful not to be seen with women at local clubs or bars. She slept with a male recruit at the academy her first year. No one suspected she was gay. She met her physical needs with one-night stands or short flings. She'd meet women at the University of Penn's gay pride center. Some she met pressured her to come out of the closet.

"It would be so great for all of us if we could point to an openly gay police officer," she was told on more than one occasion.

Great for you and other lesbians, Danai thought to herself, but never uttered the words. *Not so much for my career.*

Maybe, when she and Morales proved Aiyana Jackson had murdered her father, she would come out. Or maybe it wasn't in the cards if she wanted to advance her career.

CHAPTER TWENTY

Morales brought Danai with him the next morning to meet with Cawley. He had debated whether to do so. In all fairness, he decided, she should hear what the medical examiner had to offer. After Cawley had his say, there might be no case.

When they walked into the morgue Cawley stood transfixed by Danai. "And who is this gorgeous young woman?" Cawley greeted them. "Your daughter, Estefan?"

Morales saw Danai blush. "You're more perceptive than that, Ed," he said. "There is no resemblance between the two of us, and you know damn well I've never cheated on my wife." He paused. "She is Danai Townes. Her father is the victim from seventeen years ago I told you about. She's on the job. She brought me the case."

"My condolences," Cawley said.

"It's been a long time," Danai said.

"Yet you're still grieving," Cawley replied. "Coming to Sergeant Morales for justice speaks volumes."

"Were you able to find anything?" Morales asked. He knew it was getting uncomfortable for Danai. Cawley had hit a nerve. He was correct, of course. Danai's life had been defined by her father's death.

"Come," he said. Cawley went into his office and wheeled out a metal table, a good seven feet in length. "My ... guests usually occupy the gurney. Today a number share just one ... in a manner of speaking."

Morales saw two rows of file folders, five closest to Cawley and another five behind them.

Cawley touched the second file closest to him. Morales could see his hand shake slightly. Cawley looked at Danai. "This is your father's file. Are you sure—"

"I'm not queasy, sir," Danai said.

"Call me Ed," Cawley said. He opened the file. "A most unusual head wound," he said. "If it means anything to you, your father died instantaneously. He didn't suffer."

"It *killed* him," Danai snapped. Morales saw Danai stare at the fatal wound. "I apologize. I-I saw my father lying on the living room floor. This blow-up of his head wound ..." she began then stopped. "I overreacted."

"Quite understandable," Cawley said.

"One detective joked it could be an animal attack," Danai said, as if she hadn't heard Cawley. "What did the coroner say?" she asked.

"Only blunt force trauma. A single blow," Cawley said. "There was a question mark in the margin." He looked at Morales. "That's why I'm glad I was able to get the coroner's original report. If this was computerized the question mark would have been missing."

"What does it mean?" Danai pressed.

"Meaning, my dear, he hadn't the foggiest notion what the weapon was that killed your father," Cawley said. "He's passed away, sadly, but he was competent." He turned to another page. "He used well over a dozen items that *could* have been the weapon on a cantaloupe but *none* matched the head wound."

"Could it have been an animal attack?" Danai asked.

"An animal your father let in his apartment?" Cawley asked in return, but didn't wait for Danai to respond. "How did this animal escape?" He paused. "Let's put that question on hold for now." He looked at Morales. "Such a wound piqued my curiosity. I looked at a number of cold cases for something similar. I concentrated my search on the Southwark Towers since that was where Danai's father was murdered. I later broadened by search, to no avail." He opened the first file folder. "Lester Phillips. He was murdered four years before your father," he said looking at Danai. "Same wound."

Morales saw Danai's face turn white. She grabbed onto the table. She took several deep breaths. Morales didn't press her. "I-I know him. Well, knew *of* him," Danai said. "He had a niece … Kneisha. She was Aiyana Jackson's best friend. From what I can recall, Lester had a reputation. He … pursued young women."

"Raped them?" Morales asked.

"He was a brute of a man, I was told. I only know about him because of Kneisha," Danai said.

"And her friendship with Aiyana," Morales added for Cawley's benefit.

"*If* he raped Kneisha, she never filed a complaint," Danai added.

"Let's see if you can shine any light on the next two," Cawley said and opened both file folders. Both had the exact same wound as Danai's father and Lester Phillips.

"Anything tie the four together?" Morales asked Cawley.

"They all resided in the Southwark Projects … more than just a coincidence," Cawley replied.

"All but Lester could have witnessed Aiyana's rape," Danai said.

"A bit of a leap, but possible," Morales said. He looked at the dates of the homicides.

"Austin Pierce," Cawley said, looking at Danai. "He was killed two years after your father. And the other is Darnell Washington. He was killed three years after Pierce."

"No one noticed a similarity in their deaths?" Morales asked.

"Different detectives investigated each case," Cawley said. "A different coroner performed the autopsy on each. These were never entered into a computer. Keep in mind the killings occurred in the seventies and early eighties. Has they been entered into a computer—if we had the capability then—one of the coroners would have definitely connected the four." He paused. "Guess computers *can* be useful," he added.

"And the last?" Morales asked.

Cawley opened the file folder. "The most recent—the one you mentioned to me. Shawn Hawkins. *Also* from the Southwark Projects."

"In your opinion, were they all killed by the same person?" Morales asked.

"Victims two, three, and four most definitely," Cawley said. "The wounds are identical. The wound on Lester Phillips and Shawn Hawkins are not as deep. *Could* be the same weapon, but not wielded with the same power. But press me and I'd say the same weapon was used. By the same person, though? That I can't confirm."

"And you have no idea what that weapon was?" Danai asked.

"We have progressed over the last sixteen years, young lady," Cawley said. "Vincent Palmer was the coroner who worked the last murder—the Hawkins case. He has a list." Cawley dug through the file and showed it to Danai and Morales. "He tested twenty-four possible weapons, using a computer program, that *could* cause such damage. He rejected all of them."

"So we're back to an animal attack?" Danai asked.

Both Cawley and Morales looked at her.

"Do you have information you're not sharing?" Cawley asked Danai.

Morales saw Danai's eyes go from Cawley to him, back to Cawley and then to him again. Morales knew she was still holding something back.

"I'm just frustrated," Danai finally said. "We're getting nowhere fast."

"I think not," Cawley said. "We've identified five individuals from the Southwark Projects killed in an identical manner, possibly with the same weapon wielded by the same person. We could be looking for one killer. These cases should be reopened. Connections explored. What do all five have in common besides the victims living in Southwark? And why the inactivity between the fourth killing over ten years ago and the latest murder?"

"Point taken," Morales said, without committing himself. "What about the other files?" he asked.

"You provided a context for me, Estefan," Cawley said. "You suggested they might all be connected to Aiyana Jackson's rape. I really don't know what the connection is but I let my curiosity get the best of me. I looked for cold cases in the area of the Southwark Projects around the time of the rape. You judge for yourself if there is any connection to the other killings or to the Jackson rape."

He opened the first file folder. "Lamar Cooper, eighteen. He belonged to the Southwark Kings. He was found three blocks from the projects in an alley. He died of complete organ failure. He wasn't shot, stabbed or beaten to death. A tox screen found no discernible poisons. There was heroin in his system but it wasn't related to his death."

"No discernible poisons?" Morales asked.

"Some toxins are difficult, if not impossible, to identify," Cawley elaborated. "In technical terms, the toxin could cause a precipitous drop in blood pressure which would destroy the kidneys first and the other organs would follow." Cawley then laid out half a dozen photographs. "This young man had quite a few scars and recent cuts and abrasions. None stood out as a possible cause of death, but keep them in mind as we discuss the others."

"Now *you're* withholding something," Morales said.

"You need to discover for yourself. I don't want to poison the well, so to speak," Cawley said. He opened the second folder, the tremor in his hand evident to Morales.

Morales was stunned. Georgia Pines. He was unaware she had died. "I knew her," Morales said. He looked at Danai. "She investigated Aiyana's rape. Actually, she harassed Aiyana. She wouldn't accept unequivocally that Aiyana was raped, which I found ludicrous then and do now.

"How did she die?" he asked Cawley.

"Complete organ failure, just like Lamar Cooper," Cawley said.

Morales looked at the date of death. "Six weeks after Aiyana's rape. She couldn't have still been working Aiyana's case. There had been no arrests. A cold case."

"Where was she found?" Danai asked.

"A few blocks from her apartment," Cawley said. "She lived on Eleventh and Wharton streets in South Philly. She was walking her dog when she collapsed. Was DOA when the paramedics got her to Jefferson Hospital."

"Why did you choose to investigate her death?" Morales

asked. "She didn't live ... or die near the Southwark Projects."

"The information you provided me, Estefan," Cawley said. "I checked Aiyana Jackson's file and saw that Pines was one of the detectives who worked her rape ... along with a Detective Paul Abernathy. I used a computer," he said, with a smile, "and found that Pines had died of complete organ failure, although there were no details in the computer—no file with the autopsy report. Abernathy, by the way is still alive. He's retired."

Morales and Danai looked at the photos of the body. One mark stuck out to both. Morales began to speak. Cawley told them to hold their thoughts until he showed them the last folders.

"I'm not sure how these last three relate to the Jackson rape," Cawley began," but all three died of complete organ failure. And all had the same mark as Cooper and Pines." He let Morales and Danai see the photos.

"All five have a scratch on the back of their left wrist," Danai said. "That's what you were talking about, right?" she asked.

"Yes, indeed," Cawley said with a smile.

"Aiyana's daughter was gang raped by three men," Danai said. "None were caught."

"They were found in the Southwark area," Cawley said. "One in an alley, the other two in their apartments."

"Anything unusual about the scratches?" Morales asked.

"Initially the coroners thought a woman might have scratched them, but all three coroners eventually came to the same conclusion independently. It's more like a scratch from a cat ... a big cat, at that. There was no DNA." Cawley paused. "So, have I helped you two, or further muddied the water?" he asked.

"You've connected five deaths as a result of blunt force trauma," Morales began. "And there definitely appears to be a connection between those who died of complete organ failure." He looked at Danai. "We're going to continue our investigation." He paused. "Do me a favor, Ed, and bury these files for now."

"I need to know why," Cawley said.

"You know the politics of the department," Morales began. "A number of detectives—some since promoted to sergeant or

above—will be, at the least, embarrassed by what you've uncovered. They might want to shut down an investigation so their
reputations won't be sullied. Danai and I will stay under the
radar. We make sense of it all and *then* we'll need you to buttress
our conclusions with these files."

"You're a pretty good politician yourself, Estefan," Cawley
said.

"Perish the thought," Morales said.

Cawley laughed. "What files are you referring to?" he asked
with a wink.

Morales and Danai left. Morales left two boxes of Whoppers
on Cawley's desk. He'd buy more for the medical examiner later.
Cawley had uncovered far more than Morales had expected. It
was still hard to fathom that Aiyana was responsible for any of
these deaths but he couldn't deny the connections to her rape
and that of her daughter.

"What do we do now?" Danai asked.

"You tell me what you've been holding back," Morales said.
"I have no desire to pursue the case with one hand tied behind
my back."

"You may not believe me," she replied.

"Let me be the judge of that. Spill."

Danai nodded. They went to a park a block away from
the Roundhouse, the headquarters for the Philadelphia Police
Department. It was mid-April—a bit too early for Philly's
oppressive summer. It was in the fifties with a slight breeze.

Once seated, Danai looked at Morales. "I saw my father
murdered," she began.

CHAPTER TWENTY-ONE

(1979)

Danai had just fallen asleep when she heard someone arguing with her father. It was a woman. Her mother was at work, so it couldn't be her. Her parents seldom argued. When one was mad at the other, if they couldn't discuss it civilly they would give one another a timeout to calm themselves down. It was the same way they treated Danai when she did something that truly irritated her parents. She was told to go to her room while her parents discussed how to handle the infraction.

Danai heard bits and pieces of a one-sided conversation.

"… coward."

"… saw the attack."

"… didn't have the balls to act."

"… call the police."

"… turned away."

"Spineless."

Her father remained silent. Then the woman stopped talking. Danai heard a growl. She tiptoed out of her room and hid behind a wall that led to the living room. She saw her father. Saw a huge cat, black as tar. The cat jumped onto her father's back and bit him in the back of his head. He fell to the ground.

The cat then changed into a woman. She was naked. Danai tried to get a good look at her face but it appeared shrouded by fog.

The woman spotted Danai. Their eyes met. The woman's eyes were reddish-yellow. Danai backed away, fearful of what this woman would do to her. Several minutes later, Danai heard the front door open, then close. She waited in her room for an hour. The woman … the big cat might be waiting for her. She finally came out of her room. The woman was gone. Her father was on the floor, a pool of blood surrounding his head. Danai sat next to her father.

While only six, she had seen two boys shot by rival gangs. They bled like her father. Didn't move, like her father. She talked to her father.

"Why was the woman so angry with you?" she asked the still figure. "Why did she hurt you? Why didn't she hurt me, too?"

She held onto her father's hand. Didn't let go until her mother returned hours later and called the police. "I'll get her for you, Daddy," she said aloud as her mother pulled her away and sent her to her room.

CHAPTER TWENTY-TWO

(1995)

"Two years later, at school—I was eight then—I saw the cat in a book. It was a jaguar." She paused. "So now you tell me I was dreaming … or delusional … or a six-year-old with a vivid imagination … or I was in shock—"

"I believe you," Morales said. "I mean, it *is* impossible, but when you've eliminated all that *is* possible you're left with the—"

"Impossible … what can't be explained," Danai finished for him.

"Let's go with what you saw," Morales said. "Cawley and his predecessors have eliminated dozens of weapons that they feel could have killed your father and the others. Cawley didn't rule out an animal attack."

"He all but—"

"But he didn't," Morales cut her off. "If Aiyana or some other woman could turn into a jaguar, it would explain the wound that killed your father and four other men."

"I replay what I heard her say to my father," Danai said. "It had to be Aiyana referring to her rape."

"It could have been her mother or someone else upset that your father didn't come to Aiyana's aid. You yourself said you couldn't identify her."

"And Lester Phillips?" Danai asked. "That was three years *before* Aiyana's rape. Kneisha's uncle. Aiyana's best friend. Kneisha had moved down south before my father was killed, so it couldn't have been her. How much more proof do you need before you begin to look at Aiyana as a suspect, not a victim?"

"Suspect *and* a victim," Morales said. "There's no disputing Aiyana was raped."

"Don't forget about those who died of organ failure," Danai said. "They were murdered too. All have the same scratch on their hand. Cawley said it could have come from a cat. Cooper could have been Aiyana's rapist. Pines was giving her a hard time—suggesting she wasn't raped. And Nita was gang raped by three assailants. Three teens later found dead due to extreme organ failure with the same scratch as the others. It all adds up."

"We need to investigate further," Morales said. "We have a theory. We need to buttress it with facts. Then comes the hard part—deciding what to do."

"What do you mean? We lock her ass up," Danai said, her voice rising.

"Come on Danai. You're not naïve," Morales said. "Why didn't you tell me what you saw when you first approached me?"

"You would have thought I was delusional ... or worse."

"And what will an assistant district attorney think if we tell him Aiyana can transform into a jaguar?" Morales asked.

"I get your point," Danai said, dejectedly. "Do we take matters into our own hands?"

"And do what?"

"Put her down. Nita too," Danai said.

"Let's not go there," Morales said. "I'm no vigilante. Let's make our case first and then decide on a course of action."

"You can't let them continue to kill," Danai said. "I won't," she added.

"You kill a woman and her teenage daughter you'll spend your life in prison," Morales said. "Saying they're shapeshifters in court might get you institutionalized, but do you want to spend your life in a mental ward?"

"So your solution is to do nothing," Danai said. "She's not— may have *never* been—the victim you sympathized with seventeen years ago. She still has your number."

"When ... *if* the time comes when we have a rock solid case buttressed by facts we'll decide what to do. I'm not going to let

Aiyana and Nita continue to kill if we prove they're guilty. At the same time we can't be judge, jury, and executioner. First, though, we build our case."

"What do you want me to do?" Danai asked. She sounded defeated.

"Speak to the families of the men who died after your father. We need to know if they witnessed Aiyana's rape and if she verbally harassed them as she did your father."

"And you?"

"I want to speak to Pine's partner. Learn why Aiyana would want to rid herself of Pines so long after the case was closed."

CHAPTER TWENTY-THREE

Back in his office Morales learned that Paul Abernathy had retired two years after Aiyana's rape. He'd put in his twenty. Morales called and made an appointment with him. Before leaving, he checked with his detectives regarding the status of their cases. Morales trusted his detectives. Many had been so-called "rejects" relegated to his squad by other sergeants more in favor with the brass than he was. Nina Rios, for example, was female—one of three in his squad—and Hispanic. Some sergeants rejected female detectives out of hand. The feeling was they had been promoted to fill quotas, bypassing more qualified male officers. That she was also Hispanic meant two quotas had been filled with one promotion. Her partner, Lamar Briggs, had been transferred to his squad because some fool thought he was hot-tempered and, by being black, might lose his cool in a tense situation. It didn't help that he was a six-foot bear of a man whose shaved head made him look particularly intimidating. But beneath the gruff exterior was a teddy bear. He was also a damn good detective, Morales quickly found out. Because Briggs was a male chauvinist, Morales intentionally teamed him with Rios. She had proven herself to Briggs, and the two were more than partners—they were confidants.

Morales's "rejects" had a higher clearance rate than any other squad. Morales didn't micromanage their cases like some other sergeants. He had an open door policy when they needed his help. He demanded updates, but he didn't second-guess those who worked under him.

Morales was seated at his desk when Russ McGowan entered without knocking. "Why did you transfer a beat officer to your squad?" he asked without first uttering a greeting.

In the seventeen years since they had been partners, McGowan had aged gracefully, Morales thought. There was a bit of gray in his hair, but it made him look distinguished. He had put on some weight but still looked fit. While not a vegan, McGowan watched what he ate. He might not enjoy salads, but they were a staple of his diet. Meanwhile, the rail-thin Morales chowed down on pizza and thick, juicy burgers accompanied by fries and a shake.

"How do you stay so thin with the shit you eat?" McGowan had asked while they were partners.

"A deal with the Devil," Morales had replied.

Now he looked at his former partner. "Nice to see you, Russ," he began. "Why are you prying into my personnel?"

"It's not just you," McGowan replied. "I make it my business to know what's going on in the department."

"We're equals, Russ," Morales responded. "I don't have to explain my actions to you."

"You think you're better than me with your high moral standards," McGowan snapped. "Even as partners you refused to accept a free lunch. You didn't get it—probably still don't. By making ourselves visible at a restaurant, we were discouraging criminal activities where we ate. The owners only wanted to show their gratitude. You snubbed your nose at their offer of a free lunch. Treated it as a gateway offering that would lead to further corruption. Accept a lunch and later you're taking payoffs or turning your back on illegal activities."

"Look, Russ, I couldn't then and can't now afford to get caught up in something that could cost me my job—even something as trifling as a free lunch. A lot of people—*family*—count on me."

"So you're not going to tell me about the Townes bitch now in your squad," McGowan said.

"*Temporarily* assigned," Morales replied. He ignored McGowan's reference to Danai. McGowan had no use for female detectives. He also had no use for blacks or other minorities in his all-male, lily-white squad. "If you must know, it relates to the first major case we caught seventeen years ago—the Aiyana Jackson rape."

"You had a soft spot for that girl," McGowan said. "I have no idea why. I mean, she was good-looking enough for someone black, but you were married. As partners we caught more than our fair share of rapes, yet this one you took a special interest in. Did you end up getting something on the side with her?" he asked.

Morales knew McGowan was being serious. He ignored the remark. "Maybe it's because it was my *first*," Morales responded. "You had been on the job two years. This was another run-of-the-mill case for you."

"Did Townes get raped by the same asshole who attacked your main squeeze?" McGowan asked.

Morales knew McGowan had forgotten Aiyana's name. And he wasn't about to tell McGowan about the case. "Townes wasn't raped. She asked for my help in confidence," he replied.

"You still haven't learned how the department works," McGowan said, shaking his head. "Soon I'll be a lieutenant—*before* you. You want to be on my good side, Estefan. Look at your squad of rejects. With me as your boss you could get your pick of the litter if you play your cards right. You *don't* want me as an enemy. You collecting favors like we discussed back in the day?"

"Precious few," Morales said.

"It'll come back to bite you in the ass," McGowan said. "Me, I've gone out of my way to be helpful. Fellow cops, those higher up the food chain, ADAs, city councilmen. I kiss ass now. Later I'll collect." He shrugged when Morales didn't reply. "So, this Townes gal, I hear she's a looker. Is she going to repay you with—"

Morales glared at McGowan. He didn't finish his thought, just shrugged again. "Look, I'm not going to pry, Estefan. Helping some rookie is of no real interest to me. Watch your back, though. You're good police but I know more than a few who feel you got your promotion solely because you're Hispanic. You have enemies. You want me as your ally."

Before Morales could respond, McGowan had left his office.

CHAPTER TWENTY-FOUR

Morales sat at his desk for a while, digesting what McGowan had revealed.

McGowan was as ambitious as he had been when the two were partners. He was to be taken seriously. If you weren't with him you were against him—and he could be a powerful enemy. Morales had no doubt that McGowan would quickly climb the chain of command—that he would one day soon be reporting to McGowan and be under his thumb.

Family obligations might force him to seek a promotion to lieutenant, but it wasn't something he anticipated with any eagerness. He was already antsy being a sergeant.

He wasn't meant to be a supervisor. He had been investigating Danai's assertions for just one day and he felt more jazzed than at any time since his promotion.

He hadn't lied to McGowan. He had never contemplated a free lunch which could lead to a payoff, and worse, because he was responsible for his extended family.

(1972)

At fourteen Estefan buried his father. Enrique Morales had committed suicide—hanged himself. Estefan, the oldest of five children, had demanded to be allowed to plan his father's funeral. There were uncles who had volunteered to assist him. Estefan politely declined. He was told by a priest at the church the family regularly attended that the service couldn't be held there or at any other Catholic church. Suicide precluded a Catholic service.

There wasn't enough money to rent an auditorium. Estefan spoke to his boss at the restaurant he worked at after school, being paid under the table because he was too young to work legally. The restaurant was closed on Sundays. A deal was struck.

Enrique Morales had served proudly in the military until he suffered a debilitating back injury lifting new office equipment. He was given an honorable discharge and painkillers.

His back never completely healed and he became addicted to his pain medication. He was in and out of drug rehab facilities more times than Estefan could count. The straw that broke the camel's back was when he was laid off from a job as a janitor at a bank. The little he made plus his disability benefits, along with his wife working, barely kept the family afloat. He was soon back on his painkillers after he lost his job. Miranda, his wife, threatened to leave him if he didn't re-enter rehab. Two days later, he hanged himself.

Estefan had seen both the good and bad sides of his father. When his father died he had four sisters, twelve, ten, nine, and seven years of age. He was responsible for them—something he took quite seriously.

After Enrique returned from a rehab facility there would be weeks, sometimes months when he was a wonderful father. He particularly enjoyed baseball. He took Estefan to Philadelphia Phillies games and would play catch with his son in the front yard of their home.

He often sat with his son after dinner imparting wisdom Estefan would follow religiously when he became the man of the family. He spoke with his son days before taking his life.

"Estefan, you must continue to take responsibility for the family as the eldest of my children—as my only male child," his father told him. "I love my daughters, but girls can be a trial. Your mother does her best, but Natalia has begun hanging with a rough crowd." Natalia was his oldest daughter. "And I fear Maria will follow in a year or two. Set an example for them. Work hard, be honest and both understanding and strict with the girls."

Estefan's mother fell into a deep depression after her

husband's death. Once a vibrant woman with an infectious laugh, she now went to church daily and then spent the rest of the day on a couch watching soap operas. Estefan knew she was aware he had taken charge. She'd ask him to sit by her sometimes. She'd give him a hug.

"You're a good boy, Estefan, taking care of your sisters," she'd tell him. "You're too young to have to carry this load but I don't have the strength. I love you, my son. We're lucky to have you."

It was no easy chore for Estefan. Natalia was only two years younger than her brother and routinely ignored him. "You try to act like Papa but you're a child," she scolded him when he told her not to break curfew. "I'll stay out as late as I please."

"We can't afford you getting pregnant, Natalia," Estefan told her. He knew she was sexually active.

"You'll make a great uncle, Estefan," she told him and laughed.

"Mock me all you want, but we can't afford another mouth to feed."

Natalia gave birth to a girl two years later.

At eighteen Estefan married his long-time sweetheart, Carlita. While he was at the police academy, his mother and sisters lived with him and his wife. Estefan soon started a brood of his own—two kids the first three years of his marriage. They existed on his paltry salary and a small government check. There *was* the temptation to accept payoffs, but he knew if he was caught and sent to prison, the family would splinter and decay.

Could he say he was happy? His sisters no longer lived with his family but whenever he "loaned" them money he knew he'd never be repaid. His mother had passed away three years earlier, never having recovered from the loss of her husband. He was still very much in love with his wife and doted on his five children. But he had sacrificed more than he wanted to admit to keep his extended family from self-destruction. He didn't detest his job, but being a homicide detective had been so much more rewarding than supervising others. Working a cold case with Danai only reinforced what he had given up.

CHAPTER TWENTY-FIVE

(1995)

Paul Abernathy lived in a South Philly rowhouse. Morales had called to set up an appointment. When he arrived, Abernathy showed him into a sparsely furnished living room dominated by a television, recliner, and small folding table to eat at while watching the tube. The walls and shelves were devoid of photos. Abernathy had set up two folding chairs next to the recliner for their chat.

In the seventeen years since Morales had seen the detective, Abernathy hadn't aged gracefully. Morales surmised he spent his days watching television and drinking. The top of his head was bald with unkempt gray hair surrounding the sides and back. His eyes were bleary, his cheeks red. He had gained at least forty pounds since Morales had last seen him. His stomach, covered by an undershirt, hung over his stained slacks. He had several days' worth of stubble.

Abernathy lumbered into the kitchen and returned with two beers. "I know you're on the job, but don't insult me," he said, handing Morales a bottle.

"You retired after your twenty, like you said you would," Morales began.

"The job wore me down," Abernathy replied. "You get a punk off the streets, there's two to replace him. Me and the wife spent a lot of time in Atlantic City after I put in my papers. Sadly, I lost far more at the casinos than I won. We were also a permanent fixture at Garden State Park, the racetrack across the Ben Franklin Bridge." He paused. "You're too polite to ask, so I'll tell you. My wife got tired of having me around. We had no kids. She divorced me and married a plumber ten years younger than her. He had four kids from a previous marriage."

"You never got another job?" Morales asked.

"Did some private security gigs after my old lady left. Someone throwing a party needed some muscle. Shit like that," Abernathy said. "Did it whenever I needed money for the casinos or the racetrack. Had a hip replacement a few years ago and now spend my time here or at a local bar. Pretty pathetic, huh?" he asked.

"Are you happy?" Morales asked in return.

"I like you Morales," Abernathy said, after taking several gulps from his bottle. "Liked you when you were a green rookie and got the best of Pines. You're not judgmental. Or, at least you don't voice disapproval." He paused. "Matter of fact I *am* happy. Watch my shows. Got shelves of crime fiction to pass the time," he said, pointing to a bookcase with several dozen paperbacks. "Don't have to clean up for anyone. Don't have to be embarrassed when I fart. Got no one to boss me around or criticize what I do. One could do worse," he said with a laugh. "I heard you made sarge," he added.

"Had to take a promotion because of family obligations," Morales replied. "I'd rather be a detective."

Abernathy nodded. "So, what brings you to my humble abode?" he asked.

"Georgia Pines," Morales said.

Abernathy choked on the beer he was sipping. "Blast from the past," he said after he wiped his mouth with his undershirt.

"I wasn't aware she had died … what, six weeks after she booted me out of the hospital. I was a rookie patrolman. She wasn't killed in the line of duty, so, to be honest, I forgot all about her."

"But you're interested now," Abernathy said. "I won't ask why. Seems my curiosity left me around the time my wife did." He paused. "I know some retired cops who spend their time trying to close cases they could never solve. Me, I don't give a shit about those who got away. What do you want to know about Pines?"

"You two dropped the Aiyana Jackson rape case after a few days," Morales said.

"Officially," Abernathy replied. "We had fresh cases. I was satisfied we'd never find the girl's rapist. We had no description. No witnesses. Now Pines was another story."

"In what sense?"

"Georgia had a bug up her ass about the vic," Abernathy said. "Said the girl dressed provocatively because she planned on giving it up that night—her sixteenth birthday."

"You telling me Pines thought she wanted to be raped?" Morales asked.

"She was out that night to lose her virginity; Pines told me dozens of times. I said it was possible, but she didn't plan on being raped. As was often the case, Pines didn't hear me. She questioned if the Jackson girl was actually raped. Speculated the guy was her boyfriend and they put on a show for the residents of the towers. She'd then hold up the evidence bag with the see-through blouse." He paused got up and brought back two more bottles of beer. Morales had been milking his first. "Pines told the vic that if she could prove it wasn't rape she'd file charges against her."

"So what did Pines do?"

"Worked on the case on her own time," Abernathy replied. "Brought a sketch artist for the Jackson girl to describe the perp."

"But Aiyana said she *couldn't* describe him," Morales said.

"Pines didn't believe her, and honestly, on that I agree with Pines. Look, maybe she didn't get a real good luck at her attacker, but he didn't grab her from behind. She was holding back. You, being a rookie, believed her. Think on it, though, now that you've got experience with all manner of crimes. Anyway, Pines brought over mug books and sat with the girl while she went through them. Had her repeat her story dozens of times looking for any inconsistency."

"Isn't it possible she could identify her attacker but feared retribution?" Morales asked

"Damn, I never thought of that," Abernathy said. "Told you I was burnt out. It's a valid point, considering where she lived."

He paused and laughed. "If I *had* told Pines, she would have ignored me."

"Why the obsession? Pines had other cases she couldn't solve, right?" Morales asked.

Abernathy nodded. "She didn't like it that the Jackson girl wanted to speak to you. You don't make demands on Pines without feeling her wrath. She wasn't too thrilled with you either," he added. "I respected you for not cowering before her. She could be intimidating."

"She learned nothing new to contradict Aiyana's story, right?" Morales asked.

"It only motivated her more," Abernathy responded. "She didn't show up for work one day. That night we received an anonymous tip about a body. Cops on the scene found her still holding onto the leash of her dog."

"Did she have any enemies?"

"She wasn't the most likable person, but no one said anything to her face. Rather than chew someone's head off, she told me that when she made sarge she'd have her revenge. She held a grudge. Talked shit about you for three or four days after she kicked you off the case. Anyway, most steered clear of her. She put a lot of felons away but the detectives investigating couldn't pin her death on any of them. And, shit, the coroner couldn't call her death a murder. An unsolved homicide."

"You got along with her," Morales said.

"She tolerated me because I let her do the heavy lifting. She took the lead in every case we had. I had lost interest in the job. I had no problem playing second fiddle to her. I was the perfect partner for her. We never hit a bar together after solving a case." He laughed again. "Actually, I asked her to go for drinks ... but she refused. She thought I was angling to fuck her. I may not have been the best husband in the world, but I never cheated on my wife. I didn't particularly like Pines, but I kept my feelings to myself. She didn't respect me, but as long as I let her have her way, we co-existed."

"Was she still harassing Aiyana Jackson when she died?" Morales asked.

Abernathy nodded. "Had just spoken with her friend ... I

forget her name now, for the fourth or fifth time." He paused and thought for a moment. "Keisha ... no, Kneisha something. Pines was really pissed when the family moved down south. Pines thought she could get under Jackson's skin by pestering her best friend."

Morales asked Abernathy if there were any other cases she had been obsessed over prior to her death. Only Aiyana's rape had been on Pines' radar at the moment. There was nothing else to ask. Abernathy got both of them another beer. Morales hadn't touched the second. He answered what questions he could about others who had been on the force with Abernathy. The older man hadn't kept up with anyone from his past.

When he left, Morales sat in his car awhile. Pines was still harassing Aiyana when she died. He couldn't rule out Aiyana as a suspect. But Aiyana, a shapeshifter? A jaguar who had killed Danai's father?

At some point he'd have to confront Aiyana. How, he had no idea.

CHAPTER TWENTY-SIX

Danai decided to change before she went to interview Jameela Pierce, the widow of Austin Pierce, who had been killed in the same fashion as her father. A police uniform would be off-putting and attract the attention of neighbors. She changed to a pair of jeans and a blue dress shirt.

Jameela Pierce gave Danai a scathing look when she opened the door. Danai had never met the woman. She was a short, pudgy dark-skinned woman with slicked-back black hair. She had several moles on her face. "You're a cop. I seen you before," the woman said, not inviting Danai in. "Why no uniform?"

"I didn't want to stick out like a sore thumb," Danai said. "There's no reason for your neighbors to know you're talking to a police officer."

"You got the stench of a cop," the woman replied. "Can't hide that from neighbors. Uniform or not, you don't belong here."

"I was born and raised in the towers," Danai shot back. "I still live here, even though I could move if I wanted to. You might not like what I do for a living, but don't *dare* tell me I don't belong here," she added with more hostility than she intended.

Jameela scrutinized her. "You're a feisty one," she finally said. "I've got to get to work, so nice meeting you," she said and began to close the door.

"Five minutes, then I'm out of your life," Danai said.

Jameela smiled and moved aside. "Five minutes."

Sitting on a stained couch, watching TV, was a young man who Danai guessed was in his early twenties. He had a number of scars on the right side of his face that crisscrossed one another. Danai wondered if he had gotten stitched up at a hospital or by a blind intern who lived in the towers. The scars were jagged. Danai couldn't take her eyes off of his face.

"This be my boy, Wesley," Jameela said. "What you want? Clock's a-tickin'." She didn't offer Danai a seat. Jameela sat down next to her son, who looked at Danai suspiciously.

"I'm looking into a cold case, the death of your husband," Danai said.

"Why the sudden interest?" Jameela asked. "Cops spent all of ten minutes on it when my husband was killed."

"There's been another similar death," Danai said, without elaborating.

Wesley took out a cigarette and lit it.

"Don't you let that ash burn my couch," Jameela told her son. "And you best get a job if you want any more damn cigarettes. Twenty-two and you sit on your ass all day."

"Yes ma'am," Wesley said.

Jameela looked at Danai. "Don't want to revisit the past. I've remarried. My husband's at work. We've moved on."

"I haven't," Danai said. She decided to level with the woman. "My father was killed two years before your husband. Same manner—back of his skull crushed in."

"Sorry, but—" Jameela said and stood up.

"Did your husband witness the attack on Aiyana Jackson?" Danai asked.

"What does that have to do with anything?"

"Please, did he?" Danai asked again.

"We both did. It was horrible," the woman said.

"You didn't call the police," Danai replied.

"Did your father?" Jameela shot back.

"No, and he was killed. Did Aiyana Jackson harass you after her attack?" Danai pressed.

"The bitch … sorry, but I felt sympathy for her until she began pestering us. She'd come by ranting and raving about how cowardly we were, especially my Austin. When we stopped answering the door she shouted at us through it." She paused. "Now please, it's been fifteen years. I dwelled on it long enough after he died and the police did nothing. I've moved on," she repeated.

"Was your son—"

"I need you to leave. I've been polite, but we got nothing more to say."

Wesley stood up. He was over six feet tall and, while lean, he appeared menacing. "You heard what my moms said, lady cop. Get the fuck out of here."

Danai left. In her apartment she berated herself. She had gotten the confirmation she needed. Like her father, Austin Pierce had witnessed Aiyana's attack and had done nothing. Aiyana had targeted Pierce just as she had her father. She should have left then without further alienating the woman by having her relive something she appeared to have put behind her. But a thought had suddenly struck her. A question for Wesley. She'd have to return. She would give Wesley a day, maybe two, to cool off.

Danai took a quick shower and then went for her second interview of the day, the wife of Shawn Hawkins. She went up three floors and knocked on the door of the Hawkins's apartment.

Celia Hawkins opened the door after Danai identified herself. She invited Danai in but didn't offer her a seat. They both stood with Celia glaring at her. She was a short, heavyset woman with a puffy face and short curly hair that had more than a little gray in it. Some would think that the woman didn't care about her appearance, but Danai knew more than a few women like Celia Hawkins in the towers. They had no desire to hide their age with artificial coloring. She wore her age with pride. She also wore no makeup. *Take me as I am,* her appearance screamed. Danai guessed the woman to be in her late-forties.

"Had nothing to say to you cops the first time they came knocking after that poor girl Nita Jackson got raped. Cops had little to say when my husband was killed. Took a statement, called the …" she began and then stopped.

"Coroner, mom," a boy on a chair in front of the television said. He looked to be twenty, Danai thought. He had gang or prison tats on his neck and arms. He was dark-skinned like his mother but had shaved his head. Danai thought he looked at her oddly, then realized that he had a glass right eye.

"That be my boy DeMarius," Celia said. "Coroner come over and took my husband away," she went on. "Never saw those a-hole cops again. So why should I speak to you?"

"My father died under similar circumstances," Danai said. "We lived in the towers, three floors down from you. I still do. It's possible we'll reopen your husband's case."

"Don't do it on my account," Celia said. "Shawn was a bastard, no two ways about it. Used me as a punching bag. Did the same to DeMarius when he was young. My boy worked out at a gym, learned to fight, and Shawn decided to keep his distance. Stopped hitting me for awhile, too, until DeMarius got caught selling drugs. The eight months he was in prison, Shawn went right back to hitting on me."

"You just sell drugs or do you also take drugs, DeMarius?" Danai asked.

"Selling be all I do. Gotta help pay the bills," the young man said.

"I'll only be a minute, Mrs. Hawkins," Danai said.

Celia shrugged. "Go on, then."

"Did your husband witness the attack on Nita Jackson?" Danai asked.

"Yeah. He be real fascinated," Celia said. "Got off on seeing others fight. He'd never seen no rape. Couldn't take his eyes off of the poor girl."

"Did you and DeMarius witness the attack?" Danai pressed.

"Me, for a minute or two," Celia said. "Made me sick. I woulda called the cops but Shawn would have knocked me silly. He had no use for the police. And the girl being out late by herself, he said, she deserved what she got."

"And you DeMarius?"

"I steered clear of the window," he said. "Good chance I would have recognized those boys. Don't need more problems than I already got."

"One more question for you Mrs. Hawkins and one for DeMarius, then I'm gone." She looked at Celia. "Did Nita hassle your family after her rape?"

"Us and a bunch of our neighbors," Celia said. "She came by the first time and Shawn, fool that he was, opened the door.

The girl showed him a picture she drew of Shawn at the window. Began screaming at him. Called him a coward. He gave as good as he got, though, saying she was a skank and a whore." She gestured at DeMarius. The man went to a shelf and gave his mother a crumbled piece of paper. "She threw this picture of Shawn at him. 'Keep it, asshole,' she said. 'You think you're big and bad but you're nothing but a little turd'".

Celia handed the picture to Danai. "You can keep it. Not doing me no good. Anyways, Nita came back another three or four times. Yelled at Shawn through the door."

"Were you here, DeMarius, when your father was attacked?" Danai asked.

DeMarius shook his head. "Pops started drinking a lot after Nita's first visit. Sober, he wouldn't mess with me. Drunk, he would have come after me. One of us would have gotten hurt real bad so I steered clear of him. Hung out with my corner boys. He usually passed out around nine."

"You weren't here during the attack on your husband, were you, Mrs. Hawkins?" Danai asked.

"That's two questions for me," she said, but she was smiling. "It's like DeMarius said. I wanted nothing to do with Shawn sober or drunk. Without DeMarius here, I'd go to a friend's apartment one floor up. That's where I was when he was killed. Found him, though. Cried some and praised the Lord."

Danai gave Celia her card. "I can't promise we'll be able to link your husband's death to my father's murder, but if we do, I'll let you know."

"Ask if I care," Celia said. "I don't," she quickly added.

"He could be an asshole, but he didn't deserve to be killed the way he was," DeMarius said. "Hit from the back. *I* protected my moms. And my pops had his good days. He'd been in prison. Told me how to handle myself so I weren't no one's bitch. Advice I put to good use."

"You going soft on me, DeMarius?" Celia asked.

"Just saying he wasn't a complete asshole, mom," he replied.

Danai left, disappointed that DeMarius hadn't witnessed the attack on his father. She'd have to check with Wesley and hope he could corroborate her story. A long shot, but she was nothing if not thorough.

Danai went back to her apartment and took another shower. She normally didn't sweat much, but she had felt clammy after her two interviews. While asking her questions, she had flash-backs to seeing her father attacked.

She couldn't interview any family members of Darnell Washington, who had been murdered three years after Austin Pierce. The family had moved, leaving no forwarding address.

Danai changed back into her police uniform after her shower and went to see Morales.

CHAPTER TWENTY-SEVEN

When Danai entered Morales's office, he looked surprised. "You're temporarily assigned to homicide. There's no need to wear your uniform," he told her.

Danai laughed. "I changed out of my uniform when I visited Austin Pierce's and Shawn Hawkins's families, then put my uniform back on."

"Your instinct was to not appear as a cop when you went to see them," Morales said.

"I could bullshit you and take the compliment," Danai said. "In truth I didn't want their neighbors thinking they were talking to a cop.

"Did you wear a nun's habit?" he asked, playfully.

"Jeans and a dress shirt," Danai replied. "What—"

"Neighbors knew you were a cop," Morales said.

"Mrs. Pierce's words," Danai acknowledged.

"So, what did you learn?" Morales asked.

"Pierce and Hawkins's deaths and my father's were connected," Danai said. She told Morales of her meeting with each family. "Both saw the rapes, did nothing, and were later hassled by Aiyana or Nita." She paused. "And you?" she asked.

"Pines's death *could* also be tied to Aiyana," Morales said. He told Danai of Pines's harassment of Aiyana. "I have no proof, but my gut tells me Lamar Cooper raped Aiyana. He and Pines had the same scratch on their wrists."

"So Aiyana killed them all," Danai said.

"We still have no concrete proof," Morales said. "You want to make this investigation a sprint, to use the old cliché, when it's a marathon. We have more work to do before we come to a final conclusion, and we're not under any time constraints. We won't have a fresh case thrust upon us like my detectives, which would force us to wrap this one up."

"And when we do? When we know—"

"You try to locate the family of Darnell Washington," Morales said. "I know they moved, but they must have had friends or relatives in the towers who might know where they're currently residing." It was drudge work that would probably prove fruitless, but Morales didn't want to discuss what they'd do if they were certain Aiyana was responsible for at least six murders. He had no idea what he would agree to. "I'm going to speak to the detective who investigated Nita's rape. Then possibly speak to Nita about her rape."

"Won't that tip her and Aiyana off that we're looking into them?" Danai asked. "They might flee."

That would solve their problem, Morales thought to himself. "I've got history with Aiyana. My talking to Nita wouldn't be taken as a cop interrogating her. I won't tip our hand."

"You're the boss," Danai said, flippantly.

"Make damn sure you're aware of that," Morales said, more harshly than he desired. Before he could apologize, Danai left.

Morales sat back in his chair and ran his fingers through his thick hair. He berated himself. He had been too hard on Danai. He had to remember she was a rookie. He'd been impatient, too, when he entered the force. Danai had allowed her father's death to fester within her for fifteen years. He had to rein her in. But he should have been more tactful, he told himself. And it bothered him what he might agree to do if Aiyana and Nita were culpable. Vigilante justice was out of the question. Arresting Aiyana with Danai's story that she could shapeshift into a jaguar wouldn't fly either. He sighed. He could put Danai off for just so long.

CHAPTER TWENTY-EIGHT

Before going to speak to the detective who investigated Nita's gang rape, Morales read the file compiled by Detectives Beverly Chaffetz and Oscar Villanueva, who had handled the case. There was a notation that the day the two closed the case—unable to find Nita's assailants—Villanueva had put in for an extended sick leave. Morales checked his personnel file and saw that after six months he hadn't returned. He checked Chaffetz's personnel file and saw she had been assigned no permanent partner. She worked cases with those whose partners had taken vacation, sick days, or personal leave days.

Unlike McGowan, Morales didn't fraternize with colleagues in other units. He knew everyone in the Homicide Unit and those in his squad far better. He barely knew the sergeant of the Sex Crimes Unit and none of the detectives. McGowan would have chastised him. McGowan not only knew every detective but had probably done favors for any number of them. He would also have dirt on many of them, to use for leverage if necessary. Morales would have to win Chaffetz over so she'd freely discuss Nita's case, without probing too deeply into his motivations.

He went downstairs and saw Chaffetz at her desk working on paperwork. Television might not accurately portray all police work, because much of it was dry and wouldn't hold an audience's attention. But they got it right when it came to paperwork. It was endless.

Morales recognized Chaffetz from her personnel file photo. The picture didn't do her justice.

Chaffetz was in her mid-thirties and was not only still strikingly attractive, but looked a good ten years younger than her age. She had worked with the Sex Crimes Unit for six years. Prior to that, she had worked drugs and gangs. She was someone McGowan would have hated—a *woman* who has risen quickly in the ranks, in part due to her gender.

He had called and asked to speak to her before coming down. As a sergeant, he could have popped in without calling first. He wanted to show consideration—win her over. Yes, he was her superior in rank, but he would treat her as an equal. A different approach, he was certain, than McGowan would have taken.

When he introduced himself, Chaffetz stood up. He was surprised to see she was a good six feet tall. Unlike a number of tall women who were self-conscious about their height, Chaffetz didn't slouch to make herself appear shorter. She carried herself with pride. She was slim but had muscular arms, an indication she worked out. She wore tight jeans and a white blouse with the top two buttons unfastened, exposing cleavage. She put on a blue blazer before standing. Her breasts were the size of his wife's—a handful, she referred to them, large enough for the foreplay his wife so enjoyed, but not pillows. That was the name his wife used when pointing out big-breasted women. She was more than satisfied with what she had. Morales had a feeling Chaffetz felt the same.

She had olive skin, similar to many Italians he knew. She wore little or no makeup on an unblemished face other than a small mole to the right of her chin. She had wavy brown hair that came down past her shoulders and hazel eyes that seemed to smile.

"I'd like to talk to you about a recent case you and your partner investigated," he began after introducing himself. "How about I treat you to lunch?" he added. He had intentionally set their appointment for 11 a.m. He didn't want to discuss Nita's case in the squad room where there was no privacy.

"You're not hitting on me, are you, Sergeant Morales?" she asked with a South Philly accent. Her eyes smiled at his discomfort.

"It's Estefan or Morales, whichever makes you feel most comfortable," he responded. "And I'm happily married."

"I've been hit on by any number of 'happily married men,'" she said, using air quotes for the last three words.

"What if I said I was?" Morales asked. "You're an attractive woman, after all ... and you're well aware you are," he added.

Chaffetz blushed. "You're not, though ... hitting on me," she said.

Morales's comment had caught her off guard, as he had intended. Chaffetz, he could tell, was used to making her male colleagues uncomfortable for any lustful thoughts they might harbor. He was telling her he wasn't playing her game. "Happily married, in my case, means I'm not on the prowl. How about we get something at the carts around the park and share a bench? There's no privacy up here. And I'm not about to make advances on you in a public park."

Chaffetz regained her composure and agreed.

"What should I call you—Detective, Bev, Beverly?" he asked.

"Chafe," she said, "with a long 'a'. A partner I once had gave me the nickname and it stuck. Said I didn't look like a Bev or Beverly." She had been chewing on a piece of gum. She tossed it in the trash can and replaced it with another piece.

Morales bought two slices of pizza at one of the trucks. Chaffetz bought two hot dogs with sauerkraut. She insisted on paying for her food.

They ate in silence. As soon as she finished Chaffetz popped in a new piece of gum. She looked at Morales and anticipated his unspoken question.

"Don't get too close to me," she began. "My partner would rag on me about my diet. Hot dogs with sauerkraut, garlic on my pizza, onions on my burgers. My breath would stink. I didn't like the taste of breath mints. The gum helps, but I still reek. It works for me when I'm interviewing a perp or an uncooperative witness. I get up close and personal. On the other hand, it plays havoc with relationships."

"You're not married," he said. It wasn't a question. She wore no ring.

She shrugged. "Almost, more than once, but no. I'm a bit too intimidating for most men—a woman carrying a gun. And working sex crimes, if I discussed what I saw, men I dated

would get uncomfortable. Add to that an Italian temper I sometimes find hard to control, and not too many men would want
to marry me." She paused. "You're taking my measure. Is this a
job interview?"

"Sadly, no," Morales said. "I have no openings in my squad.
And I don't know if you'd want to work for me if you're ambitious. I'm often sent so-called misfits—those who may not
always toe the company line."

"I've heard about you, Morales," she said. "At some point I
might want to try Homicide. There are just so many rape victims or kids molested by perverts one can take. I heard you
were a fair boss."

"With little clout with the brass," he added, then paused.
"When you're tired of Sex Crimes, give me a call. There's always
turnover. You'd make a good fit in my squad. But do your homework, especially if you have further ambitions. Like I said, I'm
not given the cream of the crop. You figure out why."

"Your detectives have an impressive closure rate," Chaffetz
said.

"You did your homework after I called," Morales said with
a smile.

"Guilty as charged. Why are your detectives called misfits?"
she asked.

"They're not," he began. "It's all perception. I have more
woman than any squad in Homicide. More minorities, as well.
Too many sergeants consider their promotion to Homicide
political. They don't feel they earned their promotions, but were
handed them to satisfy special interest groups. Our closure rate,
though, speaks of their competence."

Chaffetz nodded. "So what case are you interested in?" she
asked.

"Nita Jackson," Morales said.

"Why the interest?" she asked. She seemed taken aback.

"I have history with the family," Morales replied. "Seventeen
years ago, as a rookie beat cop, I was first on the scene of her
mother's rape."

"Shit, the mother ... Aiyana, she mentioned you, though
not by name. She was initially hostile when I interviewed her.

I played nice with her and she told me about Georgia Pines—a detective before my time. She thought all female cops were alike. This unnamed male cop treated her like a human being. That's you, right?"

Morales nodded. "I saw her two times after Pines kicked me off the case. The last was six months after she gave birth to Nita. So, when I heard Nita was assaulted—"

"That was six months ago," Chaffetz said.

"I didn't want to interfere with your investigation," Morales said. He knew Chaffetz was not one to be handled lightly. He'd have to tread carefully. "And my plate was full. I want to visit Nita—see how both she and Aiyana are doing. I thought I'd find out from you what went down before I visited. If you're uncomfortable—"

"Not at all. Just curious," Chaffetz said. "It wasn't a high profile case. That's why I wondered where you fit in."

"So, what went down?"

"You've read the file," Chaffetz said.

"Cold, impersonal facts. I want your impressions," Morales replied.

Chaffetz shrugged. "It was Nita's sixteenth birthday. She was going with friends to a club. She had a fake ID. May have been sixteen, but with the makeup she wore she could have passed for twenty-one. She wore a see-through blouse with no bra that left little to the imagination. Her breasts were larger than her mother's, larger than mine." She smiled. "I caught you staring earlier."

"At all of you," Morales responded.

"You sound sincere, but—"

"Men are fixated on breasts, legs, or asses," Morales said. "You don't mind if we look," he added.

"That's presumptuous of you. Am I a tease?" she asked.

"Your top two buttons are unfastened," Morales said. "It's intentional."

Chaffetz shrugged. "I get hit on a lot by fellow detectives and patrolmen at the scene of a crime. I make a comment about them taking a peek at my tits and almost all back off—sexual harassment and all that shit. You don't scare easily."

Morales saw that Chaffetz had a tattoo on her left breast. He couldn't make out what it was. It would take unfastening a third button for him to get a good look. "What's the tattoo?" he asked, impulsively.

"Only those who bed me find out," she said. "Just how curious are you?" she added playfully.

"Back to Nita," Morales said. He wondered what she'd say if he took her up on her offer. Would she be shocked? Disappointed? Or was she attracted to him and her offer was genuine? He wasn't used to flirting. Hell, the last woman he had flirted with was his wife when they first met. He was out of his depth and decided it wasn't worth the risk of coming back with a smart remark.

"Her breasts?" Chaffetz asked, then held up a hand. "Sorry, I *do* enjoy sparring with you. Like I said most men are intimidated by me." She paused and took a breath. "Your next question is, was she inviting the attack?" Chaffetz said.

"That would be a question Pines would ask. *Did* ask Aiyana, actually," Morales replied. "Are you aware Aiyana wore a similar blouse the night she was raped?"

"Not initially, but when Nita's mother told me she had been raped on her sixteenth birthday, I dug out her file," Chaffetz said.

"I told Pines Aiyana *might* have wanted to lose her virginity that night, but she didn't ask to be raped. Could be the same with Nita," Morales said.

"There were three boys outside the Southwark Towers. They surrounded her. Two grabbed her from behind and a third raped her. Then the other two took turns. Satisfied, they fled."

"Could Nita describe her assailants?" Morales asked.

"She said it was dark," Chaffetz answered. "Two were dark-skinned, one light-skinned. She said he could have been Hispanic … or not. Her words. She told me she wasn't really looking at them when they took turns with her." She sighed. "I don't have to tell you what she was looking at, do I?"

"No, but tell me anyway," Morales said.

"There must have been two dozen—possibly more, Nita said—people looking at the attack from the towers. No one came to her aid. No one called the police until the three left."

"Just like with Aiyana," Morales said.

"Nita was more pissed at them than she was with her assailants," Chaffetz said.

"And you found someone who cooperated with you," Morales said.

"Just like you did with Aiyana," Chaffetz shot back. "I told you I read Aiyana's file. My partner and I knocked on several dozen doors, after uniformed officers came up with nothing. Just like with her mother, not one tenant admitted to seeing anything. They feared retribution." She shrugged. "I can't blame them. Gangs still rule the Southwark Projects. Police presence is minimal. Coming forward would be heroic ... and possibly suicidal."

"So with nothing to go on you had a cold case," Morales said.

Chaffetz nodded. "I brought over mug books, but I could tell Nita couldn't even pick out a type. After looking at the mug books she showed me drawings of those in the towers watching her being assaulted. Some had criminal records. Her drawings and their mug shots were pretty similar. She showed me one drawing of the three boys who attacked her. Their faces were blank ... as in she didn't draw their eyes, mouths, ears or noses. She was so damn precise with those in the towers and then literally drew a blank when it came to her rapists. I thought she might have been in shock or repressing what she saw. But with my third interview with her the boy's faces were still blank."

"Anything else not in your report?" Morales asked. "Impressions?"

"No ... wait, actually there was one thing I didn't include because it was irrelevant and made no sense," Chaffetz said. "Nita told me she was pregnant as a result of the rape. This was three days after her attack. No way she would know so soon."

"Did you go back to visit her later?" Morales asked.

"Was Aiyana your first rape case?" Chaffetz asked, not answering Morales.

Morales nodded.

"You grew attached to the victim. Went back to see her.

Went back after she gave birth, you told me," Chaffetz said. "I don't have that luxury. I close the books on one rape and there's a new one on my desk. So, I have no idea if she was pregnant."

"I'm not condemning you," Morales said. "Aiyana trusted me. She would only allow me to interview her that first night at the hospital. It pissed Pines off royally. I was a green beat cop with plenty of time on my hands so I went to see Aiyana twice. It's not something I was able to do as a homicide detective, so don't think I'm judging you."

"My bad," Chaffetz said. "Maybe I feel guilty for not following up."

"Don't," Morales said.

Chaffetz smiled. "Will you tell me how she's doing after you see her?" she asked.

Morales nodded.

"Why the cross-examination about Nita's case?" she asked. "You're only going to see how she's doing, right?"

"I didn't want to go over blind. I'm not going to talk about the case to them," he lied. "I could point out the similarities and one or both would tell me to go fuck myself—justifiably. I wasn't judgmental with Aiyana. I may have believed she was foolish going out at night wearing a see-through blouse, but as I told Pines, it was irrelevant. Aiyana didn't ask to be raped. Neither did Nita." He paused. "I really appreciate your being so forthcoming. And I enjoyed our … date," he added with a smile.

"Should we finish our … date at my apartment?" Chaffetz asked.

"If I said yes?" Morales asked in return.

Chaffetz seemed speechless. It wasn't the answer she expected, Morales knew. "I'm jerking your chain, Chafe," he said. "I *am* happily married."

Chaffetz relaxed. "You have my number … if a position opens up in homicide," she said, with a smile.

"I'll put it on speed dial," Morales responded. "To be perfectly honest, often when I have a vacancy, I'm sent someone another sarge wants to be rid of. As much of an asset as you'd be in my squad, I might be turned down if I made the request."

"You piss off someone?" she asked.

"I'm a lousy politician, if you get my gist," he responded.

Chaffetz nodded. "I feel you," she said. "Just between the two of us, I had two sergeants tell me they'd promote me if I slept with them. I want to *earn* my promotions, not sleep my way up the ladder."

"You could have filed charges," he said.

"And *never* get promoted," she shot back. "Harassment is a double-edged sword. I said no and disappointed a superior—possibly made an enemy. But filing charges would have put me in the cross hairs of far more than just the person I rebuffed. *No* one would want me in their squad."

"Agreed," Morales said. "Maybe we can have a second date after I visit Nita and her mother," he added.

"No third date, though. You know—"

"—what's expected on a third date," Morales finished for her. "You're something else, Chafe. I'm glad I came to talk to you."

"Walk me back to the Roundhouse," she said.

He nodded. "I'm a gentleman. The streets ain't safe for a poor women such as yourself," he said, attempting, not too successfully, to mimic a southern accent.

CHAPTER TWENTY-NINE

Morales sat at his desk trying to decide what his approach would be when he visited Aiyana and her daughter. His thoughts kept returning to Chaffetz. She was beautiful, intelligent, and witty. He'd never make a move on her, never betray his wife, but if he wasn't loyal to a fault he'd be tempted. She had flirted with him. *More* than flirted. If he desired, she was available.

Concentrate, he told himself, then found himself thinking of the cleavage Chaffetz had exposed. *You're not going to do anything, Estefan.* But he couldn't erase her from his mind.

Forty minutes later, he looked at his watch and shook his head. He had no concrete plan, but it was time to drive to the projects. He had called Aiyana, who had been happily surprised to hear from him. She told him to come by at two. Unprepared, he left his office.

When Aiyana opened the door Morales was shocked by the woman who confronted him. Aiyana hadn't seemed to have aged more than a few years. She was thirty-three but looked to be in her mid-twenties, at most. She was still physically fit. Still had her long black hair. Still looked at him with a penetrating stare.

She wore tight jeans and a top that clung to her body. She wore no bra. Had she dressed provocatively for him, or was this a rebellious woman who still blatantly thumbed her nose at tenants in the towers?

She invited him in and introduced him to her daughter. Nita looked at Morales for a moment, then went back to reading a magazine. She sat in a threadbare recliner that had either been purchased at a thrift shop or been found abandoned on the street. While beige in color, it was covered with stains.

Morales thought Nita looked about six months pregnant. While she had a bloated belly, her arms were toned. Her skin was a bit darker than Aiyana's tawny complexion. As Chaffetz had said, her breasts were larger than her mother's. Other than those two differences, it would have been difficult to tell mother and daughter apart. They looked more like sisters. Morales remembered Aiyana telling him that if the child resembled her she would not only keep her but cherish her. Morales could see nothing of the father in the teen.

Aiyana offered Morales a drink and returned with three glasses of lemonade. She and Morales sat on a frayed dark brown couch. Everything in the living room was mismatched, as if each item had been found somewhere and planted in the room solely for its utilitarian purpose.

"No offense, but you look far older than when I first saw you, Officer—"

"I *do* look older. Got a touch of gray in my hair," Morales said. "I can't say the same for you. You haven't aged much at all. I'm envious." He paused a moment. "It's no longer Officer Morales. I'm a sergeant now, in charge of a homicide squad. *That* has aged me," he added with a smile. "And call me Estefan. We parted as friends."

"You investigate murders?" Aiyana asked.

Morales saw Nita look up from her magazine. She was suddenly interested in what he had to say.

"Not *all* homicides are murders," Morales replied. "Homicide detectives are called to the scene of anything that appears suspicious. Suicides, accidental deaths, even those from natural causes. Only a few we investigate are actual murders."

"Are you here to investigate a murder?" Aiyana asked. She spoke softly but her eyes were full of suspicion.

Morales saw that Nita was now fixated on him. The magazine lay in her lap.

"I only just heard about the attack on Nita," Morales began. He wanted to keep them both at ease. He had decided against a full frontal assault. He would level with them—at least to a certain extent—but not be accusatory. "I wanted to see how both of you were doing."

"We're getting by," Aiyana said. "Nita has put her … attack behind her—"

"Moved on, as you did seventeen years ago," Morales cut her off.

Aiyana nodded. "Like me, if the baby resembles her she'll cherish her daughter just as I adore Nita."

Morales looked at Nita. "Like your mother, you blame those in the towers who didn't intercede more than those who assaulted you," Morales said. "Is that right, Nita?"

"Fucking cowards," Nita said.

Morales saw Nita's eyes burned with hostility. The same predatory eyes as her mother.

"I don't condone their inaction," Morales said.

"But you *understand* why they did nothing," Nita snapped at him.

Morales nodded. "They feared retribution, but that's no excuse. An anonymous 9-1-1 call was all that was required. That not one person in the towers made that call is the worst form of cowardice." He paused. "How did the detectives investigating the case treat you?" He looked from Aiyana to Nita. Nita just shrugged. "I still remember how callous Detective Pines was to you," he said, looking at Aiyana.

"Detective … Chaffetz, she was a lot more sympathetic than Pines," Aiyana said. "Pines came after me like I committed a crime. I was the victim. I can never forgive her."

"She's dead," Morales said. "Died six weeks after you were attacked."

"I'm not going to say I'm sorry," Aiyana said. "She was full of venom. Spiteful. Vindictive. Good riddance."

"You didn't know she died?" Morales asked, gently probing, wondering if Aiyana would lie. "From what I've been told, she was hard on you even after the case was closed with no arrest."

"She kept hounding me, my friend Kneisha, and my teachers for at least a month, maybe more. Then one day she stopped digging into my life. I thought she just gave up. There was nothing to uncover."

"Why didn't you file a complaint against her?" Morales asked.

"Like I needed more harassment," Aiyana said. "The gangs and the drug dealers are bad enough. I piss off the police, it would only have made things worse for me. Anyway, why would the police take a nigger from the projects seriously?"

"You could have contacted me," Morales said. "I said you could if Pines continued to harass you, when I told you the case was closed."

"At the time, you were a rookie cop," Aiyana replied. "What could you do to a detective—a superior of yours—if I had contacted you?"

"A valid point," Morales said. He then turned his attention to Nita. "Detective Chaffetz didn't harass either of you?" he asked, looking at Nita.

"She never doubted Nita was a victim," Aiyana said. "I was suspicious of her first, but … she reminded me a little of you. She didn't condemn Nita."

"For what?" he asked. He knew, but wanted to hear it from Aiyana or Nita.

"It was my sixteenth birthday," Nita said, for the first time not deferring to her mother. "I wore a see-through blouse. You could see my tits."

Morales looked at Aiyana. "The same kind of blouse your mother wore when she was raped," Morales said.

"Wearing the blouse didn't mean—" Nita began.

"You wanted to be raped," Morales finished for her. "Same thing I told your mother … *and* Pines."

"Detective Chaffetz agreed," Aiyana said. "She comforted Nita. Didn't hassle her."

"Here's my problem," Morales said, finally venturing into forbidden territory. "Danai Townes came to me. Her father was killed not long after your attack," he said to Aiyana. "Had his skull bashed in. Did you hear about it?" he asked.

Aiyana nodded. "One of those who watched me get raped. You want me to be sympathetic? The world didn't lose much."

"A six-year-old lost her father, Aiyana," Morales said.

"What's your point?" Aiyana asked. Morales could see

suspicion in her eyes. "People get killed in Southwark all the time."

"Your friend, Kneisha, had an abusive uncle," Morales went on, not responding to Aiyana's comment. "He was killed in the same manner. Then two years after Danai's father was killed, Austin Pierce was murdered—the same way. Three years after, Darnell Washington. Blunt force trauma to the back of his skull." Now he looked at Nita. "And six weeks ago Shawn Hawkins was murdered. His head bashed in." His gaze returned to Aiyana. "I'm told you ranted and raved at William Townes and Austin Pierce for not coming to your aid. And Nita did the same with Shawn Hawkins."

"I hassled dozens of cowards who peered down at me when I was raped," Aiyana said. "Are you accusing—"

"I'm trying to figure this out," Morales cut Aiyana off. "The man who is now the chief medical examiner says that all of the deaths look like animal attacks—the same animal. Hard to believe, isn't it?"

"Then look for someone with a big dog," Aiyana said.

"Danai said she saw a woman ... well, transform into a jaguar, kill her father, and then turn back into a woman," Morales said.

"And you believe her?" Aiyana asked.

"She was six at the time and had just seen her father murdered, so I have to question her credibility," Morales responded. He didn't want to paint Aiyana into a corner just yet.

"Maybe her sanity, too," Aiyana snapped.

Morales rose. "Pretty far-fetched, I admit. If I went to the district attorney with what Danai told me, I'd be laughed out of his office." He paused. "Do you have a job?" he asked Aiyana.

"I work at an animal rights shelter," Aiyana said. "I'm not on welfare."

"I worry about the two of you," Morales said. "You might consider moving away from Southwark. You've both experienced sexual assaults in the projects. It's not safe here. No place to raise a child," he said, looking at Nita. "The Townes girl is looking for a scapegoat. She became a cop to seek justice for her father. I'm at a loss for suspects—a woman who transforms into a jaguar, for Christ's sake. But even after I close this case, with no one arrested, Danai might persist."

"Are you saying she suspects me?" Aiyana asked.

Morales sensed a new confidence in Aiyana. She wasn't the teen intimidated by Pines. "Kneisha's uncle, Danai's father, and three others *all* died in the same manner. Danai connects the dots, knows you hassled those who witnessed your rape, and in her mind all evidence points to you."

"And I transform into … what … a killer jaguar?" she asked. "Did she actually see *me* or just some woman?" Aiyana asked.

"That's where her theory falls apart," Morales said. "The woman's face was shrouded. She can't make a positive ID. Look, I'll keep her at bay. Hopefully there will be no further deaths. That would only exacerbate matters," he said, looking at Nita. "There's been enough bloodshed. And leaving Southwark would be good for both of you. A fresh start, with the baby coming." He looked at Nita. "You wouldn't have to constantly look at faces of those who abandoned you when you were attacked." He turned back to Aiyana. "I could find you a decent place in a far safer neighborhood."

"Thanks for the offer," Aiyana said. "Nita and I will consider your suggestion."

"Will you call me after the baby is born?" Morales asked. "I'd love to see her."

"We'd both like that," Aiyana said.

Morales left, hoping they would truly consider his option. They *could* start over and get away from the prying eyes of Danai. As long as they remained at Southwark, Danai's quest for vengeance would never be quashed.

CHAPTER THIRTY

Aiyana went to the window and watched Morales exit the building.

"He knows—" Nita began.

"Squat," Aiyana cut her daughter off. "Yes, he's made the connection to those I killed, but my shapeshifting into a jaguar—*that* he cannot believe. And even if he did, like he said, he'd be laughed out of the district attorney's office with such a story. We have nothing to fear from Estefan."

"And the Townes girl? She's a cop," Nita said.

"With the same problem Estefan has—a preposterous story."

"What if she seeks revenge … what do they call it … vigilante justice?" Nita asked.

"What do you suggest?" Aiyana asked.

"A scratch on the wrist," Nita said.

Aiyana shook her head. "We don't kill innocents; that's our code, passed down for generations."

"Not even for self-preservation?"

"*If* she attacks either of us, then yes, the jaguar in us will respond," Aiyana said. "But that's a last resort and *only* if she attacks us. I'm going to keep an eye on her. At some point maybe even have a chat with her. The mind can play tricks on a six-year-old who has seen her father killed."

"We're not going to move … show cowardice, are we?"

"Something to ponder," Aiyana said.

"This is *our* home," Nita snapped. Your parents—"

"My adoptive parents," Aiyana corrected.

"You loved them, you told me. They treated you like one of their own," Nita said.

"And I loved them until my eleventh birthday," Aiyana said. "I didn't stop loving them, but I knew what happened to my mother, knew of our ancestors. They provided a home for me, but I no longer considered them my parents. I have no attachments to Southwark. I detest the cowardice of those who live here. You do too. I see how you look at those who watched your attack and did nothing. You have the same contempt for them as I do." She paused. "Moving from here is something to consider. Meanwhile, you take care of my granddaughter. Leave the Townes girl to me."

CHAPTER THIRTY-ONE

(ONE WEEK LATER)

Danai had been keeping track of the comings and goings of the Pierce family for four days. She had accrued a week's worth of vacation days, but she didn't go on vacations, at least not since Rain had left for the University of Maryland. Going down to Atlantic City alone had no allure to her. So she bided her time until she could speak to Wesley Pierce alone.

Danai wanted to know if, like her, he had seen who had attacked his father. Had he seen the jaguar? Corroboration from a second source could shift the scales and force Morales's hand. Wesley's stepfather worked from 9 a.m. to 10 p.m. His mother cleaned for a white family Mondays, Wednesdays, and Fridays from 10 a.m. to 4 p.m. Wesley seemed to have no job, nor was he looking for one. In the mornings, he played basketball at a local playground. There was just one court with no net on the hoop. Broken beer and alcohol bottles, used condoms, and hypodermic needles littered the ground. One of the players always brought a broom to sweep the court clean. The refuse from prior night was swept into a corner; there were no trash cans. Danai knew the city put trash cans in the playground every three months. They were always destroyed within a few days.

After his hoops game, Wesley hung with some of the players until around 2 p.m., then went home. Danai had less than a two-hour window to speak with him.

A week before, Morales had called her into his office.

"I spoke with Aiyana and Nita," he began. "They said

nothing that would lead me to conclude they were guilty."

"Did you expect them to confess?" she replied tartly. "To take you into their confidence?"

"Frankly, no, but Nita is hot-tempered. I tried to goad her into making a mistake," Morales said. "Aiyana is far more savvy than she was when I first met her. She pretty much did all of the talking."

"How did she explain the animal attacks?"

"She made no attempt to," Morales answered.

"And what I saw?" Danai asked.

"A six-year-old girl witnessing her father's murder. She didn't have to say anything else."

"Where did you leave it with them?" Danai asked.

"I suggested they move out of Southwark," Morales said. "Aiyana has a job at an animal shelter. I told her Southwark was too dangerous for them, and had too many bad memories."

"Their reply?"

"That they'd think about it," Morales said. "I offered to help them to find a new place."

"What would that accomplish?" Danai asked. "Moving a fox from one henhouse to another?"

"It would get them away from their tormentors," Morales replied. "Look, Danai, we've reached a dead end. We both know that even with the proof we've accumulated, we can't go to the DA's office with a tale about a shapeshifter."

"You never had any intention of bringing them to justice," Danai snapped. "You have this odd history with Aiyana. Regardless of what we uncovered, your mind was made up. We would do nothing."

"Look, Danai, you didn't level with me from the outset," Morales shot back. "Short of a confession, we never had a case we could take to the DA." He paused. "You had your mind made up as well. You knew you wouldn't be believed. Yes, I believe you. Cawley backs up a theory about an animal attack. But Aiyana Jackson morphing into a jaguar? That's the stuff of science fiction." He paused. "Out of the gate, your solution was vigilante justice. You want to kill both Aiyana and Nita."

"We've proved they're murderers," Danai said. "And Nita

isn't finished exacting her revenge. Any blood spilled from now on will be on your hands."

"So be it, Danai," Morales said. "I'm not about to condone, much less take part, in killing *anyone*. My history with Aiyana is irrelevant. If they were two strangers, I would have no part in killing them. If you want to go the route of vigilante justice, you'll have me to deal with. Is getting revenge worth spending your life in prison? How does that honor your father?" He paused. "I'm suspending the investigation. You can report back to your sarge for assignment."

"All of this has been a fucking waste of time," Danai replied. "I should never have told you about the jaguar. I was a fool to expect justice."

"Not a complete waste, Danai," Morales said. "You now have corroboration your theory is correct." He paused again. "We're cops, Danai. We don't take matters into our own hands when the system handcuffs us. Any number of perps walk. We live with it. If there is another killing, we'll revisit our options. As of now, though, there is nothing more to be done."

Danai had stormed out of Morales's office without another word. When she had calmed down—hours later—she admitted to herself she had put Morales in an untenable position. Regardless of the evidence, the fact that a shapeshifter had committed those murders made it impossible to work through the judicial system. Maybe—a last gasp, she knew—Wesley could corroborate her story. If not, she might pin another unrelated crime on Aiyana and Nita. Possession of drugs with the intent to distribute would make both of them face long prison terms. Or she might fake an assault on herself and blame it on them. It would be a cop's word against two women from the projects who had a history of harassing neighboring tenants. She *could* make the judicial system work in her favor. She knew that Morales would not condone her options, which is why she hadn't mentioned them to him.

She looked at her watch. It was 2:15. Time to visit Wesley. She knocked on his door and identified herself.

Wesley opened the door. He was shirtless and held a gun. Danai wasn't wearing her police uniform. By instinct, she backed up upon seeing the gun.

"I'm not here to hassle you," Danai began.

"Shut up, bitch," Wesley said, loudly. He stepped into the hall, his gun fixed on Danai. "You upset my moms. Now you're back. After my dad was killed she began to drink. She's been sober since she met my step-dad."

Danai backed up further. Her back touched the wall behind her. If anyone heard Wesley's rant they weren't getting involved. She had to stifle a laugh. This was the projects after all. No one saw or heard anything. No one wanted to get involved.

Danai glanced briefly to her left. She had caught sight of movement down the hall. Aiyana was standing by the stairwell, naked. She gestured Danai to move further to her right. As she did so, Wesley followed.

"Now she's drinking again," Wesley went on. "You had to drag up the past. You gonna pay for hurting my moms." He raised the gun.

Danai saw Aiyana transform into a jaguar. The animal sprang forward and crashed into Wesley, knocking him back into his apartment. Danai heard a crunching sound—one she had heard seventeen years earlier—then nothing. She walked into the apartment.

"Close the door," Aiyana said. She was a woman again, completely naked. Danai looked at Wesley. He was lying on his stomach. There was no question he was dead, just like her father. A chunk of the back of his head was missing.

"You killed him," Danai said.

"Saved your life," Aiyana responded.

"Why were you—" Danai began.

"Look, girl. We don't have time to chitchat now," Aiyana said. "My clothes are in the stairwell. Can you get them for me?"

Danai had questions upon questions she wanted to ask but did as Aiyana requested. When she returned, Aiyana dressed in jeans and a t-shirt. "I'll take care of this," Aiyana said. "Time for you to leave."

Danai shook her head. "We're going to talk."

"Why don't I make you some coffee and we can chat until Wesley's mother returns," Aiyana said, her voice dripping with sarcasm. She didn't wait for Danai to respond. "Come to my apartment in two hours. No one will know what happened here."

"But—"

"You have no sense of self-preservation," Aiyana said. "Want me to leave so you can explain to this kid's mother *and* the police how a woman transformed into a jaguar and killed this kid?" she asked. "Think anyone will believe you? Leave *now*. Two hours in my apartment and I'll answer all of your questions."

Danai left.

CHAPTER THIRTY-TWO

Danai went back to her apartment in the central tower. She tried to pour herself a glass of water, but her hands were shaking. Most of the water ended up on the floor. She sat on her couch and began hyperventilating. She soon began to feel lightheaded.

She awoke to the sound of a fire alarm. She was surprised to find herself in her apartment. How?—she thought to herself. What happened came back to her like the wave of a tsunami. She stood up shakily. "Put one foot in front of the other," she told herself, aloud. She opened her door. Neighbors she barely knew were running towards the stairs.

Outside were residents from all three towers. Three fire trucks were on the scene. Everyone's attention was focused on the tower to Danai's right—the tower where Wesley Pierce had lived. *What has Aiyana done?* she asked herself.

Someone bumped into her. It was Aiyana.

"What did—"

"Not now. Not here," Aiyana said. "Come to my apartment when they allow us back in."

Before Danai could respond, Aiyana had moved away from her.

Twenty minutes later the crowd was told they could return to their apartments in the towers. Danai heard what might have been rumors or facts the firemen had passed along.

"A grease fire ..."

"Defective outlet ..."

"Apartment 6G ..."

"The apartment was empty, thank God."

"For once the fire department got here quickly."

"Of course," came a reply. "The city doesn't want the towers to burn down."

"Yeah, we might move into white neighborhoods," someone responded and there was a howl of laughter from others.

Danai made her way to Aiyana's apartment. Aiyana ushered her in. They stood glaring at one another. Danai saw Nita sitting in a recliner—her eyes boring into her adversary.

"What did you do?" Danai asked.

"Saved your life, then saved your ass," Aiyana answered.

"What did you do with Wesley?" Danai pressed.

"You don't want to know," Aiyana said. "I heard on TV—*plausible deniability*—yeah, that's it. You can't be charged with something you know nothing about. You don't have to lie. His body will never be found."

"Why the fire?" Danai asked.

"The carpet was blood-soaked," Aiyana said. "Wesley's parents will report him missing but they don't know he's dead. Southwark is dangerous. He could have been collateral damage in a gang dispute. Or a witness to a crime who had to disappear. Or he just got sick of it here and bolted. I got rid of Wesley but I couldn't remove the carpet. The fire got rid of any evidence."

"You killed my father," Danai said accusingly.

"And saved your life today," Aiyana snapped in return.

"You think that makes us even?" Danai asked.

"I was an immature sixteen-year-old when I was raped," Aiyana said, without addressing Danai's question. "Your father and others watched and did nothing. I wanted them to pay for their cowardice. I was wrong. This is the fucking projects."

"Why didn't you kill me that night? I saw you. You know I did."

"You hadn't done anything to merit killing," Aiyana replied.

"You allowed your daughter to kill, *Miss Mature*," Danai said.

Aiyana glanced at Nita. "She's hard-headed. There will be no others."

"I'm supposed to believe you?" Danai asked.

"It would be in both of our interests if you did," Aiyana

said. "Give us the benefit of the doubt before you do something foolish."

"Just what the fuck are you?" Danai asked, as if she hadn't heard Aiyana's reply to her questions.

"I'm a woman. I'm a jaguar," Aiyana said. "It's kinda like the chicken/egg riddle. Am I a woman who transforms into a jaguar or a jaguar who hides within a woman? That's one I can't answer."

"Are there more of you?"

"Not that I'm aware of ... just me and Nita," Aiyana replied.

"Confess," Danai said. "What you've done is heinous," she added.

"Tell the police Nita and I are shapeshifters? Show them, as proof?" Aiyana asked. She didn't wait for Danai to respond. "We wouldn't go to prison. It would be far worse. We'd end up as lab rats in some government facility. Poked and prodded. Scientists would attempt to find out how we could transform. If they succeeded, they'd create more of us. Think of ... what do they call it ... a ... a squad of shapeshifters sent behind enemy lines. Efficient killing machines who could ... morph, yes, that's the word, from human to animal and back again. I'd rather you kill both of us now than become an experiment and possibly a weapon. You have your gun on you. Do it. Do it *now*."

"You fucking saved my life," Danai said.

"There's that," Aiyana replied. Danai heard Nita giggle.

"Your friend Morales says there's no case against the two of you. He ended the investigation. I went rogue," Danai added.

"And almost got yourself killed," Aiyana said.

"Like I need a reminder," Danai said.

"Nothing is black and white," Aiyana said. "We reside in shades of gray. I didn't think twice about coming to your aid. Nita thinks I'm a fool. That boy was going to kill you. I acted instinctively. I'm not evil. I'm no saint, but I wasn't about to let you die." She paused. "So where does that leave us?"

"I have no idea," Danai said.

"At least you're honest," Aiyana said. "Have a chat with yourself. If it's still vengeance you want, return and kill us. It's your prerogative. Spare us, and I promise there will be no further killings. Nita had her pound of flesh. It will have to do."

"You're not at all what I expected," Danai said. "You were the bogeyman of my nightmares since I was six. Now ..." she said, and shrugged. She turned, opened the door and left.

CHAPTER THIRTY-THREE

Not black or white …
   … shades of gray
But Aiyana saved my life, Danai thought.
… shades of gray
Instinctively came to her aid.
… shades of gray
Killed for her. Got rid of Wesley's body when Danai was too paralyzed to act.
… shades of gray
Aiyana killed your father, a voice within her screamed.
She saved my life, Danai argued back silently.
… shades of gray
I owe her, Danai spoke again to the voice within her.
You owe her nothing. She killed your father, the voice responded, resounding in her head.
She Saved—
She killed your—
… shades of gray
What to do? Danai asked herself. She was too tired to consider her options. She had two more vacation days. Two days to decide what to do.

She fell into a fitful sleep, two versions of herself pummeling one another in a street fight—one demanding vengeance, the other forgiveness.

She woke up surprised to see it was 10 a.m. She had slept for sixteen hours but still felt drained. She showered, then lay down to let her body air dry.

When she awoke, it was 9 p.m. She felt no better. Another

shower. A quick nap, she thought. She awoke at nine the next morning. Her two days had gone by and she had accomplished nothing. She saw a piece of paper near her door. Someone had slid it under the door. She picked it up and her knees buckled as she saw a photo of a smiling Wesley Pierce, under a banner headline:
MISSING
There was a phone number to call with information, then a notice about a meeting that night to "Take Back the Towers."

There was a knock on her door. Danai jumped, startled. *Jesus Christ*, she thought, *what's come over me?* She looked through the peephole. It was Aiyana. Danai slipped on a pair of jeans and a top. No time for underwear. She opened the door. The two women stood looking at one another.

"May I come in?" Aiyana asked.

Danai nodded.

"You look like shit," Aiyana said when Danai closed the door. "Nita and I aren't dead so I guess—"

"I've been ... passed out the past two days," Danai interrupted.

"Drinking your sorrows away?"

"Just drained," Danai replied. "My mind shut down, and with it my body."

"Because of the Pierce kid?" Aiyana asked.

"I've been fueled by hatred since I was six," Danai began, not answering Aiyana's question. "Your protector Morales told me we were out of options. He's not into vigilante justice."

"And you are?" Aiyana asked.

"I had other options ... *not* legal options, but I wanted you and your daughter to go away for a long time. Then you fucking go and save my life. I crashed. That fuel that kept me going for so long ... it was gone. A car with no gas." She paused. "Look, I'm never going to forgive you, but that 'shades of gray' shit you talked about got to me." She paused again. "You have nothing to fear from me."

She handed Aiyana the paper she had balled up after reading. "But we both might get blowback from this."

Aiyana glanced at the leaflet. "Saw one this morning," she

said. "That's why I came over. What's there to worry about? The stepfather filed a missing persons report yesterday. Cops didn't even come over to question *anyone*. A teen's gone missing from the projects. So what the hell else is new? A big yawn. That's why someone called for this meeting. We go to the meeting tonight. There will be a lot of anger but nothing will be accomplished. Been there. Done that. People here have gotten riled up for years. Like a candle, their passion melts away in a few weeks when they're faced with reality. Gangs and drug dealers *still* run the projects. Make noise and you find yourself dead." She paused. "Whatcha going to do today?" she asked.

"I took vacation days to check up on Wesley's comings and goings. This is my last day," Danai said.

"You go all out on your vacations," Aiyana said, then held up her hand. "My bad. Just trying to lighten things up. So, let's go to Center City and do some window shopping," she said.

"You and me? What, are we friends now? Bury the hatchet and all that shit?" Danai asked.

"I'm your boogeyman. I've haunted your dreams for seventeen years," Aiyana began. "Time you got to know me a bit. I'm not all that different from you other than the beast within me. You've got your own demons, I imagine. You just don't transform into a jungle creature."

"What the fuck," Danai said. "I'll meet you downstairs in fifteen minutes."

Fifteen minutes later—Danai was nothing if not punctual—she was downstairs. Besides showering, she had put on underwear. She was going to tie her curly hair in a ponytail but left it askew.

They walked up to Walnut Street. Danai felt clammy. It wasn't terribly hot for June, but it was muggy. The smell of trash that hadn't been picked up permeated the air. Several dead rats and squashed roaches littered the sidewalk for the first two blocks from Southwark.

"You were adopted, right?" Danai asked, to make conversation.

"My mother gave birth to me at the Emanuel Evangelical Lutheran Church. I-I have these dreams ... about my ancestors.

I had one about my mother. She had ... transformed. Was a jaguar. She got hit by a car. Got to the church and in her human
form gave birth. She wrote my name on my stomach in blood,
then left, having turned back into a jaguar. I had the sense she
left to die." She paused. "I-I never told anyone the story ... for
obvious reasons."

"Not even Nita?"

"She had the same dreams I had when she turned eleven.
That's the age when we learn what we are and where we came
from. I wanted her to have a normal childhood for as long as
possible. I hinted there was something that would happen to
her when she turned eleven, kind of like a mother explains a
period to her daughter to prepare her for when it arrives. We
... well, we don't began to turn ... transform, until eleven, after
we've learned who we are. The day of her eleventh birthday I
told her not to be afraid of dreams she might have that night."
She paused. "How do you prepare someone for something so
monumental? My birth mother wasn't around to prepare me. I
felt totally lost with Nita."

"Why did you kill Kneisha's uncle?" Danai asked.

"You did your homework," Aiyana said.

"You're avoiding the question."

Aiyana shook her head. "Lester raped Kneisha repeatedly.
She was considering suicide," Aiyana said. "Kneisha was my
only friend, not just my best friend. I did what was necessary to
protect her. He got what he deserved. Kneisha returned to the
land of the living." She paused. "Do you have a man in your
life?"

"That came out of left field," Danai said. "I-I don't swing
that way," she answered. As soon as the words were out of her
mouth she wondered why she told her deepest secret to her ...
adversary.

"Have a woman, then?" Aiyana asked.

Danai looked at Aiyana before answering. She wasn't
shocked by her revelation. Wasn't judgmental. She just took the
admission in stride. Danai was glad she was getting to know
this woman. At the same time it made it harder for her to consider revenge.

"I'm still in the closet," she responded. She hadn't spoken to anyone about her loneliness since Rain left for college. Now that she had opened the door she found herself eager to vent her frustrations. "Male cops are among the least understanding when it comes to lesbians. Hell, they don't want *straight* women as partners. I have ambitions—"

Aiyana cut her off. "At the expense of companionship … of happiness."

"For the time being, yes," Danai said.

"You … satisfy yourself—"

"With one-night stands," Danai, this time, cut Aiyana off. She thought Aiyana was going to say masturbating. Danai did that too, fantasizing about Rain. "No commitment. Not even an exchange of real names, at least on my part. And you?"

"Our kind have no sex drive other than when it's time to procreate," Aiyana answered.

"That must suck," Danai responded.

"It's part of my biological makeup," Aiyana said. "We're loners. We're not like dogs, constantly in heat."

In Center City the two went into a number of clothing stores, looking but not trying anything on. Aiyana picked up a see-through blouse from a rack. "It's similar to the one I wore the night …"

"You were raped," Danai finished for her.

"Kneisha picked it out for me. The store was going out of business. Kneisha waited until the sale price was eighteen dollars and insisted I buy it. We split the cost. That's how much we meant to one another."

"For a loner, you and Kneisha were close," Danai said.

"I hadn't fully come into my own when we first met and became friends," Aiyana explained. "Our sixteenth birthday is when we fully embrace what we are." She paused. "Still, we remained close until her mother dragged her down south. Since then Nita has been enough for me."

"She's a bit moody, no offense," Danai said, then cursed herself for not keeping her mouth shut.

"She's a teenager … a *pregnant* teenager," Aiyana answered, with no hostility. "She was a joy until her hormones began to play havoc with her. You've never been pregnant, so you don't know just how that adds to your moodiness."

They ate at a McDonald's on Walnut Street—Danai's treat. On the walk home Danai felt content. She wouldn't call Aiyana a friend, but she had enjoyed herself. At the towers, Aiyana asked if she could come to Danai's apartment.

"It's a mess. I've been out of it for two days," Danai said.

"Ask me if I care," Aiyana responded. "And I saw your apartment this morning ... mess and all."

They went to Danai's apartment.

"It's been ... enjoyable," Aiyana said when she and Danai were sitting on her couch. Danai had brought both of them a Pepsi. "Disturbingly so."

"Why disturbingly?" Danai asked.

"I-I had something I was going to tell you ... on our way to Center City," Aiyana said. "You would have immediately turned around and returned to the towers. Instead we got to know one another." She laughed. "We could have been friends."

"But?"

"I had to protect myself," Aiyana went on. "More important, protect Nita and my granddaughter."

"Don't keep me in suspense," Danai said with more hostility than she intended. "What the fuck have you done?"

"I have evidence you killed Wesley," Aiyana said.

"But I didn't," Danai responded.

"Look at your arm. The left," Aiyana said.

Danai saw a gash on her arm. The blood had dried. "Did you scratch me like Pines and your rapist? *Murdered* me?"

"You know about Pines and the boy who raped me?" Aiyana asked.

"Answer my question," Danai snapped. She instinctively covered the wound with the other hand.

"Why would I save your life only to kill you?" Aiyana asked in return.

"You didn't deny you killed Pines and your rapist," Danai said.

"You've obviously connected the two—"

"And the three who raped Nita," Danai added.

"I underestimated you ... or was it Estefan?" she asked.

Danai held out her arm so Aiyana could see the gash. "Why?"

"Your blood is now on Wesley's clothes," Aiyana said. "If you became a threat you'd go down for Wesley's murder. Don't cause us trouble and you have nothing to fear. I didn't save your life to see you rot in prison."

"Why won't I die like your rapist and Pines?" Danai asked.

"The jaguar's claws contain a toxin that ... kills. I scratched you with *my* nail. You're in no danger. I have no desire to harm you."

"So destroy the evidence," Danai said. "There is *no* investigation. I told you, Morales shut it down. You rein yourself and Nita in as you promised and I'll keep my word. I-I'm no vigilante."

"I wish could believe you," Aiyana said. "I know you are sincere ... *now*. But I have little faith in human nature. Those like your father to whom all I was was a sideshow. Those others who ignored Nita's torment but refused to turn away. Those like Pines who harassed me—a victim of rape. The animal within is suspicious ... justifiably. I'll heed her advice and hold on to the evidence." She got up. "I truly enjoyed spending time with you ... getting to know you." She paused. "Sadly, though, it's best if we're not seen together again."

"Could the gash you gave me have made me ill—my two days lost to sleep and lethargy?" Danai asked.

Aiyana shrugged. "As I said, you weren't injected with a toxin, but it's possible. It wasn't intentional, and you've recovered nicely."

Danai shook her head. "I want nothing more to do with you and your family. That animal within you has stolen your humanity. Get the fuck out of here."

"That's why I didn't tell you until now," Aiyana said. "You didn't disappoint. Maybe I've lost my humanity, but we're not so different. Rage has infested you for most of your life. You're not one to talk about lost humanity."

Aiyana left. Danai had been left speechless by her last comment.

CHAPTER THIRTY-FOUR

After Aiyana left, Danai unleashed her rage. She had lost control of her emotions only three times in her life. Each time, she had gone on a destructive rampage. The worst was when Rain told her she had a girlfriend at the University of Maryland—someone she was serious about. Danai had destroyed her newly furnished apartment—merely furniture purchased at a thrift store and hand-me-downs from relatives. Once in the police academy, she had left her mother's apartment and rented one of her own at the towers. The email from Rain—she hadn't had the guts to call—had set her off. She had thrown a glass ashtray at the television, shattering the screen. Thrown glasses and plates against the wall. Taken a knife and slashed her couch. She had then collapsed and awakened several hours later. She knew what she had done, but it hadn't been her. There was some demon within her that had gained control.

The next day she had replaced the television—another used one from a store on Market Street—and used duct tape to repair the couch. She had bought paper plates and plastic cups, plastic knives, forks, and spoons. She had one steak knife. Fortunately she hadn't gone to her lockbox to get her gun while enraged. She shivered at the thought of what she would have done with it. A bullet shot in the wall could kill a child in the next apartment.

Now her rage returned, though there was far less destruction. Paper cups she threw bounced harmlessly off of the television. Knives and forks thrown against the wall left marks but did little damage. She upended her mattress, tossing it weakly a few feet from the bed. She punched the mirror in her bathroom, shattering the glass. Looking at her bloody hand snapped her out of her fury.

She sat down on the bathroom floor and cried. She had let her guard down. Had trusted Aiyana, fool that she was. Told her she was a lesbian. Gotten to know her. *Liked* her. And then the betrayal. In a game of cat and mouse she was now the rodent. And unlike on television cartoons, the mouse seldom prevailed. She had no intention of seeking retribution against Aiyana. She wondered, though, if six months or a year from now her desire for vengeance—she could no longer call it justice—might resurface. Maybe what Aiyana had done was prudent.

She was also aware of the irony of her destructive rage. She had some demon within her. Aiyana had a jaguar to deal with. Were they all that much different?

She had no appetite, but she forced herself to microwave a frozen dinner after she bandaged her hand. She showered and put on clothes that didn't reek of the sweat of the day and went to the "Take Back the Towers" meeting. She would steer clear of Aiyana.

CHAPTER THIRTY-FIVE

The meeting was held in what had been intended to be a rec room in the center tower. Danai had been told that before she was born there had been a pool table, ping pong table, a sandbox for toddlers, and several dozen board games.

Since then, the tables had been vandalized and the board games stolen. Now an empty, cavernous room, it was home to meetings—Alcoholics Anonymous, a prayer group, and a gospel choir that needed a room to rehearse. Tonight over one hundred chairs filled the room. Danai had found a seat in the back. On the other side of the room, also in the back, were Aiyana and Nita. It was a standing room only crowd, much to Danai's surprise.

August Carmichael stood at the front. He had no microphone but his booming voice could be heard by everyone.

Carmichael was tall man—well over six feet—in his forties. He was a burly man with a scruffy salt-and-pepper beard and shaved head. His skin was nearly as dark as the blackboard that stood behind him. He wore a perpetual scowl. He was an intimidating man and a born leader.

Danai had heard his story. He had been dishonorably discharged from the Army after a barroom brawl sent two civilians to the hospital. It hadn't been his first such confrontation. Back at the towers, he became an alcoholic and was rumored to have been abusive to his wife, who eventually kicked him out. He'd then lived on the streets for several years. The story—possibly embellished with each telling—was he saw three teens with knives chasing a boy no more than eleven. August decked one of the teens and the others fled. Soon after he entered a rehab facility and had been sober ever since. He was now back with his wife, though he had no children. He worked as a security guard at a jewelry store.

He first introduced Wesley's stepfather, who told those gathered that his stepson had gone missing. Danai had her eyes on Jameela. She had been reduced to tears—a shell of the woman Danai had spoken with. She looked to Danai as if she had been drinking—recalling Wesley's words.

August then took over, saying that anyone with information about Wesley should call the number on the flyer. "Make an anonymous call if you want. We want to find Wesley. We don't give a shit who you are, if you can help this boy and his parents. And no, there ain't no reward. This be the towers. We're all dirt poor." There was muted laughter.

"Wesley's disappearance prompted this meeting," August began anew. Danai noticed his speech pattern constantly changed. At one moment he was articulate. He'd alternate with the patter of the streets with some profanities thrown in for emphasis. "It be time we organize. Kick the fucking gangs out of the towers. Patrol at night. Work with the police."

The last statement elicited laughter and a few boos.

"I ain't no fan of the police," August shot back, "but if they make their presence felt we can rid ourselves of the gangs, drug dealers, and riffraff who plague the towers."

A man in his seventies stood up. Danai recognized him: Ben Watson. He'd lost an arm after catching a bullet during a drive-by shooting when he was a young man. Some said he himself had been a gang member. Others just as vehemently argued he was an innocent bystander.

"Been tried before, son," Watson said. He spoke as loudly as Carmichael. "Good intentions that always fail. We good people. Those in gangs don't value life—their own or ours. Fight them and they kill the families who oppose them. They gots money to pay off the police to turn a blind eye. You be talking suicide, August."

"We must try," August responded, his eyes first on Watson and then on others in the room. "Right now we're no more than animals in cages held hostage in our rat- and roach-infested apartments. We're in a prison of our own making. We take back the towers or die trying."

"Easy for you to say," Watson shot back. "No offense, but you left your wife once. You may have no problem putting her at risk, but almost all of us gots family. These gangs don't play by the rules that got your ass booted out of the army," he went on to a smattering of laughter. "Fuck with them and they'll kill the men-folk. Rape and then kill their wives. No child will be spared. That what you want, August?"

"I won't ask you to risk your lives or those of your loved ones," August said, lowering his voice. Danai could sense he was losing his audience. "I'll take those I can get. Those with me call and we'll meet in secret to make plans." He pointed to a phone number he had written on the blackboard. "The rest of you be my eyes and ears. Call anonymously. The part you play will never be revealed."

There was more back and forth for the next twenty minutes. Many reiterated what Ben Watson had stated. People like August had tried to organize the residents of the towers before and all had failed. Blood had been spilled, mostly by residents from the towers. A small number backed August. One of their own—Wesley—had disappeared and he hadn't run away. Some were crass, saying Wesley would be found with a bullet in his head. It was time to fight back, they urged.

After the meeting, despite her earlier reservations, Danai went over to Aiyana and Nita when they were outside. Others were chatting in small groups to discuss what had been said.

"Morales was right," Danai began. "It's not safe for you here. I won't betray you, but it won't be forgotten what happened after Nita was raped. Her calling tenants out. One dying. And Ben Watson, he surely remembers what happened after your rape, Aiyana. This is a lawless mob. They might target one or both of you."

"Like you care," Nita said.

"Hush, girl," Aiyana chided. She gave Danai a penetrating stare. "After Nita gives birth," she said. "Before, if things go sideways. Right now they're preoccupied with Wesley and getting rid of the Kings. We're an afterthought."

"If I hear otherwise I'll let you know," Danai said.

"After what I told you," Aiyana said. "Why do you care?"

"It's the cop in me," Danai replied. "Vigilantes look for easy prey when they find they can't defeat the gangs and drug dealers. They want their pound of flesh. That could be you and Nita."

"We're far from defenseless," Aiyana responded.

"Which also disturbs me," Danai replied. "A cornered animal is the most dangerous. I don't want needless bloodshed." She shrugged. "Don't say I didn't try."

Before Aiyana could respond, Danai turned and walked away.

CHAPTER THIRTY-SIX

It was 8:45 that evening when Danai got to her apartment. She was a ball of nervous energy. She felt this way when she was helpless. At such times she would frequent one of the gay bars in town. A one-night stand helped her put things into perspective or at least get her mind off of her troubles. She had a foreboding feeling that violence would visit the towers. She needed an escape.

She dressed in jeans and a clingy v-neck top that exposed plenty of cleavage. A suede jacket would protect her from predatory stares outside the towers.

She went to a club at 4th and South Streets. A dive, some would call it. It had been a bar for straights that had fallen on tough times and gone out of business, as so many establishments had on South Street. Tracing previous ownership was like working an archaeological dig. Tattoo parlors, bars, and pawn shops dominated portions of South Street. Sad, lonely, and depressed stores that would often close without any notice whatsoever. There was talk of a South Street Renaissance—new stores, even chains being built to cater to tourists looking for genuine Philly businesses. Still, even when complete, some of the old ramshackle stores which gave the area its unique flavor weren't going away.

A gay couple had purchased the bar when it had gone belly-up three years earlier. It had no name, no sign. Every once in a while a straight couple would wander in unaware it was a hangout for gays. Soon, though, after seeing men dancing with other men and women with women—the dancers often kissing their partner or fondling their ass—they would get the picture and quietly leave.

The couple who owned the bar had spent precious little on their new enterprise. It had been and still was a run-down bar with a jukebox and dance floor. It was one of the few bars in Philly that gays could go to without being hassled. That seemed to be enough for the clientele.

Danai sat at the bar and nursed a gin and tonic. She recalled her day with Aiyana, which had ended in betrayal. She had always feared forming friendships with female cops. What if her glance lingered on one too long? What if one discovered she was a lesbian? Being outed wasn't an option at this point in her life. She had been candid with Aiyana. She had ambitions. She hoped to one day be a homicide detective. Possibly more. Still, she was annoyed at herself for remaining in the closet, hiding her true identity. Yes, she thought, another parallel with Aiyana, who also was forced to hide her true self. When would she be able to have a serious relationship—walk down the street holding hands with a lover?

Several women approached her. Two asked her to dance. One offered to buy her a drink. Danai was choosy with her one-night stands. She liked women her age. Women who were pretty, exotic, or sensual. The two who wanted to dance with her had been in their thirties. She had no desire to be mothered. The woman who offered her a drink was promising, but she was already plastered. Be able to hold your liquor or nurse a drink, Danai was tempted to tell her. She had no desire to wake up in the morning to someone who would blankly stare at her with little idea of their lovemaking—or voracious sex, which was more to Danai's liking.

Someone sat down on Danai's left.

"Another for her," the woman said to the bartender. I'll take what she's having."

Danai was going to politely decline. She turned to the woman and was taken aback. Her companion was wearing jeans, a denim shirt and a cowboy hat. Danai looked at her shoes—cowboy boots. She seemed completely out of place at the bar—like someone who had been on her ranch just hours before.

Danai had to admit the woman was attractive. She figured she was in her late-twenties, though it was difficult to tell with her weather-beaten complexion. She could have been in her forties—a young-looking, fit fortyish, if so. Words were all but out of her mouth politely declining the drink, but they remained unuttered. This stranger exuded sexuality that Danai rarely encountered. Danai felt drawn to her.

She was tall and full-bodied—muscle, not flab. She had wavy brown hair, engaging blue eyes, and a mischievous smile. She spoke with no discernible accent.

"You're not from around here," Danai said.

"Perceptive, aren't you," the woman responded. "Bobbie-Joelle" she went on. "That's my first name, with a hyphen. Everyone calls me B.J." She stuck out her hand.

"Danai," she responded. "With no hyphen," she added, then laughed. She shook the woman's hand. "You're not from the East Coast. No accent. Not from the South either."

"No accent," B.J. said, mimicking a southern drawl.

"Nor Texas. Somewhere in the Midwest or Southwest," Danai said, fishing. "Just where ..."

"Colorado," B.J. said.

"You live on a ranch?" Danai asked.

"So, everyone in Colorado lives on a ranch?" she asked, but didn't wait for an answer. "I have a horse," B.J. said. "No other animals. No vegetables or fruits growing on my land. My house isn't quite a cabin from the Old West, but it's not one of those cookie-cutter homes I see being built not far from where I live. Place has personality and often needs repairing."

"Which you do yourself," Danai said. It wasn't a question.

"Of course," B.J. said. "I live off of the land for the most part. You're not a vegan, are you?"

Danai laughed. "Had a burger at McDonald's earlier today."

"Big spender," B.J. replied.

Danai laughed again. "What do you do for a living?"

"This and that," B.J. said. "And you?"

"The same," Danai said with a smile.

"You've got a pretty smile," B.J. said. "Don't smile much, do you?" she added.

"How would you know?" Danai asked.

"Been sitting watching you for the past twenty minutes. You

come to a gay bar, then send three attractive women packing. You seemed … distracted, I guess I'd call it. Lots on your mind."

"Maybe I just came here for a few drinks," Danai said.

"Or the atmosphere," B.J. responded. "Been nursing that watered-down drink in front of you since you got here."

"So that means—"

"You're here to get laid. No emotional commitment. A one and done. Tell me I'm wrong," B.J. said.

"And I should go home with you," Danai said. "No offense, but I prefer younger women."

"You could do worse," B.J. replied. "And age is just a fucking number. Do you turn me off because you're black?" she said, then went on. "I'm staying at a fleabag motel while I'm in town. You're toned. Whatever the hell you do, you keep yourself in shape. Too many here, even at your age, are soft. They work in an office, if they work at all."

"Got me figured out, don't you?" Danai said, feeling a bit irritated.

B.J. shook her head. "No, you got layers. Your pretty exterior covers up pain, anger, maybe even rage … and secrets. But you're a demon between the sheets."

"Hardly," Danai said without feeling. She didn't elaborate.

"Well, I'm not here for the ambiance," B.J. said. "You want no-strings-attached sex, you can come to my motel. You want to continue your pity party, tell me to go on my way."

Danai finished the drink B.J. had bought for her. She was tempted to ask the woman's age—late twenties or early forties—but she didn't. It didn't matter if this woman was not her normal type. Maybe that's why she was attracted to her. She had a presence—that was the word that came to Danai. Self-confident and sensual. There were no other women in the bar as enticing, regardless of age.

"Why me?" Danai asked. "I'm not the most gorgeous girl in here and, like you said, I looked distracted—*am* distracted. Hardly your first choice for a hookup."

"Insecure much?" B.J. said, then waved her hand dismissively and went on. "Many of the women here have piercings—rebelling against the world. You removed yours."

"How do you know?" Danai asked, suspicion in her voice. Had they met some other time? Maybe when she wasn't wearing her cowboy outfit? She was preoccupied with her thoughts, so only belatedly became aware B.J. was touching her eyebrow.

"They left a bit of a scar," B.J. said. She gently touched Danai's ear, her nose, then her lip. "Could be your job frowns on piercings." She then glanced at two women dancing. Both had piercings. "Their jobs may also reject piercings, but they put them back in when they get home ... or go on the prowl. You've decided to forego them for good. I *do* wonder if you've removed those from your nipple, navel, and ... *possibly* your clit."

"So my permanently removing my piercings is why you're attracted to me," Danai said, ignoring B.J.'s last remark.

"Piercings and tats don't make them real women—more fuckable than you," B.J. said. "You wore them at some point—maybe a rebellious phase. Striking back at a world that has been unfair to you. But you've clearly matured." She paused. "Look, you intrigue me. You have this brooding demeanor. And you're clearly selective, what with those you've rejected. It's your call," she said, then went silent.

Danai scrutinized B.J. again, then shrugged. "Lead the way, cowboy," she said.

In B.J.'s motel room, Danai was initially hesitant. She removed her top but not her bra. "I-I'm not all that experienced," she began. "Had one girlfriend in high school. We kind of fumbled and stumbled around when it came to sex. Pretty vanilla. Since she ... left, I've had one night stands with girls my age—most as green as me. What I'm trying to say is, I don't want to disappoint you. I'm not quite the demon between the sheets you described."

"Let me be your teacher," B.J. replied. She removed Danai's bra. "Beautiful tits," she said, fondling Danai's breasts. "Like low-hanging fruit from a tree."

Danai recalled how Rain loved playing with her tits. She'd refer to her breasts as water balloons, not for their size but the way they hung from her chest. She would tell jokes to make Danai laugh and watch as her breasts swayed to the left and right.

B.J. now grabbed them, then began sucking and pinching her sensitive nipples. "You *had* nipple rings," she whispered to Danai, then pinched her left nipple again.

They were both soon naked on B.J.'s bed. Danai had shaved all but a vertical sliver of her pubic hair, which she had trimmed. Rain hadn't liked getting Danai's hair in her mouth during oral sex. Shaving had pleased her lover. Now whenever Danai went on the prowl for a one-night partner she honored her lover by shaving.

B.J. put her hand between Danai's legs and gently touched her clit. Danai shivered. "You didn't get a ring for your clit," she said. "At least I don't think so. I won't know for sure until I can peer into your pussy," she added.

"Couldn't get a piercing there," Danai said. "Even us rebellious types have limits." She put her hand between B.J.'s legs. B.J. pushed her hand away.

"Put yourself in my hands," B.J. told her. "I'm gonna rock your world." She was naked except for her cowboy hat.

For the next forty minutes Danai allowed herself to be putty in B.J.'s hands. Danai was a loud lover. She found herself uttering God's name again and again as B.J. brought her to the brink of an orgasm with oral sex, only to stop when Danai was about to cum.

"What kind of game are you playing?" Danai breathlessly asked. "You knew—"

"Trust me," B.J. whispered. "One orgasm now and another in twenty minutes is what you're used to. Multiple orgasms, one after the other, is something else altogether." She put two, then three, then four fingers in Danai's vagina and pumped in and out. She steered clear of Danai's clit. "When you feel you're going to cum, hold back."

"For God's sake why? This is torture," Danai said as she gasped.

"Patience. You'll be rewarded."

Danai did as B.J. demanded. When Danai was about to explode B.J. removed her fingers. She continued to alternate between sucking and licking Danai's vagina and probing with her fingers until Danai told her she could no longer control herself. Only then did B.J. lick Danai's clit.

Danai convulsed, her orgasm stronger than it had ever been. B.J. gently touched her clit with her thumb and Danai came again. She then spread Danai's legs and eased herself into a scissor position so her clit touched Danai's. The two rocked back and forth. Danai kept coming like waves of an ocean crashing against the shore. Exhausted, Danai finally lay limp on B.J.'s bed. B.J. wasn't finished yet. She rubbed the palm of her hand against Danai's clit. Danai moaned. Her hands and legs began to spasm.

"What the fuck?" she asked with difficulty. "It's like I'm having a seizure!"

"Silly girl," B.J. said. "It's your nerve endings. Your brain is saying *enough* but ... well, it's like aftershocks of an earthquake. Touch you here," she said and brushed her hand against Danai's clit, "and it's like mini-orgasms one after the other."

Danai finally sat up, dripping with sweat. "Let me reciprocate. It's not fair for me to—"

"You don't think I enjoyed myself?" B.J. asked.

"Not like I did," Danai said. "Let me—"

B.J. put her finger to Danai's lips. "Shush. I gave you pleasure you'll try to replicate with others." She was playing with Danai's breasts. Danai moaned again. "There *is* something you can do for me."

"Anything," Danai said.

"Tell me about the shapeshifter," B.J. said calmly.

It was like a slap in the face to Danai. She swatted B.J.'s hand off of her breast and sat up in bed. She had been blindsided. "What are you talking about?" She asked. She was playing for time trying to get her wits about her. "You didn't randomly pick me up," she finally said.

"I gave you something you can use to seek sexual pleasure for the rest of your life. I'm asking for little in return."

"How did you know I was a lesbian? That I frequented *that* bar?" Danai asked.

"You're a cop. You tell me."

"How did you know I was—" Danai began.

"Are you going to question me ad nauseam?" B.J. asked. "I

thought there was more substance to you."

Danai glowered at B.J. She was tempted to cover herself with the bed's sheet but thought better of it. B.J. had explored her entire body. Covering herself up now would be childish. And angry as she was with B.J., she loved the way the woman looked at her. With her other one-nighters, she seldom felt sexy or appreciated; it was just two animals getting it on. B.J.'s eyes gobbled her up, even as she betrayed her. Even as she talked, they were fixated on Danai's breasts. Danai closed her eyes for a moment and the elusive answer to her question wormed its way within her. "Rain," she finally said. "My being a lesbian. *That* bar. Only Rain knew."

B.J. nodded. Her hands were on Danai's breasts again. Danai didn't resist. "I read an article about the two of you when you were in high school. The dynamic duo, it called the two of you. A little snooping and I learned she was openly gay. A month ago, she had just broken up with her girlfriend—"

"Really?"

"You haven't gotten over her, have you," B.J. said. It wasn't a question. "FYI, she's in no mood for a relationship right now. She feels burned by her ex at college. Like you, she's into one-night stands with no emotional attachment. I picked her up, taught her what I showed you, and we ended up talking about you … without my even having to probe. The two of you never broke up. You just took two different paths. She told me the two of you often went to the bar I found you at with fake IDs. You were both in the closet. I've been going to the bar for over two weeks." She paused. "You could easily rekindle your—"

"Relationship advice from *you*," Danai cut her off.

"You're right. We're off topic. Now tell me—"

"Are you even a lesbian?" Danai asked. She recalled B.J. didn't want her to reciprocate. B.J.… *fucking*—it certainly wasn't lovemaking. "When we scissored your orgasm—"

"I'm bisexual, though I prefer men to women. I've never had an orgasm. Yours, though, were genuine—*plural.*"

"So you'll fuck anyone to get what you want?" Danai asked. "I could deny knowing anything about this shapeshifter you're asking about."

"*Could.* You're not denying you know the shapeshifter," B.J. said.

"How did you latch onto me in the first place?" Danai asked.

B.J. shrugged. "The answer will only lead to another question," she began, then paused. She shrugged. "Have it your way. We're nearing the end of our journey anyway. Computers have greatly simplified my search. Before I had access to them I had to rely on television and newspaper reports. Sixteen years of frustration. I saw an article, quite short, actually. I almost missed it. Three gang members in Philly died within two days of one another from complete organ failure. I hacked into your medical examiner's records and found out about the scratch on the wrist." She showed Danai her wrist.

"*You* were scratched ... and survived?" Danai asked.

"A tattoo. A reminder," B.J. replied. "Your name and a sergeant were listed as having accessed the data. I then did a search for your name. Read about you and what happened to your father. Killed by a shapeshifter. *That* wasn't mentioned in the article, just the unusual wound. But you know what killed your father. Where is Bly?"

"I know no Bly," Danai said. Danai could see B.J. eyeing her carefully. B.J. sighed. "She must have had a daughter. *Another* shapeshifter. Who is she?" Where can I find her?"

"Why are you after her?" Danai asked.

"So full of questions," B.J. said and sighed again. "I'm a bounty hunter by trade, but this is personal."

CHAPTER THIRTY-SEVEN

(1978 / OUTSKIRTS OF LA JUNTA, COLORADO)

Milos brought Bly home. "Get your ass down here, B.J.!" he yelled.

B.J. came downstairs. She was eleven. She hated her stepfather, and knew that if she looked him in the eyes he would see her disdain. He was a handsome man when he smiled, which wasn't often. Even though it was chilly that night, he wore a sleeveless undershirt which exposed muscular arms.

She looked at the new arrival. A teenager, B.J. knew, but had no idea how old she was. She had a swarthy complexion, a wide nose, and thick lips. Her brown eyes bore into B.J. as if she was reading her mind. She had straight black hair that almost reached her butt.

"This is Bly," Milos said. "She sleeps with you in your room. There's a mattress in the basement for one of you. I don't give a fuck who gets the mattress and who gets the bed." He looked at B.J. "Teach Bly the house rules. I'm parched. Gonna get me a cold one."

B.J.'s father had died a year earlier from a brain aneurysm. B.J. had no idea what that meant—only that the man she adored was no longer a part of her life. Her mother had married Milos five months later. B.J. had cried when her mother told her the news. She had sat her daughter down.

"You know how much I loved your father, B.J.," she told her. "The love ... the *only* love of my life besides you. Your father and I were best friends at your age and got married when we turned eighteen. You have to understand, B.J., that I'm not built to live alone. And there are bills to pay and I've pretty much gone through your father's life insurance. Milos will provide for us. Just obey him. He has a temper."

"Do you love him?" B.J. asked.

"Love has nothing to do with it, something you'll learn when you're older. Most men don't want to be tied down with another man's child. I didn't have a whole lot of ... well, options. None actually, other than Milos."

"So it's my fault you had to marry him?" B.J. asked.

"No, baby. It's just a fact of life."

In the cramped bedroom, Bly unpacked the one small suitcase she had brought with her.

"You can have the bed," B.J. said.

"Not a chance, B.J.," Bly told her. "Consider me a guest. All I need is one drawer and the mattress in the basement. This is your room. What are your father's rules?"

"Stepfather," B.J. corrected her. "I despise him. You'll learn to hate him, too." She paused. "Do your chores. You got to get up early, like five in the morning. Do the chores you can while mom makes breakfast. Walk to school. Don't cause no fuss there, 'cause Milos doesn't like to be called away from work. Come right home after school and complete your chores. No sassing Milos. And steer clear of him after dinner. He watches TV and drinks a lot. Has a bad temper when he drinks."

"When he gets drunk," Bly corrected.

B.J. nodded.

"Does he hit you or your mother?" Bly asked.

"My mom, sometimes. When I'm bad I have to sleep in the basement. There are rats in the basement," she said and shuddered.

Three days later, Bly snuck out of B.J.'s room when Milos and his wife closed their door.

When she returned she sat on her mattress. She sat with her knees pressed against her chest, her arms cradling her knees.

B.J. sat down next to her. "What's wrong?"

"Milos took me in as a foster child so I could have his baby. Told me so on our way here. He wants his own kid. You and I ... we mean nothing to him. The monthly check he gets as a foster father doesn't hurt either."

"What do we do?" B.J. asked.

"You do nothing, girl," Bly said. "I'll make him regret the day he brought me here."

The next day Bly broke Milos's curfew. B.J. had no idea where she went or what she did. Milos had Bly sleep in the basement … the dirt floor since the mattress was now upstairs. Bly broke curfew the next three nights and cut school.

"What's wrong with you, girl?" B.J. heard Milos yelling at Bly the third night she came home after 2 a.m. "You got a boyfriend sticking it to you?" he asked. All B.J. heard was silence from Bly.

The next morning, Bly sat at the kitchen table wearing only her bra and panties.

"Aren't you going to school?" B.J. asked her when they were back in their room.

"Milos burned my clothes. Left me with what I'm wearing. Said if I was cutting school I didn't need clothes."

"I can borrow some from—"

Bly shook her head. "He'll burn those, too, and punish you for helping me."

Bly still snuck out at night. Where she would go in her bra and panties, B.J. had no idea. When she returned home Milos slapped her. She went out the next night. When she returned, Milos was drunk. He burned her stomach with his cigarette.

"Keep on defying me and it will be your face I'll burn."

Bly was taken to the hospital on three separate occasions. A broken arm. Broken ankle. Broken ribs. With Milos by her side, she told the ER doctor each time she fell off one of three horses Milos owned. The police came to the hospital after Bly's second accident. "I never lived on a ranch," Bly told the officer. "Riding a horse isn't as easy as they make it appear on television." The cop left, satisfied Bly was accident prone.

B.J. finally went to her mother. "You know what Milos is doing to Bly, don't you?" she asked.

B.J.'s mother untied her bathrobe. B.J. saw black and blue marks on her torso. "I don't fare much better," she said.

"Kick him out," B.J. said.

"And lose the ranch? Have us living in a shelter, or worse,

on the streets? Have social services place you in a foster home? No, baby, I can take what Milos doles out. Bly can, too. There's a strength to the girl. I wish I was more like her."

On Bly's sixteenth birthday—two years after he had first brought her home—Milos came into B.J. and Bly's room. "You're a woman now, Bly," he told her. "You're gonna have my baby. Someone I can mold." He looked at B.J. "Close your eyes, girl. Us grownups are gonna … play."

B.J. didn't close her eyes. She saw Milos remove his clothes then take off Bly's bra and pull down her panties. Bly didn't resist. Didn't utter a word as Milos entered her. He then got up, dressed, and left.

He returned the next two nights and raped—that was the word Bly told B.J.—Bly. Bly remained silent. Didn't cry. Didn't fight back.

The morning after Milos had raped her the third time, Bly told B.J. she was pregnant. B.J. didn't know better until much later. She believed Bly. And Bly looked content. "It ends tonight, B.J. Stay in your room after I leave."

B.J. wasn't much more obedient than Bly. At midnight with all asleep, Bly slipped out of the room. B.J. waited a few moments, then opened her door and peeked out. Bly had opened the door to her mother's and Milos's room. She changed into a big cat— B.J. would later find out it was a jaguar. B.J. saw the animal toss Milos out of his bed and bite him in the back of his head.

B.J.'s mother screamed as the animal jumped on the bed. It peered at B.J.'s mother, reached out with one of its claws and scratched her on the back of her left wrist. It hopped off of the bed, gave B.J. a long look and padded out the front door which had been opened.

CHAPTER THIRTY-EIGHT

(1995 / PHILADELPHIA)

"It was the last time I saw Bly," B.J. told Danai. "I ran after her, fell over a fallen tree trunk and hit my head. I was taken to the hospital. When I recovered, I could no longer feel pleasure or pain. Still can't, which is why I faked my orgasm when we scissored. Anyway, I didn't tell the doctors or police what I saw. I heard a doctor say I had sustained a concussion and it might be a while, if ever, before I recalled the attack on my family. I learned how to fake physical pain and emotions."

"Didn't your mother tell the police what occurred?" Danai asked.

"That my foster sister turned into a jaguar and killed her abusive husband?" B.J. asked. "She was afraid they'd think her crazy and put me in a foster home." She paused. "I don't blame Bly for what she did to my stepfather. Milos was a brute of a man—a monster who got what he deserved. But my mother was another story. Three days after Bly scratched her, she died—extreme organ failure. My mother was scared shitless of Milos. What could she do? Bly had no excuse to kill her. The irony is I ended up in the foster system anyway. When I turned eighteen I bought my mother's house. Because of the murder, no one had lived in it since I was placed in foster care. It was a ramshackle mess. I got it for a song—money I had saved from jobs I had for a down payment. I fixed it up and lived in it ever since. And I've been on the prowl for Bly."

"What do you want to do to her?" Danai asked.

"Make sure she hurts no one else. Has no children who will

do the same. Looks like I've failed on both counts so far. She killed your father. Had a child. Now, where is she?" B.J. asked.

"I've never met Bly. God's honest truth," Danai added, evading B.J.'s question.

"Then her daughter," B.J. said. "Don't tell me you don't know your father's murderer."

"I can't tell you," Danai said.

"Can't or won't?"

"It's complicated," Danai responded.

"Bullshit," B.J snapped.

"She saved my life. And she has evidence to prove I killed the man she saved me from," Danai said. "If anything happens to her, I end up in prison." She explained how Aiyana had saved her life and then betrayed her. "So if I tell you who she is, you get your revenge and I get screwed," Danai finished.

"An empty threat if she's dead," B.J. said.

"It's not your ass that's on the line," Danai said.

B.J. shrugged. "There's no need to tell me. You've filled in all of the blanks other than her name. I'll check to see who was raped in the Southwark area around the time the three teens died. They would have died several days after the rape. That would be Bly's granddaughter. Find her and I know who the mother—Bly's daughter—is. I end them for my mother and to prevent other innocent people from dying."

"The rapists were innocents?" Danai asked. "Like Milos?"

"The collateral damage is unacceptable," B.J. shot right back. "My mother, your father and others killed that I'll learn about. And the rapists should have been tried and punished accordingly."

"Like Milos?" Danai countered. "I'm not defending him, but Bly was no longer a minor. You said she didn't protest when he raped her. Didn't say 'no'—the magic word. Didn't fight back. What if the courts believed the sex was consensual? Hell, you're a witness for the defense."

"Bly told me she was raped," B.J. said.

"And a decent defense attorney would punch holes in your testimony. Bly didn't say no. Bly didn't fight back."

"You'd make a good defense attorney. They pay for my

mother and your father. Or do you feel they were culpable?"

Danai shook her head. "You can't go after them," she said.

"Because if they die, the evidence she supposedly has that could land you in prison will surface," B.J. said. "It will be assumed she killed the boy who went missing. You have nothing to fear."

"I disagree, but that's not what I meant," Danai said. "You'll stick out like a sore thumb if you venture into the projects, is what I was referring to—even if you get rid of your hat and put on clothes to blend in. You're white and a stranger. The tenants have organized to protect themselves from the gangs and drug dealers. Eyes will be on you. Will follow you. You may even be confronted. She will then know you are coming. I doubt you'd prevail. Even if somehow you do, you'll be easy to identify. Is killing them worth spending the rest of your life in prison? It's a question I had to confront before Bly's daughter saved my life."

"That's sweet of you to care about me," B.J. said. "I'm not planning on a frontal assault. Stealth will be my approach. I'm a trained hunter—a damned good one at that." She paused. "Look, we've exhausted this discussion. Let's part on good terms."

Before Danai could respond B.J. brushed her hand against Danai's clit.

Danai felt a surge of electricity tear through her body. "What are you doing?"

"Your call, but you told me who my prey is. The least I can do is repay you."

Before Danai could object, B.J. had climbed on top of her and was grinding her pussy into Danai's. Despite herself, she let B.J. have her way with her and lost count of the orgasms she experienced. B.J. had her change position. On her hands and knees she fingered Danai from behind, then anally. Both had been foreign to Danai. She was surprised she enjoyed anal sex.

Afterwards the two slept. Danai woke up in the morning to the smell of bacon. There was a robe on the bed. She put it on. She saw B.J. naked in a small kitchenette that was part of the room.

"Breakfast is served," B.J. said. "Can I have my robe?"

"I'll put my clothes—"

B.J. came over and opened the robe Danai was wearing. She gently grabbed Danai's hanging breasts and held them in her hands as if they were eggs.

"Water balloons, Rain used to call them," Danai said aloud this time.

"A good description," B.J. said. "We'll both eat naked. I like the looks of you."

A question—a crucial one suddenly occurred to Danai. "Did you spend the night with Rain, showing her everything you taught me?"

"Rain was a means to an end, Danai," B.J. said. "She was part of the job. We fucked, I taught her a few tricks but, well, like I said, she spent a hell of a lot of time talking about you. I didn't spend the night."

"Did you tell her you weren't there for her, but to learn about me?" Danai pressed. She was close to tears.

"I'm not a monster, Danai," B.J. said, sounding hurt. "*She* talked about you before I pumped her for information. I had no desire to hurt either of you. Look, I may be out of line but the girl's in love with you. You might want to think on that."

B.J. had toasted bagels. She set cream cheese next to them. She had heated cinnamon buns, cooked bacon, and poured orange juice. "When do you have to go to work?" she asked as they ate.

"I'm on the four to midnight shift," Danai said.

"Then we can fuck once more. I haven't showed you fisting yet. It's not for everyone, but we can try it. If you're uncomfortable all you have to do is tell me to stop."

"Why, if you don't enjoy it?" Danai asked.

"But I do," B.J. said. "Not in the classic sense. I wasn't lying when I told you I don't feel physical pleasure or pain. I'm not emotionally stunted. Rage has driven me in my search for my mother's killer. I *do* get off seeing you cum."

"You didn't need to seduce me," Danai said. "You could have found your prey without me. So, why pick me up?" Danai asked.

"You lost your father. I thought you might want to join me in ridding the world of these monsters," B.J. said.

"She saved me," Danai said, knowing she was repeating herself over and over. "That changed everything for me."

"And you're a cop—not a vigilante. I envy you in a way," B.J. said. There are lines you won't cross. I have no such ethical dilemmas." She was silent for a moment. "I sometimes wonder what I'll do when I've had my vengeance. What the fuck will I have to live for?"

Danai left a little before noon. "Will I see you again?" she asked before she left.

"Am I growing on you?" B.J. asked.

Danai blushed.

"When I'm finished, if I'm alive and not in prison, I'll be at the bar we met for three nights. You want more of me, I'm yours. You want nothing to do with me, don't show up. Three nights and I'm gone." She paused. "I wish I didn't have to deceive you," she said.

"But you did," Danai replied. "I'm not a very forgiving person. I waited until I graduated from the police academy to go after … the killer of my father."

"And I gave you something in return," B.J. answered back.

"An education in lesbian sex?" Danai asked.

"There's that … but far more," B.J. responded. "I told you Rain had broken up with her girlfriend. Told you she's still in love with you. Come out and you have her back again. It's up to you whether you want to pursue your true love." She paused. "Yes, I deceived you—but you got a hell of a lot more back in return."

"There's that," Danai said, repeating what B.J. had told her. She smiled. "I won't hold your deception against you." She shook her head. "Looks like I've been doing a lot of *forgiving* lately."

"Going soft," B.J. said. "Not a bad thing."

CHAPTER THIRTY-NINE

Back at her apartment Danai was going to take a shower. She smelled of sex that morning with B.J. Smelled of B.J., which wasn't altogether unpleasant. She decided to put off showering until later. B.J. had opened up an entire new world of sexual satisfaction to her. And, she had told her that Rain had broken up with her girlfriend—Rain had in fact spoken to B.J. a lot about her. On the other hand, B.J. had also told her she would ruthlessly kill Aiyana and Nita. The last disturbed her, and not because she was a cop. Vigilante justice had been on the table for her, though she wondered now if she would ever have resorted to its use.

What couldn't escape her was that Aiyana had saved her life. But, it was more than that. Aiyana hadn't hesitated. She saw Danai in dire trouble and reacted immediately. She *knew* Danai might cause her trouble. That was why she had been following her. Could Aiyana really be the monster she had built her up in her mind if she had come to her aid without a second's thought? It would have been far easier to have allowed Wesley to shoot her. Aiyana's problem would have been solved. Yet, she didn't take the easy way out.

That the two had gotten to know each other just added to her sense of malaise. For seventeen years she had created this monster in her mind and allowed her rage to fester and grow. When her investigation with Morales began, in her mind Aiyana had no redeeming qualities. She and Nita were rabid dogs to be put down.

But now, she had gotten to know Aiyana. Even if Aiyana had an ulterior motive—making herself more human to Danai—the fact was that Aiyana wasn't all that different than she was. *She* had a beast within her—the mounting rage of her father's murder. *Was the jaguar within Aiyana all that much different?* she wondered.

The cynic within Danai considered the possibility that Aiyana's befriending her had been intentional. She recalled a detective giving a guest lecture at the academy. He dealt with kidnappings when he had been with the FBI. Unlike most, he had left the FBI to become a cop. He talked of press conferences where the victim's family was encouraged to mention the victim's name numerous times. How they were told to humanize the child by telling stories of the youth.

"You get the kidnapper to identify with his victim," he told them. "Personalize the child. It can sometimes dissuade the kidnapper from killing his victim … if only for a little while. Every minute we gain can literally be the difference between life and death. You can apply the strategy to other situations. Make it personal."

Had Aiyana made herself into a sympathetic figure so Danai would abandon her desire for vengeance? And then added another layer of protection with the evidence she had of Danai's involvement in Wesley's death?

Did it really matter? Whether a ploy or not, Danai no longer had a thirst for vengeance.

Now Danai had information vital to Aiyana and Nita's survival. She could leverage it to get the evidence Aiyana possessed. She had never promised to keep her knowledge of B.J.'s desire for retribution confidential. She called Aiyana.

"I'm coming over," she said, then disconnected before Aiyana could respond.

Aiyana and Danai sat on the couch of her apartment. Nita, as usual, sat on the recliner, eyeing Danai with hostility.

Danai glared at Nita. "You got a problem with me, girl, or were you born with a sour disposition?" she asked, even though Aiyana had already explained Nita's moodiness. Danai would be the first to admit that she was often impulsive, prone to say something and later regret the remark.

"You mean to harm us," Nita said.

"Bullshit," Danai responded. "I've come to terms with my father's death."

"Now who's spewing bullshit?" Nita asked, tartly.

Danai looked at Aiyana. She had a wry smile on her face. "I'm not getting involved," Aiyana said.

"There's no convincing you," Danai said to Nita. "Ask me if I give a fuck." She turned to Aiyana not waiting for Nita to answer. "There's someone after you. Someone who *does* believe in vigilante justice. Someone who *will* find you. Might be a match for you."

"And you're telling me this out of the goodness of your heart?" Aiyana asked.

"That's all you get from me unless …" she began but didn't finish.

"Unless what?" Aiyana asked. She sounded exasperated to Danai.

"You've got to be kidding," Danai said, herself now exasperated. "You're usually two steps ahead of me." She paused. "What I know in exchange for the evidence you're holding over my head."

"No way," Nita snapped. "She's bluffing, mom. We can't trust her."

"Your daughter has issues, and it has nothing to do with her raging hormones," Danai said, her eyes on Nita.

"We *all* have issues, Danai," Aiyana said. "I don't believe you are devious enough to try to scam us." She looked at Nita. "Go get it," she said.

"But, mom—"

"Don't sass me, girl," Aiyana cut her daughter off. "You can be rude to … to our guest, but you'll do as I say without another word."

"But—"

"Without *another* word," Aiyana repeated.

Nita got up and stormed out of the apartment.

"I take it you've never been pregnant," Aiyana told Danai when Nita had left.

"I'm a lesbian, as you know, and I don't believe in immaculate conception," Danai responded.

"Nita's irritable. Her back hurts. Her second trimester has been a trial," Aiyana said and paused. "The worst is that we can't transform during our second trimester. I have no idea why. It's not like there's a book that explains us," she said with a tight smile. "Part of her feels imprisoned and is screaming for release. Think of it as a pregnancy on steroids. As moody and bitchy as a normal woman gets, it's two, three, or four times worse when she can't release the jaguar within her."

"You ... transform? Go out ... as a jaguar? To do what?" Danai asked.

"I told you before I don't know what I am—a woman with a jaguar within or a jaguar imprisoned in the body of a woman. Regardless, I can't deny the jaguar the freedom she requires. I go to Fairmount Park and let her loose. She just prowls around mostly in wooded areas of the park. When the park is completely empty the ... other me races through it. Sometimes if there is a stray dog, she chases it. And, yes, sometimes she goes for the kill. Feasts and then drags the dog's carcass to the woods."

"And if a two-legged animal appears?" Danai asked.

"She doesn't kill humans for sport or sustenance," Aiyana said. "You should do some research on predators. Few kill except for sustenance. It's man who kills for pleasure. Kills our kind and others for their skin or ivory or to hang a head on a wall. Kills their own kind, like here at the towers, for no good reason at all." She paused. "If a human appears she hides in the forest. Have you heard any reports of a mangled man or woman found in the park?" she asked.

Danai shook her head. "So, Nita is a bitch because she can't transform during her pregnancy?" she asked.

"Like I told you, she was a good-natured teenager, meaning she had mood swings before her rape as every teenager does, but there's a decent person lurking beneath. Neighbors chalk up her moodiness now to her rape. One even gave me a card for a therapist. She noticed the change in Nita. So cut her some slack ... or don't. I kind of like how you two spar with one another. Neither of you backs off. Like two sisters who never got along. She'll be better in a week or two when she can transform again, and be a loving mother after she gives birth."

She paused. "Now: who is after us?"

"The evidence," Danai said.

"I've never lied to you," Aiyana shot back. "You'll get your evidence. I want to know why some stranger is after us. How this person knows of our existence."

"She was after Bly," Danai said. "She's your mother, right? You never told me your mother's name. So there's my evidence I'm not lying. Too bad Nita isn't here."

Aiyana nodded. "Bly was my birth mother. I never got to see her."

"She was a foster child with a family in Colorado," Danai said. "The stepfather raped her when she turned sixteen. Your dad, I guess. He was abusive the two years previous when he brought Bly into his home. Raped her three nights in succession when she turned sixteen. The mother had a thirteen-year-old daughter. Too young for the stepfather. Bly then told the daughter she was pregnant. She killed the stepfather like you did my father. She then scratched the mother like you did your rapist and Pines—"

"You held something back from me," Aiyana began. "No, Estefan did. He never mentioned my rapist or Pines."

Danai shrugged. "The mother died in three days. B.J.—the daughter—saw Bly transform. Saw her kill her stepfather, which didn't bother her at all, then scratch her mother, which now drives her. She was placed in a foster home. She's now a bounty hunter. She came looking for Bly. With her gone, she wants to end you and Nita."

"And you told her about us?"

"She knew all but your identity," Danai said. "She's a hunter … a predator equal to, if not better than, the jaguar within you. I didn't give up your identity but it won't be difficult for her to locate you."

"Why is that?" Aiyana asked.

"Patterns," Danai replied.

Nita returned. She gave a bag to her mother then sullenly went back to her recliner. Danai looked at Nita and then turned back to Aiyana.

"This *might* interest your daughter," Danai said. "Nita led

B.J. to the towers. The three boys who gang raped Nita all died within three days from complete organ failure, just like B.J.'s mother. All three had a scratch on the back of their left wrist. B.J. found that out by hacking into the computer of our medical examiner. B.J. has a tattoo on the back of her wrist identical to the scratches we found on Nita's rapists—and your rapist and Pines. It won't be difficult for her to locate the name of the girl who was raped three days earlier at the towers. Nita's name is confidential. It was never released to the press, but as I said, this B.J. can easily hack into police files to find the identity of the victim. She gets Nita's name and it leads to your door. Bly's daughter and granddaughter."

"How did she meet you?" Aiyana asked.

"It's irrelevant," Danai said.

Aiyana lifted the bag. "I need to know how good this … this bounty hunter is."

"She picked me up at a gay bar I frequent," Danai said.

"There's only one gay bar in Philly?" Aiyana asked.

"She slept with my former girlfriend," Danai said. "She's at the University of Maryland. B.J. tracked her down, bedded her, and got her talking about me." She paused. "It was the day you betrayed me," she said, and pointed to the bag Aiyana held. "This woman did her homework. She knew how my father died. Checked me out and then went to the bar for … I think she said for two weeks and waited for me to show up."

"Describe her," Aiyana said.

After Danai had finished Aiyana nodded. "Anything else we should know?" she asked.

"Don't take her lightly," Danai said. "She knows you're dangerous. That there are two of you. She hunts humans for a living. She won't come knocking at your door."

"Does she suspect you'd warn us?"

Danai shook her head. "I wouldn't put anything past her, though. She might assume I'd warn you. She's like you. She plans two moves ahead … maybe more. I told her you had evidence to hold over me if I went rogue and came after you myself."

"Why did she need you if she had all the information you say she has?" Aiyana asked.

Danai saw Nita sit up straighter in the recliner. "She hoped I would join her," she said. "You killed my father, so we would both get our vengeance. I told her you saved my life. That I no longer seek vengeance."

"Bullshit," Nita said.

Danai smiled at Nita but didn't reply. She was tempted to give the girl the finger, but controlled herself.

Aiyana took a shirt out of the bag. She held it out to Danai.

"Wesley wasn't wearing a shirt when he came after me," Danai said.

"It was on the couch," Aiyana said. She pointed out a stain on the shirt. Danai knew it was blood. "Your blood." She put the shirt back in the bag and handed it to Danai. "I have nothing more," she said.

"I should believe you?" Danai asked.

"Believe what you want," Aiyana said. "You warned us. I honor my word. My promises. Nita's pissed," she said with a slight smile, "but now we can prepare."

"You'll kill her," Danai said.

"We'll defend ourselves," Aiyana said. "You would do the same if attacked. But we won't go looking for her."

Danai left. She would burn the shirt and hope Aiyana had been truthful about there being no other evidence.

CHAPTER FORTY

Danai went back to her apartment. She thought her mind would be on B.J.—they had spent an incredible night together, after all. Or on the battle between Aiyana, Nita, and B.J. that would surely ensue. Instead, it was on Rain.

Rain, her first lover. Rain, who had taken a lover in college. Danai had told her she understood. Rain had come out, after all, and pretty as she was, there would be no shortage of suitors. Still, Danai had been disappointed. Now, though, Rain and Amanda had broken up. But Rain, into one-night stands? Danai couldn't wrap her mind around the notion. Rain with B.J.? Danai blushed at the thought. She looked at her watch. It was 4:40 p.m.

She called Rain.

"Hi, it's me," Danai said when Rain answered. Would she recognize her voice?

Rain was silent for a moment. "Is that you, Danai?" Rain asked, her voice rising.

"I-I should have called sooner," Danai began. "But with you and basketball, college classes, and Amanda—"

"Amanda and I broke up," Rain said. "Three weeks ago."

"I'm so sorry," Danai said, not feeling sorry at all.

"We were together four months and … I kept thinking of you," Rain said.

"No way," Danai responded. "She must have been better in bed than me."

"She was," Rain said, then laughed. "We were both novices in high school. Amanda had an affair with a woman twenty years older than she was. It ended badly but Amanda knew a

hell of a lot more than you and I about how to pleasure one
another." She paused. "Still, my mind was on you ... when we
weren't in bed." She paused again. "You and I were inseparable,
but we spent time alone. *Me time,* I remember both of us saying
it at the same time. I didn't feel the need to call you ten minutes
after you left. I didn't wonder what you were doing. We had
each other but we had a life apart from one another. Know what
I mean?"

Danai nodded, then felt foolish. "Everyone needs me time,"
she said.

"Not Amanda. With her it was like we were tied at the
hip," Rain said. "She bought me this clunky cell phone with an
antenna that looked like a penis. I'd go to the library and ten
minutes later she'd call. I could never figure a way to end a conversation with her. We'd end up talking thirty minutes."

"She loved you," Danai said.

"Wanted to *possess* me," Rain responded. "Anyway, like I
told you, we met on the basketball team. I ended up starting
and she was on the bench. She quit the team but came to our
practices. She had a jealous streak I wasn't aware of. I'd be talking to one of my teammates about basketball and later Amanda
accused me of flirting with her—fucking her, if I took a shower
after practice that she thought was too long. It all became too
stifling." She paused. "Look at me monopolizing the conversation. Are you seeing someone?"

Danai imagined Rain crossing her fingers or holding her
breath in anticipation of her answer. "Yeah, there's room for two
of us in my closet," she answered.

"Two of you—"

"I'm still in the closet, Rain. I'm not seeing anyone," she
said and hesitated before going on. "I go to that no-name bar
on South Street and hook up with someone for the night sometimes. Remember that place?" she asked. She wondered if Rain
would lie to her. Then she wondered what kind of game she was
playing with her first love.

"Of course I do," Rain said. "I-I remember everything about
us." Now she paused. "You thinking you might come out of that
closet?"

"You know I have ambitions. Know if I come out, making detective will be that much harder," Danai said, then quickly went on. "But—" she began then stopped.

"But what?"

"It's damn lonely in my closet," Danai said. "A few days ago I inadvertently told someone I was a lesbian."

"Who?"

Danai sighed. "The woman who killed my father," Danai said. Shit, she thought to herself. She hadn't meant to mention Aiyana to Rain, but she had always confided in Rain without first thinking if what she said was appropriate or wise.

"Is she in prison?" Rain asked. "Why would you—"

"It's a long story and not one I want to talk about over the phone," Danai said. "To whet your appetite, I've kinda forgiven her. And she saved my life, which complicates things."

"Holy shit," Rain said. "I thought my life at college was complicated. Me and Amanda is *nothing* compared to the shit you have going on."

Danai laughed. Rain could always make her laugh no matter how gloomy Danai was. "You coming home when the semester ends? Or staying—"

"I-I was going to call you … *seriously* … about something I've given a lot of thought to," Rain began. "I spoke to my coach. Yes, I'm starting as a freshman but there's no way I can make a career in basketball. You know how they talk about the ceiling of a player?" Rain asked, but didn't wait for Danai to respond. "Well, my floor, as they call it, is my ceiling. Coach agrees. So, I was thinking of transferring to Temple. I could still be on the team there, but I'd concentrate on figuring out what I want to do with my life. Basketball ends for me when I graduate."

"That would be fabulous. What's stopping you?" Danai asked.

"You," Rain said. "I'm not homesick. Like anyone could miss the towers," she said with a weak laugh. "I miss *you*. I'd only leave here for you."

"You'd have me," Danai said.

"Not if you're in the closet," Rain said. "Being out has opened my eyes to possibilities. Going to dinner with Amanda. To the movies … even making out in the theater. If I was with you I'd want to show you off. Walk down the street holding hands. Put my arm around you at the movies. Kiss you at a concert. Go to Atlantic City like you suggested, even when you knew you couldn't."

Danai was silent.

"Look, Danai, I don't want to pressure you," Rain said. "Hell, I wasn't going to even bring it up until I came home after the semester. But hearing your voice… I'm sorry. I sure know how to fuck—"

"Hush, girl," Danai cut her off. "I won't lie to you. I'm more than a little blindsided. Can I have some time to mull it over? It's a really big step." She paused. "There's a cop … a *male* cop. Actually, he's a homicide sarge. I'd like to talk it over with him. Maybe I'm making a mountain out of a molehill. Maybe coming out won't ruin my career. Give me a time frame. I won't drag this out."

"I'm home in three weeks," Rain said. "I'm either staying for a week and coming back here for summer school or—"

"Staying for good," Danai finished for her. "Four weeks, then."

"Do what's best for you—" Rain began.

"You're what's best for me," Danai interrupted. "What we had wasn't puppy love. You know, a first love that burns hot and fast leaving only embers."

"Jeez, you studying poetry on the side?" Rain asked.

Danai laughed again. "I've laughed more during this phone call than since you left." She was silent for a moment. "You know what I mean. You'll be on my mind until you return home."

When Danai disconnected a few minutes later, she considered her quandary. You came out in the Philly Police Department and there was no going back. She knew she would face prejudice and hostility. Some—probably many—men and women would refuse to partner with her. It would most definitely take longer to make detective and longer still to get into the elite homicide unit. But a fast climb *alone* had no appeal to her. A slower ascent with Rain by her side had its allure. Then again, Rain might dump her like she had Amanda. Both had changed in the nine months they'd been apart. What if she came out and a few months later Rain tired of her? She had a lot to consider. She wished she could talk it over with B.J., then laughed. *Going to B.J. for relationship advice*, she thought, then laughed again.

CHAPTER FORTY-ONE

Danai met with Morales the next day before her shift. She had spent the evening and a good part of the night debating with herself. There were two questions to answer. Did she want a serious relationship with Rain regardless of how long it lasted? And would she come out of the closet to make that relationship occur? She no longer wanted to be alone. Even if she and Rain eventually went their separate ways, with Danai being openly gay there would be chances for further relationships. Still, she worried about her career. She decided to solicit advice from Morales. How pitiful was her life, she wondered, that the *only* person who could advise her was a heterosexual male she had known for just a few weeks.

She called Morales in the morning and made an appointment for 10 a.m.

Sitting across from Morales, everything she had rehearsed—a dozen times in front of a mirror—was forgotten. Morales looked, as always, like he'd worked through the night. He had removed his suit jacket, loosened his tie, and unfastened the top button of his wrinkled shirt. He ran his hand through his hair.

Morales began the conversation. "Have you reconciled yourself to the fact that Aiyana will never be prosecuted for your father's death?" he asked.

"Grudgingly, at first," Danai replied. She shrugged. "I'm tired of living in the past, Sar-"

"Just call me Morales," he said. "All my detectives do."

Danai nodded. "My father's ... murder had defined me for sixteen years. I decided I have to move on if I'm to have any kind of life. Which is why I'm here," she said and smiled. "May I ask you for advice?"

"Of course," Morales answered. He returned Danai's smile and ran his hand through his thick hair again.

"I'm a lesbian," Danai began. *There it's out,* her mind screamed at her. "I've been thinking of coming out of the closet," she added, then fell silent. *What do I do next?* she wondered.

"Are you wondering if doing so will harm your career?" Morales asked.

"Hearing you say it makes me sound so cowardly," Danai said.

"It shouldn't," Morales responded. "There's not a lot of tolerance in the department. Minorities and women have a hard enough time climbing the ladder. Blacks, women, even Hispanics have advocacy groups putting pressure on politicians who in turn make demands of the department. Gays … not so much yet. You're a black woman, which makes advancement tough enough. A black woman who is also a lesbian is tougher still. What are your career aspirations, Danai?" Morales asked.

"To be a detective," Danai answered. "One day in homicide," she added.

"You don't want to move further up the chain of command in a supervisory or policy-making role—sergeant, lieutenant, captain?"

"Maybe someday in the way distant future, but no offense, I've no desire to be a bureaucrat," Danai replied.

Morales smiled. "I didn't either, but that's a story for another time." He went silent for a moment. "I'll be honest with you. Coming out may be a stumbling block, but it's no deal breaker. By that I mean it may take you two or three years longer to make detective, but if you're a good cop, sergeants like myself will take notice and welcome you. And if the gay community starts exerting pressure, your being openly gay might become an asset. So, if you're staying closeted for fear it will adversely impact your advancement, personally I don't believe it will hurt you. May I ask why now?"

"I was in a relationship in high school," Danai began. "My girlfriend went to the University of Maryland on a basketball scholarship. I entered the police academy. She came out in college, even had a relationship. But it ended recently and she's interested in transferring to Temple … to be with me."

"But only if you go public," Morales said.

"Not an unreasonable request," Danai replied. "And I *do* want to go public. I'm not ashamed of who I am."

"For what it's worth, I think your happiness is more important than how fast you ascend to detective. If this woman makes you happy, you might one day be sorry if you lose her to your career."

Danai visibly relaxed. She had been unaware that she had been sitting on the edge of her chair as Morales spoke.

"She could be my everything," Danai said. "My chance to put the past behind me."

"Then you have your answer," Morales said.

"I'd like to work under you one day, but by the time I could make homicide you'll be a lieutenant or captain," Danai said.

"I don't know about that," Morales said. "I'm no politician and honestly I miss being a detective. There are other considerations, but I have no plans to move up the chain of command."

"Then maybe one day I can repay you … for believing what I told you when we first met and the advice you offered today."

"My door's always open, Townes," Morales said.

CHAPTER FORTY-TWO

After Danai had left with the incriminating evidence Aiyana had given her, Nita and Aiyana had one of their more bitter arguments which had become frequent of late. Aiyana knew Nita's combativeness was due to her pregnancy. She remembered, as if it were yesterday, the hardship of the second trimester of her own pregnancy. It had been worse for her than for Nita. Aiyana didn't have her biological mother to calm her fears. Not being able to transform into a jaguar—her true self?—had been torment. She worried something was wrong with her. Would she be unable to transform after she gave birth? She could feel the big cat within her trapped and definitely not happy being unable to emerge. The jaguar was as frustrated, and possibly as fearful, as she was.

During her third trimester, however, she had been able to shapeshift again. She had told Nita what to expect, but Nita had only grown more irritable and argumentative in the fourth, fifth, and sixth months of her pregnancy. It finally came to a head the day Aiyana gave Danai the evidence that could have sent her to prison.

"What is it with you two?" Nita asked when Danai had left. "She's *not* your friend. It's all pretend. She'll stab you in the back at the first opportunity. And now you have no leverage."

"You're wrong, Nita," Aiyana said, calmly. She knew better than to get into a shouting match with Nita as this time in her pregnancy. "I saved her life."

"Which was also a mistake," Nita shot back. "You could have been rid of her for good. You killed her father. You've always said blood is thicker than water. A cliché, but it's true.

You're nothing to Danai. Her hatred towards you will fester. Yes, you saved her life, but you killed a member of her family. She'll have her revenge. Probably sooner than later."

"I'll be on my guard," Aiyana said to placate her daughter.

Against her daughter's wishes, Aiyana went out at midnight to unleash the jaguar within her at Fairmount Park. Nita feared that B.J. might be lurking and attack her from behind.

(TWO DAYS LATER)

Whenever Aiyana went out at night, Nita did the laundry. Being pregnant came with its challenges. The worst was not being able to be her true self. Unlike her mother, who equally shared herself with her human body and that of the jaguar, Nita felt her human self was just a protective façade. She was a jaguar first and foremost. Trapped during her second trimester, the jaguar gave off a smell which most would have found revolting. Both Aiyana and Nita bathed in the aroma, finding it both soothing and intoxicating. Nita had to change her clothes and shower before she went outside for air. The apartment, with just a single fan to cool it, was stifling. She sometimes changed her clothing up to four times a day. Those nights her mother went off to the park, Nita did the laundry. She had done one the day Danai told them about the bounty hunter. Now, two days later, her mother had gone off again.

The laundry room was in the basement. Nita went down with her mother in the elevator at midnight. Neither spoke to the other. There were four washing machines in the room, only one of which worked. Roaches skittered across the room when Nita turned on the light. She put the clothes in the washer. Two days earlier, there had been a folding chair in the room to sit. At the projects, you didn't go up to your apartment while your clothes were in the washer or dryer. You'd return to find them stolen. The chair was good for her aching back. Tonight it was gone. *Stolen or vandalized*, Nita thought.

Nita thought of those who lived in the towers as animals. Not jaguars—stealthy predators—but prey who allowed themselves to be beaten into submission. Unlike her mother, she had no respect for any of them. She wished she lived somewhere where she could dispose of her human shell and wander about as the predator she was. Her mother had gone soft, Nita felt, because she had had no one to guide her other than her dreams. Bly would have toughened her up, Nita thought. But Nita agreed with her mother that Bly had most certainly died after giving birth to Aiyana. She would never have left otherwise.

Nita sat in a corner while the washer did its work. Roaches approached her but veered away. Nita knew it was her stench that repelled them. Forty-five minutes later, it was time to transfer the wet clothing to one of the two dryers that were operable. As she opened the washer door she heard a sound behind her. She was about to turn around when she was hit on the side of her head. She fell to the floor. She stared for a second at her attacker, recognizing her, before a second blow struck her. Blood dripped from her forehead into her eyes. She could see nothing as she was hit a third then a fourth time.

CHAPTER FORTY-THREE

Morales heard of Nita's murder when he arrived at work the next morning. Word of a confirmed murder spread especially quickly within the Homicide Unit. Chompsky, one of McGowan's detectives, caught the case. Chompsky, in Morales's opinion, was a barely capable, not overly innovative detective. Without the knowledge of what Aiyana and Nita were, within a few days the case would be pushed to the detective's back burner, a new one beckoning.

Moreover, that the murder occurred in the Southwark Projects meant it would receive the *Daily News* front page headline treatment for just a day. Within a few days, if news broke, a small article might appear. Crime in the projects didn't sell papers.

Morales also thought that Chompsky, like his mentor McGowan, was a racist and a killing in the projects would never be given priority. A perfect storm, thought Morales, for a "who the hell cares?" quickie investigation. If no obvious suspect presented itself, the culprit would never be apprehended.

Hat in hand, Morales went to McGowan. While the two had been partners, Morales could never call McGowan a friend. They had different core values. McGowan demanded team play and loyalty. He micromanaged his detectives. He had disdain for minorities and even greater vitriol for women detectives.

Morales, on the other hand, cared only about his detectives' ability regardless of their race or gender—and in the case of Danai her sexual orientation. He gave his detectives free rein to pursue cases as they saw fit. To keep him in the loop and consult him if they hit a roadblock was all he asked.

McGowan took credit for the success of his detectives. Morales allowed—even encouraged—his detectives to take the accolades that came with solving a high profile case. During a press conference on such a case, he often gave a perfunctory opening statement, then deferred to the detectives who had solved the case. He'd rather remain in the background, with those who did the real work given the spotlight.

Morales was no soft touch, though. If two of his detectives had problems working together, he demanded they work to resolve their differences. Changing partners or transferring a detective from his squad was a last resort.

Morales knew McGowan wouldn't give him Nita's case without exacting his pound of flesh, even though McGowan had no desire to pursue a low profile case in the Southwark Projects.

McGowan told Morales to sit when he entered.

"Did you learn anything about the death of the father of the rookie cop?" McGowan asked.

Morales knew this was McGowan's way of reminding him he hadn't stood in his way when Danai was temporarily assigned to his squad. "We hit a dead end. Townes is back on patrol."

"Hate to beat a dead horse, but I told you so," McGowan said. "Even if there was a case, you don't bring a rookie beat cop on board to help solve it. Even I'll admit I needed those years on the beat to get the lay of the land. And working as a detective in other units prepared me for Homicide. You just can't pluck some green rookie off the streets to investigate a homicide." He paused. "So, Estefan what can I do for you?" he asked.

"I'd like to take over the Nita Jackson murder," Morales said.

"Is it that you don't trust my detectives to solve this murder?" McGowan asked in return. He glared at Morales. "Chompsky—"

"That's not it at all, Russ," Morales cut him off. "You know I'm invested in Aiyana Jackson, the victim's mother."

"*Invested*," McGowan said. "Again, that first rape case of yours. You got a thing for her? Or, did you have a fling for her back in the day? Or did she offer a pity fuck because you treated her decently?" He waved his dismissively before Morales could answer. "I know I broached this with you before. At the time, I was jerking your chain. Now ... well, I'm being serious. Just what is it with you and this Jackson woman?"

Morales knew McGowan was baiting him. The man could be coarse and crude when provoked. McGowan was trying to get under his skin. Have him overreact. Why? Because McGowan got off on making others feel uncomfortable. Then *if* he gave Morales the case he would be even more indebted because he had lost his temper. Morales, though, didn't bite. He knew McGowan from way back. He had seen him play this game numerous times before, and knew not to respond with an angry outburst or even a denial. "I'd be handling the investigation myself, Russ. I'd be under no time constraints, like your detectives, who will have other cases piled on their desk in a matter of days."

"Sergeants don't investigate," McGowan replied. "You delegate. Won't your detectives be pissed—infer you don't trust them?"

"Everyone in my squad has cases they're working," Morales began, then changed tactics. "Look, Russ, I do feel an obligation to Aiyana Jackson. She bore the child of a rapist. Now that child *and* her granddaughter have been taken away from her. This has nothing to do with anyone's competence. I have the time to devote to the case. Three days, a week. More if necessary."

"You know the trail will go cold in three days," McGowan responded.

"If that's the case I'll have an unsolved case on my board," Morales said. "Another reason to let me handle it. I might even be doing you a favor," he added. He suppressed a smile.

"No, I think you'll *still* owe me," McGowan replied.

"I already do," Morales said. "Add it to my bill."

McGowan nodded. He left his office and returned with a file folder which he gave to Morales. "Chompsky tried to speak to the mother," he began.

Morales noted McGowan wouldn't even mention Aiyana's name.

"She said she was too distraught other than to tell Chompsky where and when she found her daughter," McGowan went on.

"We're still waiting on the autopsy. Chompsky thought the mother might be good for the murder. She was evasive, he told me. Defensive. And a bit hostile." He paused. "Just something for you to ponder. You know stats say someone close to the vic is often the doer. What I'm telling you, Estefan, is don't let what you and this woman may have had in the past cloud your judgment. Think with your head, not your cock," he added.

"I'll keep that in mind, Russ, when I interview Aiyana," Morales said. "I won't go easy on her either." He sighed at what came next. "I really appreciate this, Russ."

"We gotta have one another's backs, right Estefan," McGowan said.

Morales nodded and left. *A knife in my back is what you want,* Morales thought to himself, but remained silent.

CHAPTER FORTY-FOUR

McGowan remained at his desk after Morales left. He wondered why his former partner wanted the Nita Jackson case. He knew Morales hadn't screwed Aiyana Jackson. He was a devoted family man who kept his dick in his pants. His accusations had been made just to get a rise out of Morales—anger him so he would blow up. To his credit, Morales had kept his composure. He reminded himself not to underestimate the man. At some point, though, he'd squash him like a bug. A Hispanic sergeant was a threat to his climb up the chain of command. His politically correct superiors were under enormous pressure to promote minorities. *At my expense.* It was totally unacceptable.

Now, in the span of less than two weeks, Morales had wanted two cases involving Aiyana Jackson. What was so special about this project dweller who could do nothing to advance Morales's career? It had to be more than the *I am invested in Aiyana Jackson* crap he'd spewed. He'd keep an eye on his adversary. He was reminded of his father's advice. "All is fair in the battle to rise to the top."

CHAPTER FORTY-FIVE

(1972-1995)

At fourteen, Russ McGowan gave a short eulogy at the funeral for his father, who had died from a sudden massive heart attack.

"My father was a badass," Russ began. There was an audible gasp from a number of those gathered in the crowded church. But his father had taken no prisoners and said what was on his mind no matter whom it offended. He would have liked his son's approach. "You were with him or against him. You know who you are," he went on, his eyes scanning the assembled group. "He didn't give a crap if you liked him. He demanded respect and loyalty. Anything else was gravy, and my father *never* put gravy on his meat or potatoes."

He went on for another three minutes then sat down. He hadn't said it, but his father was also a fan of brevity.

Ron McGowan—not Ronald—had been a teacher and then a high school principal. When a student misbehaved, Ron would walk up to him. "Why did you do it, William? Tell me in one sentence, not a word more." Teachers who drew his ire received the same treatment. "You deviated from the lesson plan. Why? Short and sweet or you'll bore me to death." If the explanation took more than thirty seconds he'd interrupt with his famous, "Now tell me in one sentence, not a word more."

Ron McGowan had served in the military for eight years. He returned home intent on becoming a cop, but due to a leg injury sustained in battle he couldn't pass the physical.

He and Russ, his only child, were close. Ron took his son

hunting and fishing in the Poconos. He shot animals for sport. "Don't listen to those animal rights assholes who rant that hunting is barbaric. *We* are at the top of the food chain. Those below us are fair game." His home was filled with the heads of animals he had killed that had been mounted on the walls.

He also took his son to Philadelphia's college and professional sporting events. Whether hunting or fishing, they wouldn't return home empty-handed regardless of how long it took. During these trips he imparted wisdom to his son—values Russ made his own.

"Son, there's a lot in the army not to like, but it made me the man I am today," he told Russ. "I learned discipline, loyalty, and the importance of a clear chain of command."

He had been a principal at a predominantly black inner-city high school. He would tell his son about the students at his school.

"These black students come from fatherless homes where they learn no values. They're raised by a mother on welfare snorting cocaine up her nose or shooting up on heroin. They don't want an education. They sass their teachers and constantly get into trouble."

He thought even less of women. "The girls at my school are what you call loose. Of the two hundred girls at school no more than a handful are virgins." His school had a strict dress code which Ron vigorously enforced. "You should see the way they dress, Russ. Those with big breasts flaunt them with tight tops. I send a dozen home a day. They think they can sleep their way to good grades." He also forced any girl who was pregnant out of his school. "Let them have a teacher home school them. They set a poor example for others."

Russ's mother was the perfect wife and mother, according to his father. She was a stay-at-home mom. She took care of Russ when he was young, kept the house spotless and had meals prepared at 6 p.m. without fail. "The male is the provider, Russ," his father told him. "Women shouldn't work outside of the home. When a child comes home from school, even when they are in high school, they need guidance and supervision."

Ron also had ambitions which had been cut short by his heart attack. "I have no plans to be a principal my entire life," he told his son at weekly dinners just the two of them went to at local restaurants. "District Superintendent in a few years and eventually Superintendent of Schools. You see, Russ, I do favors for other people. They owe me and I damn well mean to collect. And, I gather dirt on my colleagues. If a promotion is between me and another guy, there's a good chance my adversary will have done something to make him vulnerable. I know one man who is cheating on his wife with *two* other women. I tuck the information away until it's needed. Another recently got pulled over for a DUI. Not a career-breaker, but character is important. If it's between the two of us, that DUI can come in handy. And one bastard is into kiddie porn. He trades photos with others like him. He hasn't harmed children, so there's no sense turning him into the police. But … he's on the school board. If it ends up being between me and another for Superintendent of Schools, I'll have his vote or he'll go to prison."

After his father died, Russ became the man of the house. He applied to Stanford but didn't get in due to affirmative action quotas. He ended up going to Temple University for a year but he had no interest in a liberal arts education. He had no desire to join the military, to go overseas and fight for foreigners who didn't hide their disdain for Americans.

The police force intrigued him. He could follow the path his father had set for himself before he failed his physical. And once on the force, Russ followed his father's advice to the letter. "Don't waste your talent," his father told him shortly before his death. "Whatever you strive to become, your ultimate goal should be to command *all* those below you. Superintendent of Schools. A general in the military. Chief of Police. Second place is for losers."

Russ would have made his father proud. Minorities and women far less competent than him received promotions they didn't merit. His team play philosophy had earned him advancement. He had collected favors without having to owe anyone himself. He had dirt on many of his superiors. There was no way he'd allow Morales—a *Hispanic*—to surpass him. He'd keep an eye on Morales. He said he wasn't ambitious, but Russ didn't believe the man. All was fair in the rise to the top. When the time came, he'd cut Morales's legs from under him.

CHAPTER FORTY-SIX

At 1 p.m., Morales knocked on the door of Aiyana's apartment. Aiyana looked like she had been crying, Morales thought. She appeared subdued.

"I-I was going to call you, Estefan," she told him when they were seated. "That Detective Chompsky who came by earlier is an animal—"

"Strange term for you to be using, isn't it, Aiyana?" Morales interrupted. "But go on. Why?"

"He as much as accused me of murdering my daughter," Aiyana continued. "I was—still am—hurting and he asked about arguments we had and my lack of *responsible supervision*—his words—when I let her go out late the night she was raped. He attacked me … my parenting, then asked if I had killed her because she'd become too much of a burden with her pregnancy."

"Sound a lot like Pines," Morales said. "He really shouldn't anger you. He might end up like Pines or your rapist."

"Why the hostility, Estefan?" Aiyana asked. "You're treating me—"

"It's Sergeant Morales, Aiyana," Morales said. "I'm now in charge of Nita's case. I won't be easy on you. I want the truth. No bullshit. You're not at all who I thought you were. You played me for a fool."

"I've never lied to you, Este—Sergeant Morales," Aiyana said.

"Not when you were raped, but over the years you've killed any number of people. Nita, too. I have proof. My problem is, I can't convince an assistant district attorney you can transform into a jaguar. It sounds ludicrous even to me when I say it out loud. But what Danai Townes saw wasn't the imagination of a youngster who just saw her father murdered. You killed Kneisha's uncle, Danai's father, and two others. You poisoned your rapist and Pines. Nita poisoned her three assailants and one of you killed Shawn Hawkins. Am I forgetting anyone?" he asked, but didn't wait for an answer. "I have proof, but it's all contingent on your being a shapeshifter. I'm no threat to you, Aiyana, so let's lay our cards on the table. There's no way in hell you would kill Nita. I'll do my best to find her killer. At some point, though, we *will* discuss your future—one where no one else loses their life."

"Neither one of us are who we were seventeen years ago," Aiyana responded. "Rage consumed me when I was sixteen. My rapist and Nita's got what they deserved. So, too, did Kneisha's uncle. The others ... not so much. But without a confession, you're helpless. And I'll confess nothing to the authorities." She paused. "My rage returned after that beast Chompsky—"

"Another word that could apply to you," Morales cut her off again.

"You *want* me to snap. To hurt you. Maybe even kill you," Aiyana said. "No, Estefan, you *won't* bait me," Aiyana shouted. "My rage returned, but I have no idea who would kill Nita. I'm not going on a rampage. I'll—"

"You'll be patient while we investigate," Morales interrupted. "Rein in your anger. Play the victim. Don't be a deterrent to our investigation. And once we find Nita's killer, the judicial system will decide his or her fate ... *not you*."

"Is Danai going to help you?" Aiyana asked.

"Danai is what we call a person of interest," Morales said. "She won't be involved in our investigation. I hope to enlist Detective Chaffetz, who followed up on Nita's rape. She's no Pines."

"I liked her," Aiyana said. "She was sympathetic to Nita."

"First, though, I have some questions for you," Morales said. "I need complete honesty. You can spin your answers for Chaffetz so you don't sound delusional. Why was Nita doing the laundry at midnight?"

"Two or three times a week I go out at midnight … to stretch my legs," Aiyana said.

"You're not the jogger type," Morales replied.

"I let loose the jaguar in me. Are you happy … *Sergeant?*" Aiyana asked.

"I asked for honesty," Morales said. "So, yes. Why didn't Nita join you?"

"During her second trimester, she couldn't transform," Aiyana replied. "It was incredibly frustrating for her. So rather than sit in our apartment she did the laundry."

"Where did you go?"

"To Fairmount Park where I wouldn't be seen," Aiyana said.

"Leave any carnage in your wake?" Morales asked.

"Damn it, Estefan, that's beneath you," Aiyana said.

"Not in light of your past activities," Morales shot back. "I honestly need to know."

"Have you found any mutilated bodies in the park?" Aiyana asked in return, responding as she had to Danai earlier.

"Point taken," Morales replied.

"A stray dog once in a while, if you must know, but I don't transform for sustenance or to hunt prey of any kind. The jaguar within me needs release."

"When did you return the night Nita was murdered?" Morales went on.

"Around 4 a.m.," Aiyana said. "I assumed Nita was in her room sleeping. I wasn't going to wake her. Without a means of release she doesn't get the sleep she needs. I couldn't sleep. I had this foreboding something wasn't right. At around five I checked Nita's room. She wasn't there. Her bed hadn't been slept in. I … I found her in the laundry room. I wanted to call you. I didn't want a stranger—a Chompsky, making light of Nita's death. This is the projects, where life isn't worth shit." she said, her voice rising. "Just another nigger killed. I expected the apathy and scorn I received." She shrugged. "But I didn't call you. I let it play out."

"Before, with your rapist and the others, you decided to take matters into your own hands," Morales shot back. "Don't tell me you didn't consider doing the same now."

"I have no idea who killed Nita," Aiyana responded. "Do you think I was going to kill everyone I suspected?"

"The thought crossed my mind," Morales said.

Aiyana hit Morales in the chest with the palm of her hand. Then she hit him again with her other hand. "*I'm not a monster—* an indiscriminate killer," she yelled at him.

Morales grabbed her hands. She collapsed into him unable to say anything more. Overwhelmed, she began to cry uncontrollably.

"I had to be sure," Morales said. "I'm so sorry for your loss."

"Are you?" Aiyana asked.

"I saw Nita when she was six months old. Saw a devoted mother. Whatever you are, you're not a monster, and no mother should see her child and grandchild die."

"What now?" Aiyana asked, brushing tears from her eyes with the back of her hand.

"I convince Chaffetz to take the case," Morales said. "Then she and I come up with a list of suspects. The number of times Nita was hit with the bat—the medical examiner says it was eight, though she was dead by the fourth blow—indicates that this was personal. She still had her wallet in her jeans pocket with a little cash, so it wasn't a robbery gone wrong. There was no sexual assault. What those two things mean is that someone didn't just come into the laundry room and attempt to rob or rape Nita. And there were no defensive wounds on Nita's hands—no skin from her attacker under her nails. Until proven wrong, I don't believe this was a random attack. Whoever killed Nita intentionally targeted her. Struck with fury. Someone you or Nita angered to the point of murder. It's a working theory, Aiyana. The facts will either back it up or tell us to go in another direction." He paused. "Watch your back, Aiyana. This person may come for you."

"Unlike Nita, I'm not helpless. Nita couldn't morph into a jaguar when attacked. I can," Aiyana said. She sighed. "I appreciate the warning."

"Is there anyone you consider a suspect?" Morales asked. "Someone you or Nita antagonized or angered?"

"Nita called out a lot of those who watched her rape without doing a thing," Aiyana said. "She ... she killed Shawn Hawkins, but that was more than five months ago. From what I hear, his wife wasn't too distraught over his death. I can't think of anyone else."

"Don't do anything rash, Aiyana," Morales said. "Keep a low profile while we investigate." He wanted to say more, but nothing came to him. He got up and let himself out of her apartment.

CHAPTER FORTY-SEVEN

In his car, Morales chastised himself. He had been harsh and relentless, unlike the detective he had been prior to his promotion. McGowan's chiding him had made him become a bully.

At the same time, he had to admit that Aiyana had been incredibly frustrating. She admitted she had committed the murders he and Danai had uncovered. She said she had changed, but he couldn't forgive her for what she had done after her rape. And she hadn't reined in Nita after her attack.

He was more disappointed than angry, he had to admit. Which was why he had been so hard on her. Subconsciously, he had wanted to see if she'd lash out at him in anger, as she had with Pines. Wanted to see if this more "mature" Aiyana was a façade. She had acted like any mother who had lost a child to senseless violence. He hoped she still had within her a semblance of humanity. When the case was closed—solved or not—he would have another talk with her to decide upon her future.

He looked at his watch. It was 2 p.m. He had spoken with Chaffetz's sergeant after McGowan gave him the case. The sergeant had agreed to let him have Chaffetz to work the Nita Jackson murder. Another favor Morales owed. At some point he'd have to earn a few favors from his colleagues, much as he detested the thought. His debts were piling up. McGowan would most definitely come collecting. Sykes, Chaffetz's sarge, probably would, as well.

He sighed and called Chaffetz. "How about a late lunch?" Morales asked after exchanging pleasantries.

"Isn't it a bit late in the day for lunch?" Chaffetz replied.

"That's why I referred to it—"

"As a late lunch," Chaffetz finished.

"I have an offer I don't think you'll want to pass up," Morales said.

"Does it involve a motel room?" she asked.

"You gonna make me grovel?" Morales asked in return.

"I'm always up for a hot dog," Chaffetz said. "An afternoon snack," she added.

"Meet me in fifteen minutes at our bench in the park," he said.

"*Our bench*. Romantic," she replied.

Morales laughed despite himself. "Grab me two hot dogs, without the sauerkraut, and a Pepsi. Just mustard on the dogs. I haven't had lunch." He disconnected before Chaffetz could respond with a witty retort.

CHAPTER FORTY-EIGHT

Chaffetz was sitting on *their* bench when Morales arrived. She handed him two hot dogs and the Pepsi he had asked for. Morales saw she had finished her hot dog and was chewing gum.

"I was hungrier than I thought," she told him. "And it was getting cold."

"Want a bite of mine?" he asked.

"Without sauerkraut? I think not," she responded. "What's this offer—"

"You're not going to allow me to enjoy my lunch?" he asked in return.

"Add impatience to my many vices," Chaffetz said.

Morales held up a hand and gobbled down his two hot dogs. He took a long gulp of soda but didn't finish the can. Once he was done, it was time to lay out his offer. "How would you like to help me investigate a murder?" he asked, but went on before Chaffetz could reply. "It could take a week or more, if necessary. Like most in the projects, the media has ignored it after a single day of coverage. There is no pressure to solve it quickly."

"Nita Jackson," Chaffetz said.

"There are no secrets within the department, are there?" he said.

"I wouldn't go that far, but in this case I heard about Nita's murder this morning and your taking over the case just before lunch … my *first* lunch," she said with a smile. "Aren't your detectives looking into the murder?"

"I'm handling this one personally," Morales said. "My detectives are knee-deep in their own cases and they could spend just so much time on Nita's murder before we got slammed again. As I told McGowan, I have no other cases. I'd like you to be my lead investigator."

"Why me?" she asked.

"I could say something witty ..." Morales began then stopped. "When I first spoke to you I may have misled you a bit," he said, starting over.

"A bit?"

"Let me finish and then you decide," Morales said. "I have a conflict of interest now that I didn't before Nita's death. Danai Townes asked me to look into her father's murder—from fifteen years ago. There were similarities between his death and that of Shawn Hawkins, who was murdered in the projects five months ago. Danai's father had witnessed Aiyana Jackson's rape from the safety of the towers. Hawkins had a similar view of Nita's assault. Both were murdered in an unusual fashion. Both cases went unsolved. Which makes Danai a suspect in Nita's death—my conflict of interest. You've also established a good rapport with Aiyana. She had no use for Chompsky when he tried to interview her. Bully her is more like it. The man wouldn't know subtle if it hit him in the head."

"So, Aiyana is calling the shots," Chaffetz said.

"Not so," Morales snapped. "Full disclosure, I just came from speaking with her. We *do* have a history and I wanted to offer my condolences. I told her the case was mine but I would cut her no slack. I had already spoken to Sykes, so I threw your name out to her. She'll be forthcoming with you. Chompsky handled her clumsily, like Pines did. You won't confront her like a bull in a china shop."

"And if Danai killed Nita?" Chaffetz asked.

"She made her own bed," Morales said. "I told her our initial investigation was a process. We hit a dead end. She was disappointed, but I don't believe she's a vigilante. If she jumped the gun I gravely misjudged her. Personally, I don't believe she did it, but I need someone without blinders to interrogate her like any other suspect. Again, full disclosure, I want to speak to her first. Living in the towers, she can lead us to other possible suspects."

"Or have you running around following your tail," Chaffetz said.

"Granted, but I'll be having an informal chat with her," Morales said. "You'll interrogate her on the record, and if you feel she's a viable suspect, I won't interfere."

"Any constraints?" she asked.

"You're all business with my offer on the table," Morales said. "I don't micromanage my detectives. You'll have the same leeway."

"And could it lead to a promotion to Homicide?" she asked.

"I wish I could say yes, but I wasn't bullshitting you when we first met. I seldom get to pick my detectives. I get what others consider rejects—minorities and women. Most turn out to be fine detectives. However, if you solve Nita's murder it goes in your file. At any press conference held you would in the forefront and I would remain in the background. It certainly couldn't hurt with other homicide squads where there's a vacancy. No guarantees, though."

"Who have you pissed off?" Chaffetz asked.

"It's more what I don't do that puts me in this position," Morales said. "And I pose a threat to those like McGowan because I'm Hispanic. He, and I'm sure others, feel I'll get preferential treatment when it comes to a promotion. It's unwarranted, as I have no desire for advancement at this time. But I can say that until I'm blue in the face and I still won't be believed."

"Elaborate. What won't you do?" Chaffetz asked.

"You're interrogating me," Morales said.

Chaffetz remained silent.

"I'm not an ass-kisser or a brown-noser," Morales said. "I don't do favors for others to put them in my debt. A superior asks me to turn the other way when *he* is asked to intervene by a friend, relative, or special interest group … well, I politely decline to let a perp walk. I can count the favors others owe me on one hand with a finger or two remaining. I'm not a politician, and as I told you, I have no desire for further advancement right now."

"So even though you don't have the ambition, those like McGowan see you as a threat solely because you're Hispanic," Chaffetz said.

"Ironically my race works against me," Morales said. "I'm happy where I am. Was *happier* as a homicide detective. But I may very well be offered a promotion due to pressure on the department. I'd probably decline, but my white colleagues still see me as a threat."

"At least you're honest," Chaffetz said. "Maybe I should make myself known to McGowan."

"You'd live to regret it," Morales said. "First, he wouldn't allow you into his squad. He has no desire for women on his team. And you're not his type of cop."

"Are you saying I lack ambition?" Chaffetz asked. "Or the opposite?"

"Neither. First, you're a free thinker. McGowan wants his detectives to be in lockstep with him. And he wants only team players—ones who will fall on their sword if he fucks up and needs someone to blame. And, unlike me, he micromanages his detectives."

Chaffetz smiled. "Your honesty is refreshing." She shrugged. "I'll work your case."

"There are things you're going to have to find out on your own," he said, "just as I did when Danai Townes came to me."

"Handcuffing me already?"

"You won't believe me unless you uncover certain things for yourself," he said, shrugged, then added. "Let's leave it at that. I know I'm being cryptic—"

"No offense, but anything you uncovered I'll make it my business to learn," she cut him off. "Got somewhere for me to start?"

"Where I did," Morales said. "Go see Ed Cawley—"

"The Chief ME?" Chaffetz asked.

"Bring a box of Whoppers along with you and leave it on his desk when you leave. And treat him like a human being." He held up his hand before Chaffetz could respond. "You can't imagine how many detectives make demands on him and treat him condescendingly. Anyway, I'll call him and tell him you have access to whatever you require. Look into Danai's father's murder. Georgia Pines' death. Shawn Hawkins' murder. That's more than I started out with. Connect the dots. You come up with an outrageous theory, lay it on me."

"This is like one of those Russian nesting dolls," Chaffetz said. "A doll within a doll, etc. Here it's one mystery that, if solved, may lead to success in finding out who killed Nita. It would be a hell of a lot easier if you leveled with me now."

"Danai Townes led me on initially," Morales said. "If she had opened with what she knew I don't know if I would have taken her seriously. Just go into this with an open mind. I really don't want to influence you. Unless I'm mistaken, you'll end up with the same conclusion I did."

"So, do we go to a motel now?" Chaffetz asked.

"If it seals the deal," Morales answered.

"I really should call your bluff," Chaffetz replied.

"Maybe it's no bluff," Morales responded.

Chaffetz shrugged. "I don't sleep with my boss. As of now I'm working for you."

"Convenient isn't it?" Morales said, with a smile.

"You're too much," Chaffetz said. "Walk me back to the Roundhouse. Call Cawley on the way. You going to speak with Danai Townes today?"

Morales nodded.

"I'll pick Cawley's brain while you do," Chaffetz said. "Tell Townes to meet me at 8 a.m. tomorrow. I may not have solved your first puzzle by then, but I want a crack at her before she has time to concoct tales to lead me astray."

"She's not like that, but you'll have to find that out for yourself," Morales said. "*If* you clear her and want another pair of hands, I can have her transferred again."

"A threesome. Getting kinky on me," Chaffetz said.

"Busting my balls again," Morales replied.

"Always."

"I'll let you have the last word," Morales said with a smile.

"Always," Chaffetz replied, and returned the smile.

CHAPTER FORTY-NINE

Morales saw Danai at 3:25 p.m. He knew her shift began at four, and he was glad there was no time for small talk. "You've heard about Nita, I assume," he began.

"This morning," Danai said.

"I have to ask—did you kill her?"

"Is this an interrogation?" she asked.

"Did I read you your rights?" Morales asked in return.

"You think I went rogue?" Yet another question.

"Look, Danai, we proved our case but we could do nothing. It's possible—"

"I've made peace with not being able to get justice for my father," Danai said. "I have an alibi if—"

"Someone else will officially interview you—"

"You mean *interrogate* me," Danai shot back.

"Will question you," Morales said. "I had to look you in the eye and ask. I don't believe you killed Nita, but I have to consider you a person of interest until you're not."

"Fine …" Danai began irritably, then paused. "I-I understand. Aiyana killed my dad. I guess I would consider me a suspect, too. But Aiyana and I have become … well, not exactly friends, but we now understand one another. We went to Center City together a few days ago. We stopped at Jolene's Clothing Store. They have cameras to spot shoplifters. That's proof the two of us were there. We ate at McDonald's on 18th and Walnut. Any number of the staff should remember us. And like I said, I have an alibi for *all* of last night."

"Let's assume Chaffetz clears you," Morales said. "I brought her on board to lead the investigation. Personally, as I said, I don't see you as a vigilante. You had fifteen years to avenge yourself. And your beef was with Aiyana, not Nita. You live in the towers. Who should we be looking at?"

"*I'm* a suspect and you want my help," Danai said. "I could lead you astray—"

"You didn't kill Nita," Morales said. "Chaffetz has to clear you, but I've gotten to know you. Even if you would kill Nita to make Aiyana miserable, I can't see you taking the life of an unborn baby—Nita's child. So, get over yourself and tell me who we should look at."

Danai pondered the question for a few moments. "Wesley Pierce went missing," Danai began. "You should look at his step-father. Then there's August Carmichael. He leads the Towers Watch—it's a newly formed group to rid the towers of gangs and drug dealers. He's an angry man. He might have acted for Wesley's parents. And, there's DeMarius Hawkins, son of Shawn Hawkins, who Nita killed. The thing is, both he and his mother despised the man. He was physically and emotionally abusive, so they weren't terribly broken up by his death."

"Anyone—"

"Yes, but not someone from the towers," Danai said. She stood and walked around the cramped office. "After I went to Center City with Aiyana that day, I attended the towers meeting. Afterwards, I went to a gay bar. I was distracted. I considered hooking up for the night. My heart wasn't really into it. Then this woman hit on me. Billy-Joelle Cuthbart. Goes by B.J. She caught me off guard. She was dressed as a cowboy—hat, boots, and all. We went to her motel. After … well, while lying in bed, she asked me about a shapeshifter."

"She set you up," Morales said. "How—"

"A long story, which I'll tell Chaffetz, if I must," Danai cut Morales off. "The gist of it is that Aiyana's mother Bly killed both B.J.'s stepfather and mother. Bly was a foster child. The stepfather abused her—cigarette burns on her skin, and when she turned sixteen, he raped her. Bly killed him in the same manner as my father. Three days later, her mother died of complete organ failure. B.J. saw Bly turn into a jaguar. She's a bounty hunter. She's been looking for Bly ever since she got out

of the foster care system. The three rapists Nita killed caught
her attention. She hacked into Cawley's computer and saw I had
accessed their deaths. She's thorough. My name led her to my
father's murder."

"So she has sex with you and puts you into a false sense of
complacency, and you told her about Aiyana," Morales said.

"I didn't give Aiyana up, but she told me it was simple for her
to identify Aiyana and Nita. She had the date when those boys
died. She knew the rape occurred at the towers. All she had to do
was check police reports to find out the name of the rape victim.
That gives her Nita, who leads her to Aiyana. I got the sense … no,
she *asked* me to join her to avenge my father's death. I declined."

"But she's after Bly," Morales said.

"Who was never in the picture," Danai said. "Aiyana says
she left to die after giving birth to her. B.J. wants to end the family line."

"Why kill Nita first?" Morales asked. "It would alert Aiyana.
And Aiyana was far more dangerous than Nita *before* Nita was
killed."

"It's only conjecture, but B.J. went through hell when her
mother died—being placed in a foster home. Maybe she wanted
to put Aiyana through the same pain. Plus B.J. is a bit arrogant.
She feels she can take Aiyana on even if Aiyana is aware of her
existence."

"Our prime suspect," Morales said.

"One more thing I touched on before," Danai said, not
answering his question. "B.J. saw Bly transform into a jaguar.
It's not like she could testify against Bly even if she was in the
picture. You were right, I'm no vigilante. Can't say the same for
B.J." She paused. "Still I have my doubts. B.J. is no butcher. I
heard Nita was hit in the head with a baseball bat eight times.
Was unrecognizable. That's overkill. B.J.'s anger was directed at
Bly. Ending the family line is her goal, but, personally, I can't see
the brutality."

Morales stood. "Thank you Danai," he said. "I wasn't
bullshitting you when I told you I believed you had nothing to
do with Nita's death. You didn't have to tell me about this B.J.
It's appreciated."

"Now I have to tell Chaffetz I'm a lesbian," Danai said glumly.

"You still haven't made up your mind about coming out?" Morales asked.

"I'm coming out, but I want it on my terms. Now—"

"Chaffetz is discreet," Morales said. "A confidential informant pointed us to B.J. We're not going to out you."

"Not going to let me help with the case either, are you?"

"That's up to Chaffetz," Morales said. "I've given her the option to bring you on board. I won't dictate to her, though."

Danai looked at her watch. "My shift begins—"

"Go," Morales said. "Be straight with Chaffetz. She's not your enemy."

"Tell her about Aiyana transforming into a jaguar?" Danai said.

"You now have B.J. to corroborate your story, so why the hell not?" Morales said. "I sent her to Cawley. She's going to come to the same conclusion as I did *before* you confided in me. Your father and others died from what more than one coroner thinks was an animal attack. You didn't see Aiyana's face, but B.J. saw Bly morph into a jaguar. If Chaffetz doesn't believe you, she's not the cop I think she is."

Danai shrugged, got up and left.

CHAPTER FIFTY

BLY

(1962)

Bly woke up and attempted to sit up. A sharp pain in her hip wracked her body. She lay down until the pain subsided. She then sat up again, this time more slowly. She was lying on a cot. Her right hand was handcuffed to a metal rod beneath the mattress. She removed the sheet that covered her. She was naked, her breasts ponderous from milk she would have fed her newborn child. Her hip was black and blue. Her leg from her toes to her hip was enclosed in a cast.

She recalled that she had gone to Fairmount Park to die after having given birth. Only she wasn't dead. She was a prisoner.

A woman entered the room.

"Thought I heard something," she said, in a strong South Philly accent. She was a husky, diminutive woman. Bly guessed her to be in her late forties. She had a bright smile and kind eyes. Her red hair looked to be colored.

"Am I your prisoner?" Bly asked.

"I'm Madeline," the woman said, ignoring Bly's comment. "And you're ... ?"

"Bly. Am I—"

"I heard you, child. Don't get your panties in a bunch," she cut Bly off. "I'll answer your question in due time." She paused, then laughed. "You don't have no panties to get in a bunch, do you now?" She laughed again. "I apologize. It's just ... Never mind. Anyway, my husband, Henry, and I found you in Fairmount Park. Only you weren't human. A big black cat—"

"A jaguar," Bly interrupted.

"Whatever," the woman said. "You were hurt real bad. Lucky for you, Henry is an ER doctor. He poked and prodded you a bit—doing doctor things—and you … well … you transformed into a woman. A pretty young thing, at that. Kind of threw us a bit. Well, we couldn't very well take you to a hospital, could we? What if you changed into that … jaguar again in front of a bunch of doctors and nurses? So we brought you here—South Philly—to our home. We didn't know if you'd change back into a … jaguar. Didn't know if you'd attack us if you did. You know, we didn't know if you were dangerous."

"Hence the handcuffs," Bly said. "I would have done the same," she added. "I won't change back. And I'm not dangerous." She paused. "What were you doing in Fairmount Park in the middle of the night? You said you're from South Philly."

"Neither Henry or I sleep well at times," Madeline said. "Teens these days stay out all night drinking, throwing bottles against walls and making a nuisance of themselves. I woke up and couldn't fall back to sleep. If I can't sleep, Henry can't sleep either. We've often driven to Fairmount Park when it gets too hectic here. It's like another country there. We walk, and other than crickets, you don't hear a thing. That's how we came upon you. It could have been the police, which would have made things difficult for you."

Bly nodded then held up her hand with the handcuff.

"I'll get Henry," Madeline said and left.

The two returned five minutes later. Henry towered over his wife, though he was no more than five foot nine. He was stocky. His thick hair was mostly gray with a bit of black remaining. His eyes mirrored his wife's.

"Am I going to survive?" Bly asked the man.

"You got a broken leg, as you can see," he said. "Hip looks only bruised, though I'd like to take an x-ray. I'd also like to win the lottery, if you get my drift. We'll have to do without the x-ray. There's no internal bleeding that I could tell. Do you recall giving birth … like tonight?" he asked.

Bly nodded.

"All in all I'd say you're damn lucky. What happened to you?" he asked.

"It doesn't disturb you that you found me as a jaguar who transformed into a woman?" Bly asked.

"All in due time," Henry said. "Please answer my question. I'm obviously concerned most about your health right now."

"I got blindsided by a car," Bly said.

"Where is your baby?" he asked.

"At a church," Bly said. "I thought I was dying. I had to get away from her. If I was found in either of my forms there would be questions, especially if I died as you found me."

"Want us to contact hospitals to find out how she is?" Henry asked.

Bly shook her head. "There are questions I obviously don't want to answer that the authorities would have if you began asking about her. It's the same reason you can't take me to a hospital. They'd draw blood and become real interested in me." She went silent for a moment. "How can the two of you be so calm after what you witnessed?" she asked.

"I was a medic in World War II," Henry said. "Saw things that were truly horrific. Saw men who should have died that didn't. Others who were hardly wounded didn't make it. Our troops captured some *real* monsters—vile creatures who ran or worked in concentration camps. Saw ... well, some of their *experiments* on humans. Bastards were proud of all the Jews they mutilated and killed. You, my dear, don't compare to them. You transforming into a ... jaguar, my wife told me. That doesn't make you a monster."

"I've got blood on my hands," Bly said. "Self-defense," she added, a half-truth.

"Should we put you down?" Henry asked.

Bly smiled for the first time. Maybe she had found a home.

BOOK THREE

CHAPTER FIFTY-ONE

CHAFFETZ

(1995)

Danai was supposed to meet Chaffetz at 8 a.m. Her phone rang at seven.

"Come in at one this afternoon," Chaffetz said after identifying herself.

"Any reason—" Danai began.

"I'll be asking the questions," Chaffetz interrupted, then disconnected.

Bitch, Danai thought, then reconsidered. Danai was a suspect. Chaffetz didn't have to tell her a damn thing. She had already set the ground rules for the interrogation. Chaffetz would be asking the questions.

Danai was seated across from Chaffetz a bit after one. She thought Chaffetz might let her stew in the interrogation room for fifteen minutes, maybe more—a common police practice she had been taught at the academy. Chaffetz, though, wasn't playing games.

"I'm not going to ask you softball questions to gain your confidence or throw you off balance," Chaffetz began after she had entered the room. "You've been taught the tricks that we use with suspects. So, tell me your alibi—from midnight the day before yesterday until 5 a.m."

"I was on the four-to-midnight shift—" Danai began.

"That's no alibi. My question was *from* midnight on," Chaffetz cut her off. "I don't give a flying fuck what you did before midnight. Nita was killed between one and four that morning."

So that was the tactic Chaffetz had decided to use, Danai thought to herself. Constant interruptions to make it difficult for Danai to adhere to any rehearsed narrative. And, yes, Danai had rehearsed what she was going to tell the detective a number of times the night before.

"I didn't go right home," Danai said. It wasn't quite as she had rehearsed. Score one for Chaffetz. "My partner and I, Kyle Abbott, have a decent rapport. He must have known I'd been preoccupied ... distracted the entire day—"

"Why were you distracted?" Chaffetz pounced.

"Aiyana and I had gone to Center City," Danai said. "Didn't Morales give you notes from our ... meeting?"

"I want to hear everything firsthand. Go on."

"I had this picture in my head of Aiyana. A cold-hearted killer," Danai went on. "I found her far different than my perception. Likable, you could say. I was dwelling on our time together the entire shift."

Chaffetz opened a manila file folder. She glanced at the first page for a moment, then closed it. "Go on."

"I went over to Kyle's for a drink," Danai said. "I have no love for the Southwark Towers. No desire to hurry back to a home I loathe."

"You and Abbott an item?" Chaffetz pressed.

"I'm a lesbian, but you know that," Danai shot back.

"There was something in Morales's notes about you fucking a bounty hunter who was after Aiyana and Nita. Could be you're bi," Chaffetz added.

"A lesbian, though I'm still in the closet. I'm thinking of coming out," Danai said. She knew Chaffetz was baiting her with her description of her night with B.J. *Fucking her.*

"So Abbott doesn't know you're a lesbian, right?" Chaffetz asked, but didn't wait for an answer. "Maybe he hoped to get lucky."

Danai shook her head, still angered by Chaffetz's reference to her and B.J. Why? Because Chaffetz was right. She and B.J. had spent over an hour fucking. There was no other euphemism for it. Not *making love* or *sleeping with*. They were *fucking*.

"Will Abbott be disappointed if you come out?" Chaffetz continued.

"I told him the day we were teamed together that I don't go to bed with my partner. It can only lead to problems," Danai said.

"A clever way of hiding your sexual identity," Chaffetz responded.

"My only other partner was female," Danai said. "Straight, as far as I know. If she had hit on me I would have told her what I told Kyle. Besides, Kyle has a girlfriend. He's not the type to betray her for a hookup."

"What time did you leave his apartment?"

"That's just it. I *didn't*," Danai said. "One drink led to a second and a third. I soon lost count. Kyle refused to let me drive home. I slept on the living room couch. Got up at 6 a.m. He was making breakfast. Afterwards I went to the towers. Got there a bit after seven. That's when I heard Nita had been killed."

"You slept on the couch? Not too chivalrous of your partner," Chaffetz said.

Still baiting me, Danai thought. "I've never asked for preferential treatment because of my gender," Danai replied, reining in her anger. "He offered me his bed. I told him I'd take the couch or walk home. He knew I wasn't busting his balls. Knew where I lived and walking home would be dangerous even for a cop. So, yes, I slept on the couch, and not because he's an asshole."

"You and Abbott tight?" Chaffetz asked.

"To the point he'd lie for me?" Danai asked, but went on before Chaffetz could make an insulting remark. "We're partners. We go out for a drink once in a while. Sometimes hang with other cops at a bar. That's the extent of our relationship. We don't confide in one another. Like I said earlier, he doesn't know I'm a lesbian. If we were *tight*, as you say, I might have confided in him. Only you and Morales, in the department, know I'm gay."

"I'll verify your account with Officer Abbott," Chaffetz said. "Let's say I believe you. Why didn't you bring this B.J. you hooked up with to Morales's attention before yesterday?"

"I'd been reassigned to beat patrol," Danai said. "We had no case."

"This B.J. was clearly a threat to Aiyana and Nita," Chaffetz continued. "Didn't you have a responsibility, as a police officer, to report the threat to *someone*?"

"I had outed myself to Morales. I wasn't ready to go public," Danai said. "The proper channel would have been to tell my sarge. I wasn't prepared to tell him I got picked up by a *woman* at a gay bar."

"So you gave a pass to a possible murderer to stay in the closet," Chaffetz said. "Either you're a coward or maybe this B.J. doesn't exist. It's pretty convenient of you to come up with another suspect out of the blue."

"Why would I lie? I have an alibi," Danai said.

"Too bad you *didn't* sleep with Abbott," Chaffetz replied. "You both had too much to drink—or so you say. He's in the bedroom passed out. You *could* have slipped out, killed Nita, and returned well before he woke up. Then, to bolster your alibi, you created another suspect. There's something you're not telling me. This B.J. was a threat to Aiyana and Nita. So, tell me again you remained silent," Chaffetz said.

"I didn't," Danai said. "I told Aiyana about B.J. Nita was in the room, but she had no use for me. I warned Aiyana. She could take better care of herself than the police. Aiyana would never accept police protection."

"I thought you only told Morales, and now me, that you were a lesbian," Chaffetz said.

"I blurted it out to Aiyana when I wasn't thinking … on our way to Center City," Danai said.

"So Aiyana *and* Nita also know. Since Nita had no use for you—your words—maybe you were fearful she'd reveal your secret," Chaffetz said.

"Think what you want," Danai said. "You want to find out the truth? Speak to B.J." Danai gave her the name of the motel and room number B.J. was staying at along with her description.

Chaffetz left the room and returned five minutes later.

"Your pal checked out of the motel the morning after you

two hooked up," Chaffetz told Danai when she sat down. "Made the reservation by phone. Registered under the name Cynthia Knox. The woman who checked in looked *nothing* like the person you described. I almost believed you. So, who was this B.J.—a figment of your imagination?"

"She's a bounty hunter," Danai said. "Everything you said can be easily explained by someone who is a professional. I spent the night with her. I don't know if she was bullshitting me, but she told me that when she was finished she would go back to the bar for three nights before leaving Philly."

"A second hookup? Are you that good in bed?" Chaffetz asked.

"Go fuck yourself," Danai snapped, then silently cursed herself. Chaffetz had gotten to her. Sexually, she had been a novice until her night with B.J.

"How could she be done with Aiyana still alive?" Chaffetz went on, ignoring Danai's comment.

"She's no fool," Danai said. "She'd draw too much attention going after Aiyana now. She's had seventeen years for her hatred to fester—"

"Just like you," Chaffetz interrupted.

"She can leave and return in six months or a year," Danai said. "Or maybe killing Nita set her free. What I'm saying is, she *might* be at the bar tonight. You don't have to believe me, but if I'm telling the truth, you want to get B.J. before she leaves the city. Maybe she fed me a false name. Maybe she's not from Colorado. And maybe she'll just disappear. But can you afford to *not* check out the bar?"

Chaffetz spent another thirty minutes asking about the other possible suspects as if she was finished with B.J. After telling her about DeMarius Hawkins, Danai was spent. There was nothing left to tell. "Are we finished?" Danai asked.

"Morales had a puzzle to solve," Chaffetz said. "Told me I had to figure it out myself or I'd never take the case seriously. I had you come in at one because I had to speak to Ed Cawley. Had to look at evidence of a significant number of murders. I've drawn conclusions, but they lead me nowhere. You're the last piece of the puzzle."

"What have you uncovered?" Danai asked. She wasn't about to talk about a shapeshifter without knowledge that Chaffetz had all her ducks lined up in a row.

Chaffetz told Danai what she had found. "So we have five blunt-force head traumas causing near-instant death, over a period of twenty years. Neither Cawley nor any of the other coroners who examined the bodies could find a weapon that could have caused the injury. And he feels it was the work of one person. You have five other deaths due to complete organ failure. Each victim had an identical scratch on the back of their wrist."

"Your conclusion?" Danai asked.

"The first to die of complete organ failure died several days after the rape of Aiyana Jackson. Detective Pines had been investigating Aiyana Jackson—harassing her. And the three who died most recently correspond to the gang rape of Nita Jackson. But no toxins were found in their systems to indicate murder."

"And those with their skulls caved in?" Danai asked.

"All residents of the Southwark Towers," Chaffetz went on. "Three, including your father, occurred within five years of Aiyana's rape. And another was five months after Nita's rape. The first was three years prior to Aiyana's rape. That one has me stumped."

"He was the uncle of Aiyana's best friend, Kneisha," Danai said. "Her uncle raped Kneisha. She was considering suicide. Aiyana solved the problem."

"You're implying these ten killings were perpetrated by Aiyana and Nita Jackson," Chaffetz said.

"I'm stating a fact," Danai replied. "I saw who killed my father," Danai said.

"You never told the police."

"They wouldn't believe me. I was a six-year-old kid who had just seen her father murdered," Danai responded.

"What didn't you tell them?" Chaffetz asked.

"Aiyana transformed ... shapeshifted—pick whatever word you want—into a black jaguar. The jaguar—an animal with powerful jaws—bit my father in the back of his head. The jaguar then transformed back into a woman. I couldn't positively identify her as Aiyana. There was a fog surrounding her face. But all Morales and I uncovered, and all you discovered, points directly to Aiyana and most recently Nita. Morales said the district attorney's office would kick us out on our asses if we made that assertion. I concur. What's your verdict?"

"A shapeshifter?" she said, sounding incredulous.

"Find B.J. and she'll confirm my story," Danai said. "Her stepfather was killed by a jaguar—by Aiyana's mother. B.J.'s mother died from complete organ failure three days later. B.J. has a tattoo of the scratch on her wrist as a reminder."

"Morales believes in this shapeshifter—"

"Shapeshifter crap?" Danai finished for her. She nodded. "Go ask him."

"It's inconsequential whether I accept your conclusion," Chaffetz said. "I don't have to believe in this jaguar you refer to. It's irrelevant to Nita Jackson's murder."

"I disagree," Danai said. "I had motive because I saw Aiyana transform into a jaguar. B.J. saw Aiyana's mother transform. My father, Austin Pierce, and Shawn Hawkins were all killed because they watched Aiyana's and Nita's rape and did nothing to intervene. I believe one of those I suggested as suspects killed Nita."

"I think we're done, Danai," Chaffetz said.

"You going to the bar tonight?" Danai asked.

"We're done, Danai," Chaffetz repeated and stood up. "You're free to go."

CHAPTER FIFTY-TWO

BLY

(1963)

Bly sat in a rocker, cradling her infant child.

The first four months after her rescue had been incredibly painful. She was bedridden for a month, tension within her mounting as she was unable to free the jaguar within her. At the end of the third month, the cast on her leg was removed. Henry introduced her to a personal trainer who undertook her rehab. During therapy, she learned she would always walk with a pronounced limp.

When she was finally able to transform into her true self, the jaguar was likewise hobbled. She could run, but only for short, painful bursts. Chasing dogs in Fairmount Park late at night became a humiliating exercise in futility. She lacked speed. She could no longer cut to the left or right, blocking the way of the petrified animal she pursued. Her mind screamed at her. Her body refused to obey. She often wondered if it would have been better if Madeline and Henry hadn't found her in the park. Better if she had been left to die.

She began to drink as despair engulfed her. Madeline eventually told her she couldn't stop her from drinking, but there would be no alcohol in the house. Bly began spending her nights at local bars, stumbling home at two or three in the morning. Men often made passes at her, but she was quick to rebuff them. She received no physical pleasure from sex. Her foster father had savagely raped her. He'd had no desire to pleasure her, just impregnate her. When she had known she was pregnant, she had rid herself of the brute.

One night a man in his thirties hit on her at a bar she seldom frequented. She had had far too much to drink when the man—she never learned his name, or if she had, she couldn't recall it later—sat next to her, bought her a drink, and chatted with her.

The next thing she remembered was waking up in his bed. Her genitals ached, as did her leg and hip, but she couldn't recall having sex. She smiled as she stretched. She had gotten what she wanted. She dressed and left while her partner was in the bathroom.

Days later, she knew she was pregnant. When she delivered her daughter, the pain was excruciating. Henry, who administered to her, told her it was her hip which was causing the discomfort.

And now she rocked her child in a chair Henry had made for her. He told her several days after giving birth that having another baby would be dangerous. She didn't listen as he rambled on in technical terms how close both she and her daughter had come to dying. So, any further sex was out of the question, not that Bly really cared.

She had stopped drinking once she knew she was pregnant. Pills for her pain were also off limits. But holding her child, she knew it had been worth a horrendous nine months. She had held Aiyana for just a few moments. She now had a daughter she could mother. She was finally content. In appreciation of her benefactors, she had taken Henry's last name, which she gladly passed onto her daughter.

CHAPTER FIFTY-THREE

(1995)

After Chaffetz had finished with Danai and corroborated her alibi with Kyle Abbott, she went to see Morales. She felt miserable. She had been brutal with Danai—poking holes in her alibi and doubting the existence of B.J. She had questioned Danai as she would a pedophile found raping a child. Danai had somehow brought out the worst in her. She felt like a shit.

"Do you believe Danai's story?" Chaffetz asked Morales when she was seated.

"Which one?" he asked.

"The jaguar—Aiyana a shapeshifter," Chaffetz said.

"She told you?" Morales asked.

"After I told her the evidence I had uncovered. You had me chasing my tail, if you recall," she said.

"I needed you to see the evidence Danai and I uncovered so you could approach the murder with an open mind. Cawley and other medical examiners could find no weapon that could have caused the injury that killed Danai's father. She says the wound was that of a jaguar. Cawley said that, yes, it could have been the bite of a jaguar."

"You told him of Danai's shapeshifter theory?" Chaffetz asked.

"No, but he and others had mentioned the possibility of an animal attack," Morales said. "All tossed it aside. How could the animal have gotten in and, more importantly, left the apartments after the kills? So, do you have an alternative theory?" he asked.

"You know I don't," Chaffetz said. "An animal attack I could run with, reluctantly. I mean, *five* animal attacks over the course of twenty years? The logical me is skeptical. But the evidence points to an animal attack. I've got to deal with it. A *shapeshifter*, though. Where do I go with that?"

"You don't," Morales said. "That case is closed. I had you explore it to put Nita's murder in perspective. Believe it or don't, but how could you investigate Nita's murder without the knowledge of what Danai believes she witnessed? Backed up, by the way, by this B.J. she mentioned."

"The elusive B.J.," Chaffetz said. She explained to Morales what she had found when she tried to locate Danai's bed partner.

"Finding out if this B.J. exists shouldn't be too difficult. How would you go about it?" Morales asked.

"Go to the bar and see if the bartender had seen a woman who fit her description," Chaffetz said. "I mean, according to Danai, she would easily stand out in a crowd."

Morales nodded. "Have you cleared Danai?"

"Reluctantly at first, but I admit her alibi is airtight," Chaffetz said. "I told her I could punch holes in it, but it was a stretch. I do want to check out her claim that she and Aiyana have come to an understanding. I seriously doubt she lied. And while it wasn't in your notes, I can't see Danai killing an unborn child. The viciousness of the attack also doesn't fit Danai." She paused. "I came at her hard, Morales. Some part of me wanted to break her. I don't know what came over me," she said, and shrugged. "Maybe it was how outrageous her story was. How the hell would I prove Aiyana is a shapeshifter? It's something I'd have to take on faith, and that's not how I roll in Sex Crimes. And bringing up this B.J. chick made me even more combative. She, *too*, saw a shapeshifter. I suggested to Danai this woman was a figment of her imagination, or worse, someone she fabricated to take the heat off of her."

"Were you rough on her because she's a lesbian?" Morales asked.

"I don't care who she fucks," Chaffetz began, "but I'll admit this remaining in the closet irks me. I mean, she likes women. Screws women. Who the hell cares? Why hide—"

"Potential partners would care," Morales interrupted. "The brass would care. This department is hard enough on straight women. It would be worse for a lesbian. Look at the military with its 'Don't ask, don't tell' policy. The military is hardly tolerant of women. The police department forces gays to remain in the closet if they want to advance. The police department doesn't have an official policy like the military, but we're not an enlightened bunch. Danai is as ambitious as you are. All else being equal, would Sykes rather have you or Danai in his squad?"

"Putting me in my place," Chaffetz answered.

"No, pointing out a reality," Morales countered. "If you find this B.J. exists, are you going to try to locate her?" Morales asked.

Chaffetz nodded. "I'm not passing on any lead. *If* she exists, she's a viable suspect."

"Don't be so hard on yourself, Chafe," Morales said. "Danai will replay your interrogation in her head over and over again. How you handled her will make her a better cop when she makes detective."

"So you agree with my approach?" she asked.

"I didn't say that," Morales replied. "She will consider your approach and then counter it with other ways you could have handled her. *That* will make her a better cop."

Chaffetz smiled. "You're a glass half-full guy, aren't you?" she said.

"I have my detectives' backs. You were tough on her but you didn't cross any lines."

"What does one wear to a gay bar … to blend in?" Chaffetz asked. She had been speaking to herself, but she said it aloud.

"Ask Danai," Morales said. "It's your first step in reconciling with her. You could use her input on the tower suspects. And her insight *if* you find this B.J."

"You had this in mind the whole time—partnering me up with Danai," Chaffetz said.

"If you cleared her and if you agreed," Morales said. "I wouldn't force her on you."

"You're a devious man, Morales," she said. "I'll have to be on my toes around you," she added with a smile.

CHAPTER FIFTY-FOUR

BLY

(1974)

Bly's daughter sprinted ahead of her mother in the moonless night in Fairmount Park. Bly was favoring her bad leg. Her daughter had turned eleven the previous day. With her birthday came the dreams that spoke of their shared heritage. Bly wondered how Aiyana had coped with the knowledge spewed at her. Her eldest daughter had no one to help her interpret her dreams. Bly would be there for her younger daughter to answer questions that could otherwise overwhelm her.

Bly was twenty-eight, but she knew her health was failing. Having been hit by a car must have caused internal damage that was now wracking her body. Often her urine was bloody. She'd be constipated for days, followed by bouts of diarrhea four or five times a day. She had intense headaches and her vision was blurred. Henry chastised himself for not taking her to a hospital when he and Madeline found her. Bly argued it was something he could never have done.

"You've analyzed my blood," she told the man she considered her father. "You know it would have raised red flags at any hospital. I would have ended up a lab rat, trapped in a cage like animals at the zoo. I'd rather be free. I've had eleven good years with my little one because of you. And it's not like I'm going to die tomorrow," she added.

"You've made Madeline and me incredibly happy," Henry said. "We despaired when Madeline couldn't bear children.

We'd go to a playground and Madeline would be heartbroken. I tried to be strong for her, but I was as despondent as she was. Then you came into our lives. Someone Madeline could talk with as if you were her child. And your daughter ... what a blessing for us. I just don't want to lose you."

Bly was intent on surviving at least until her daughter turned sixteen. When *her* dreams had begun, she had realized that with her sixteenth birthday her life would change forever. It would be the same with her daughter.

CHAPTER FIFTY-FIVE

(1995)

At 9 p.m., Chaffetz entered the bar where Danai had said B.J. would meet her. She had reluctantly asked Danai what she should wear.

"I usually go topless," Danai answered. "Go in with a jacket or blazer and toss the coat away."

"You're kidding. I—" Chaffetz began.

"Busting your chops," Danai replied. "You earned it, coming at me like you did today."

Chaffetz remained silent.

"Us lesbians are like everyone else," Danai continued. "Go to a straight bar and you'll see businessmen in suits. Others will wear gaudy shirts unbuttoned to their navel. Some women don't wear a bra, even if they have saggy breasts and one is called for. Many just wear casual attire. My point is there is *no* lesbian dress code. But, if you *don't* want to scare B.J. away, I'd suggest tight jeans and either a blouse or top that accentuates your breasts without it appearing you're trying to look too sexy. Show cleavage but not too much. Little or no makeup. You don't need makeup anyway. You'll get hit on or offered drinks if you have to wait for her. Be polite, but rebuff any advances. Accept a drink and you're sending out a vibe a hookup is possible. There's always the excuse you're waiting for someone. Someone *special*, if you want to sound mysterious."

"I asked how to dress and you gave me an entire tutorial," Chaffetz said.

"Too much information?" Danai asked.

"Not at all," Chaffetz replied. "I hadn't thought about how I'd act at the bar. The furthest thing from my mind was whether I'd get hit on if I had to wait for your B.J."

"You're an attractive … exotic-looking woman who will draw stares," Danai said. "Just as you would at a straight bar. And, no I'm not hitting on you, just stating the obvious."

Chaffetz wore jeans and a V-neck top to the bar. She felt like all of the women's eyes were on her when she entered. She sat at the far end of the bar—not far from the ladies' room, so she could see those who entered the bar. B.J. might have dressed as she had when she hit on Danai, or she could be a chameleon looking totally different. Danai had described B.J. to a police sketch artist. Whatever she wore, Chaffetz was confident she would recognize the woman.

She waited until she had nursed her first drink, then asked the bartender if she had seen B.J. as Danai had encountered her. The bartender told her she recalled such a woman—with her unique attire she stood out—but hadn't seen her recently. At least Chaffetz had been able to corroborate Danai's story that the woman existed.

As Danai had predicted, several women approach her. Some wanted to dance, others offered to buy her a drink. She politely declined and finally began using the line Danai had suggested.

A little after ten, B.J. entered. She was dressed as Danai had described her—complete with cowboy hat. She sat at the bar and ordered a drink which she nursed for fifteen minutes.

Chaffetz waited another five minutes and then took a seat next to B.J. "A refill for my friend," she told the bartender. "Same for me," she said, using the same line B.J. had on Danai.

"I'm not looking for a hookup," B.J. said, after scrutinizing Chaffetz.

"Danai isn't coming," Chaffetz responded. She lifted the bottom of her blouse which covered her badge. "You're a person of interest in a homicide. How about a friendly interview at the Roundhouse?"

"And if I say no?" B.J. asked.

The bartender brought Chaffetz and B.J. their drinks.

"I toss the drink on myself, get in your face for disrespecting me, and take you out in cuffs—assaulting a police officer."

"Aren't you the clever one?" B.J. said. She took a long sip of her drink. "A friendly interview it is, I guess," she said. "Will Danai be joining us?" she asked.

"She's a person of interest as well," Chaffetz lied. "It will be just the two of us."

"I was so looking forward to a threesome," B.J. said.

At the Roundhouse, Chaffetz took B.J. to an interrogation room. "Can I get you some coffee?" Chaffetz asked.

"So I have to pee during our ... interview? Or so you can get prints or DNA off of the cup I use?" she asked. "I'll pass. Are you going to read me my rights?" she then asked.

"We're just having a conversation," Chaffetz replied.

B.J. shrugged. "Whose homicide are you referring to?" she finally asked.

"Nita Jackson was murdered last night," Chaffetz said. "Found by her mother this morning."

"Maybe there is a God," B.J. said.

"That's cold," Chaffetz snapped. "Nita was pregnant, so it's a double murder."

"Crime prevention, then," B.J. responded. "The child would have been a carbon copy of her mother. I take it you think I might have killed Nita."

"You top my list of suspects," Chaffetz said. "Danai was very forthcoming. You have motive—"

"Not to kill Nita ... or even Aiyana," B.J. shot back.

"To end the family line," Chaffetz replied. "Wasn't that what you told Danai?"

B.J. remained silent.

"If you weren't interested in Aiyana or Nita, why remain in Philly? Certainly not to hook up with Danai a second time. Or was she that good in bed?" She didn't wait for B.J. to respond. "Danai said you were disappointed that Bly might have been dead, but you'd go after Aiyana, Nita, and Nita's unborn child."

"Killing Nita first would be foolhardy," B.J. replied. "The mother is far more dangerous, especially now with Nita dead. If it were me, I'd go after the most dangerous one first. Nita would be easy pickings, being six months pregnant."

"Not if you wanted Aiyana to suffer like you did when your mother was killed," Chaffetz said.

"A valid point," B.J. responded. "Still, strategically not the right move."

"Where were you from midnight until 4 a.m.?" Chaffetz asked.

B.J. smiled. "With Aiyana, in a manner of speaking. I admit I was interested in her. I stayed hidden in an abandoned car—a rusted Chevy that had once been red. The wheels had been stripped."

"Why hidden?"

"I was keeping tabs on Aiyana and her daughter," B.J. said. "I had a hunch one or both might be going out at night."

"Like Bly when she was at your house?"

"Danai does have some mouth on her," B.J. said. "Anyway, two days before Nita was killed, Aiyana left the towers alone at around midnight. I followed her on foot to Fairmount Park. Lost her there—"

"Give me a break," Chaffetz interrupted. "You're an experienced bounty hunter. You telling me you lost her in the park? I don't buy it."

B.J. shrugged. "I don't know if you believed Danai, but Aiyana shapeshifted into a jaguar. I was then at an extreme disadvantage ... even *with* my experience."

"You saw her mother, Bly, transform. Go out at night," Chaffetz said.

"Just once. The night she killed my stepfather and mother," B.J. replied. "She had gone out almost every night, but that was the only time I saw her turn."

"Go on," Chaffetz said.

"Aiyana made the same trek last night," B.J. continued. "The result was the same. Each time she eluded me I went back to my hiding place. Aiyana got back to the towers at 3:45 the first night and 4:15 last night."

"Why didn't you stake her out tonight?" Chaffetz asked.

"She had established a pattern—never two nights in a row."

"Tell me what happened to your stepfather and mother," Chaffetz said.

"Didn't Danai tell you?"

"I want to hear it from you," Chaffetz said.

B.J. told Chaffetz her tale.

"What were you going to do to Aiyana and Nita?" Chaffetz asked.

"End them," B.J. said, "if you want to know the truth. Far too many have died at their hands. The family line ends with Nita … at least that was my plan."

"So Nita *was* more important to you than Aiyana," Chaffetz pounced.

"You're twisting my words, Detective," B.J. said. "Aiyana could have had another child. Getting rid of Nita would be a temporary setback for her. Aiyana is now aware she might be stalked. And I have no desire to spend the rest of my life in prison. Aiyana's in your crosshairs. Attack her and I get caught."

"So you plan on leaving Philly not having accomplished your goal?" Chaffetz asked.

"Which is why I didn't kill Nita. I've accomplished *nothing*," B.J. said.

"You'll be back, though—six months, maybe a year from now. Danai is certain," Chaffetz said.

"She has the makings of a good cop," B.J. responded.

"Are you threatening to make good on your vow?" Chaffetz asked.

"Please, Detective, give me some credit. Aiyana has nothing to fear from me," B.J. said. "Nita's death puts me on your radar if something should happen to Aiyana. I've already told you I have no desire to spend my life in prison. I won't be leaving empty-handed. I now know Bly is dead. With Nita and her unborn daughter dead it will be another seventeen years, at least, before any child Aiyana has is a threat. And I assume you'll be keeping a tight leash on Aiyana so she doesn't kill any of your suspects. All in all, I won't leave disappointed."

"Pardon me if I don't believe you," Chaffetz said. She pushed a legal pad over to B.J. "Write down the name of the motel you're staying at. Don't leave Philly until I tell you you've been cleared. Return later at your own risk," she added.

CHAPTER FIFTY-SIX

BLY

(1979)

Bly lay in bed knowing within a week, two at the most, she would be leaving. She was dying and hoped she had the strength to make it into the woods of the Northeast Extension which led to the Poconos. There, she wouldn't be found until all that remained was her carcass.

The last two years had been particularly excruciating. She had willed herself to recover from one setback after another so she could be there for her daughter when she turned sixteen.

One of her lungs had collapsed on three separate occasions. Henry had administered to her each time, cursing to himself for not being able to take Bly to a hospital. She had fought off two bouts of pneumonia. And recently she had had a series of nosebleeds. Henry told her that her autoimmune system was compromised.

"Each time you go to the park with your daughter you're in danger of contracting an illness you won't recover from," he told her. He never even hinted, though, that she stop going to the park where she could transform into her true self.

"I know you worry," she'd respond each time she was bed-ridden. "I've had a good run. I was prepared to die seventeen years ago. You and Madeline not only saved my life but allowed me a second chance at motherhood. I never had a father, Henry," she continued. "*None* of my ancestors had a father—only Aiyana because she was adopted as a newborn. We were all raised by our mothers. I've had you and my little one had a grandfather. I've been blessed. I have no regrets." A coughing fit stopped her from continuing.

Her hair had begun falling out a month earlier. She had finally cut it short, close to the scalp so she wouldn't further upset Madeline, Henry or her daughter. When she transformed she noticed large hairless areas on her body.

Her daughter had grown into a beautiful young woman—almost a mirror image of Bly's younger self. She had the same luxurious long black hair as Bly had before she cut it. Her hazel eyes were incredibly expressive. At school she was on the cross-country team. She was lean and muscular and spent time daily exercising at a local gym to prepare for upcoming meets. The major difference between the two was she was far taller than Bly. Her long stride helped make her a stellar long-distance runner.

After she turned eleven, dreams of her ancestry pelted her like a persistent thunderstorm. She'd often awaken in the middle of the night and fall asleep with Bly in her bed. In the morning she would tell her mother what she had discovered. Bly would put the dreams into perspective.

Three weeks earlier, after Bly had recovered from her latest bout of pneumonia, her daughter came to her.

"We were never meant to be," she told Bly. "We could exist in isolation, but this city is no place for our kind. You were hit by a car. Aiyana is a monster. Soon I'll be a monster, too."

"You're not a monster," Bly told her.

"I will be when I turn sixteen if I follow Aiyana's path."

Bly had located her firstborn shortly after Aiyana had been raped. There had been a small article in the *Daily News* that dwelled on the apathy of those living in the Southwark Towers who had watched a teen get raped without coming to her aid. Little had been mentioned of the victim of the rape. There had been no follow-up stories.

A year later, the worst of Bly's fears were confirmed when she read another short article about a murder in the same projects—a man felled by a single blow to the back of his head.

Bly had tied her hair in a bun, donned a hat, and gone to the projects. She had sat on one of the benches outside of the towers. With her tawny complexion, no one questioned her presence. She had seen Aiyana walking with her daughter in a stroller. She stifled a gasp when she saw Aiyana. The long black hair was a dead giveaway.

More than once, Bly wanted to interject herself into Aiyana's life, but she knew she had forfeited the right when she abandoned the newborn at the church. She told her daughter about Aiyana. Life had been cruel to her—growing up as a shapeshifter with no guidance. And Aiyana had gone astray, killing men whose only crime had been fear of retaliation if they had come to Aiyana's aid when she was raped.

When her daughter turned fifteen, Bly had cut her hair so it was now shoulder length. With rollers she had added waves and had dyed her daughter's hair brown with a tinge of red. Her daughter had looked in the mirror with a look of distaste on her face. She had asked her mother the reason for the makeover. Bly had never lied to her child and wouldn't now. She told her, for the first time, about locating Aiyana and what she suspected her of doing.

"One day your paths may cross," Bly told her. "With your long black hair, the two of you look similar. I-I don't know how she would respond to you. She thinks I'm dead. You would remind her of the truth that I had abandoned her, though it had never been my intention. Once she was placed in the foster care system, there was nothing I could do, especially while recovering from my injuries." Bly paused. "I feel horrible that she had no one to guide her when she began having her dreams and was able to transform. You had me and she might be terribly jealous and bitter if she found out. So, we change your hair and the two of you don't look so much alike."

"The cycle must end, mom," she told Bly. "I'm not going to have children. On my sixteenth birthday I won't let myself to be raped or give myself to a stranger to impregnate me. I hope you're not disappointed."

"You never disappoint me," Bly said. "Missing out on being a mother, though, is too much of a sacrifice for you," she added.

"One I can deal with."

"The cycle will continue," Bly said. "Nita will have a child."

"Would you hate me if ... if something were to happen to Nita ... so the cycle would end?"

"Wouldn't you then be the monster you never want to be?" Bly asked in return.

"I'd be saving others if Aiyana and I were the last of our kind."

"A rationalization for the violence you would commit," Bly continued.

"Do you see another path?" she asked her mother.

Bly thought for several minutes. "You want me to condone your killing my granddaughter?" she finally asked.

"I'm not asking for permission. That would be cruel of me. I just need to know you won't hate me if that's what I decide."

Bly sighed. "Do what you must. All I ask is that you let Aiyana live out her life. By the time Nita is sixteen, Aiyana will be too old to give birth to another child. Our kind will end with you and her."

Bly would wait for her daughter's sixteenth birthday to make sure she kept her vow. Her child was strong-willed, but the jaguar within her would demand she procreate. With two such powerful forces clashing, Bly had to be there for her daughter. And fate might also intervene. Her daughter *could* be raped when she turned sixteen. Would she have an abortion? Clinics would draw her blood just as hospitals would, so abortion might not be an option. It might be left up to Henry to conduct the procedure, as much as he might detest doing so.

An abortion might be out of the question for another reason. Bly embraced the jaguar within her. She wondered if her daughter's jaguar might rebel if she didn't commit to her biological imperative. No one in her line had defied the animal within. This was unknown terrain that soon her daughter would have to traverse alone. Bly would will herself to remain for her daughter's sixteenth birthday. More than that, she couldn't promise. Soon she would be permanently bedridden and that was unacceptable.

CHAPTER FIFTY-SEVEN

(1995)

DAY TWO OF THE INVESTIGATION

Before reporting to Morales, Chaffetz tried to wrap her head around her interview with B.J. The woman had no solid alibi. Following Aiyana without someone else's corroboration just didn't cut it as an adequate alibi for Chaffetz. But Chaffetz couldn't see B.J. killing Nita without also taking Aiyana out at the same time. She was a seasoned professional bounty hunter. After phone calls that afternoon prior to meeting B.J., Chaffetz had ascertained she had brought in at least thirty fugitives who had fled after posting bail. Several had been high-profile defendants Chaffetz had read about in the papers. Others had long rap sheets as violent felons. B.J. didn't go after shoplifters or small time hustlers who skipped town after posting bail. She had an impressive résumé.

With Nita murdered, there was no way B.J. could get to Aiyana now. She *could* have killed Nita to make Aiyana suffer, as Danai had suggested. And she could return in six months or a year to complete her task. If she did and Chaffetz could prove she had been in Philly, B.J. would be more than a person of interest. Yet returning a second time seemed like wasted effort for a professional like B.J. Lastly, Chaffetz hadn't mentioned to B.J. the brutality the killer had exhibited—which suggested to Chaffetz that there was a personal nature to the attack on Nita. That didn't seem to be B.J.'s style. She didn't lose control. This wasn't Bly, who had taken her mother's life. An attack on Bly might be impassioned. Killing Nita—a mere substitute for Bly—wouldn't have been personal; wouldn't have been so brutal.

Chaffetz sighed. When all was said and done, B.J. still couldn't be ruled out as Nita's killer.

Morales agreed with her assessment when they met. He also suggested that she take Danai with her when she interviewed suspects at the towers the next day. Danai knew these people, Morales told her, even if she didn't associate with them often or even at all. She could spot a lie more easily than Chaffetz. Danai had been at the Towers Watch meeting, for example. Her impressions could prove invaluable. And Danai knew a good deal of the gossip and rumors that swirled around the Southwark Projects.

The day proved incredibly frustrating. First up was August Carmichael, organizer of the Towers Watch. Chaffetz experienced his rage firsthand when she and Danai interviewed him at his apartment.

"You fucking cops are intent on pinning Nita's murder on a brotha," he yelled at Chaffetz when she began.

Danai quickly interceded. "Or a sista, August," she countered, using Carmichael's street vernacular. "Nita was killed in the damn laundry room. You saying someone *white* snuck in and did the deed? With the Watch on the prowl? Give me a break, August."

August gave Danai a look of contempt. He simmered for a while, but seemed to understand this wasn't a crime perpetrated by a white hate group or bigoted white individual.

"All I'm asking for is an alibi," Chaffetz told him.

"Why would I want to kill the girl?" August asked instead.

"Is that your alibi?" Chaffetz asked. "You have no motive to kill Nita. That will get you nowhere."

"I could—*should*—ask for a damn lawyer," August said. "You tryin' to railroad me?"

"Jesus, August, do you have to be so difficult?" Danai cut in again. "If you have an alibi—"

"I was doing planning for the Towers Watch from midnight until three in the morning," August spat out. "With six others," he added. "When we broke up I went to Buffalo Bob's apartment for a few beers. Didn't get to my place until after four."

"Buffalo Bob?" Chaffetz asked. She couldn't help herself. She was curious.

"As a kid—well, a teenager—he went down to Texas or some such state and shot a buffalo," August said. "He has this big-ass picture on the wall of his living room showing him standing next to the buffalo he killed. Someone started calling him Buffalo Bob and it stuck."

"Was that so hard, August?" Danai asked. She slid a pad over to him. "Write down the names of the others at the meeting with you and their apartment numbers. Phone numbers, too, if you know them."

"You don't believe me?" he asked, looking at Danai. "You know I'm a straight shooter."

"It's procedure, August," Danai said. "We have to verify who you were with. And, if you were all together it excludes them as suspects, as well."

In the elevator, Chaffetz had complimented Danai. "I thought you were going to be a ball and chain on me. You know Morales suggested I take you with me. I wasn't too thrilled. I was wrong. You defused a volatile situation. These are *your* people—not because they're black, but you share life with them in the towers. You can relate to them, and even though you're a cop, they trust you. I misjudged your value, is what I'm saying."

"Is that an apology for how you came at me yesterday?" Danai asked.

"Hell, no," Chaffetz responded. "At times yesterday I thought you had been sniffing glue. First the shapeshifter crap and then this B.J. you created as a suspect." Chaffetz had already told Danai she had found and interviewed B.J. the night before, and apologized to Danai for doubting her existence.

"Do you believe me now?" Danai asked. "About the shapeshifter?"

"I find it difficult to believe in … shapeshifters," Chaffetz said. "But B.J. corroborated your story. Two different sources with the same tale. Bly being Aiyana's mother adds credibility." She was silent for a moment. "It takes a breath to accept the existence of such … things."

"Is B.J. still a suspect?" Danai asked.

"She had no credible alibi," Chaffetz said. "Killing Nita without also killing Aiyana makes no sense to me, but she's not exonerated."

"Am I?" Danai asked.

Chaffetz laughed. "I spoke with Officer Abbott. He seemed embarrassed … or it could have been he was scared his girl-friend would find out you slept over at his place, but you have a solid alibi. I also saw the video at Jolene's with you and Aiyana getting along famously. Spoke to some of the staff at the McDonald's you mentioned who also saw the two of you together. Did my due diligence and cleared you."

They spoke with Buffalo Bob and two others from the Towers Watch organizing committee. Chaffetz was satisfied August could be eliminated as Nita's killer.

They next went to see Jameela Pierce. It was eleven in the morning and she seemed already hammered. Chaffetz saw her bloodshot eyes. Saw how she wobbled as she led them to a couch. Saw a three-quarters empty bottle of whiskey on a table next to the couch along with an empty glass. She wore a house-coat, and her hair was askew.

Danai had told Chaffetz of the fire. Chaffetz saw Danai take in the apartment when they entered. There seemed to have been precious little damage.

"You were lucky you could return here," Danai said. She pointed out some changes for the benefit of Chaffetz. "Your car-pet is gone and one corner of your couch is … scorched."

"Had to throw out the carpet," Jameela said. "What wasn't burned was soaking wet. The couch, I could salvage. Them fire-men got here quickly. The stink is the worst." She pointed to an open window. "In this weather, opening the window don't do a hell of a lot of good, but it's way better than it was when we were told we could move back in."

"Where is your husband?" Chaffetz asked when they were seated. "We'd like to talk to him as well."

"Good luck with that, honey," Jameela said. "He was arrested around eleven the night the Jackson girl was killed. Fool beat up a gang member at a pool hall on 7th and Wharton.

He got a hot tip the clown knew something about Wesley's disappearance. Now he's jammed up with the cops *and* the gang the boy belonged to."

"He hasn't be released on bail?" Chaffetz asked.

"*Bail. Bail,*" Jameela repeated. "We hardly have enough money for rent and food. I can't afford a new rug. *Bail* … got no money for damn bail."

"Where were you that night … when Nita was killed?" Chaffetz went on.

Jameela picked up a bottle. "With my friend here. Then had my neighbor Martha Jenkins take me to the police station when Carl called and told me he was arrested. A wasted trip. Had to wait two hours to be told Carl wasn't going nowhere until he was arraigned the next day. Suggested I go home and scrape up what I could for bail."

Chaffetz and Danai went to see Martha Jenkins, who vouched for Jameela. Chaffetz called the station that Jameela's husband had been taken to, and his alibi was verified.

"Let's do lunch—my treat—and this afternoon we'll tackle DeMarius Hawkins," Chaffetz said. "Where do you want to go?"

"How about Pat's or Geno's?" Danai asked. The two restaurants were world-famous for serving original Philly cheesesteaks—and they were literally across the street from one another. There was no indoor seating at either, but each had several rickety metal tables outside that customers could use if they didn't want to take their food home.

"You choose which," Danai said.

They each ordered a no-frills cheesesteak, fries, and soda from Pat's. Steak and Cheez Whiz with no other toppings. Chaffetz was tempted to order onions on hers but didn't want her breath to reek when they interviewed DeMarius Hawkins.

Seated, they ate in silence for a few minutes.

"Why are you thinking of coming out?" Chaffetz asked.

Danai had been chewing her steak and almost choked. She looked around.

"It's just us two ladies," Chaffetz said. "Your secret is safe with me."

"Next you'll ask if I'm a carpet muncher," Danai said, barely above a whisper.

"A carpet muncher?" Chaffetz asked.

"You *are* naive … and a good ten years older than me," Danai said. "A carpet muncher is a woman who goes down on another woman." She saw Chaffetz look puzzled. "*Oral sex.* Eats her pussy. A hairy one at that," she clarified.

"I-I wasn't asking what you did," Chaffetz said.

"Want to know about grinding, scissoring, rimming?" Danai asked, her anger rising.

"You're fucking oversensitive," Chaffetz said. "And maybe a coward," she added.

"For staying in the closet?" Danai asked, but didn't wait for an answer. "You must have ambition. You're a detective, after all. But you've been held back because you're a woman. Well, it's worse yet for a black woman. And a black woman who likes pussy … how many obstacles should I throw in my path?"

"But you're thinking of coming out?" Chaffetz said. "With all of these obstacles, I was only asking why come out *now*. Look, you don't have to—"

"But I do," Danai said. "Yes, I'm overly sensitive, but I'm no coward. I'm not into gay-rights politics. I don't want to set an example for others. And I certainly don't want media scrutiny. Who I spend my time with in bed is no one's business. The truth is I'm in love—"

"With B.J.?" Chaffetz asked.

"*God*, no," Danai said. "Why…" she began, then stopped. "Never mind. Look, I never got over my first girlfriend. I might be deluding myself but I considered her my soulmate. She went to college out of state. I became a cop. Now she's thinking of transferring to a school in Philly, but she's outed herself and has no desire for the two of us to spend all of our time at one of our apartments or skulk around fearful of getting caught."

"So your choice is whether to come out for love or remain in the closet for career advancement, right?" Chaffetz asked.

"In a nutshell, yes. What would you do?" Danai asked.

"You want my advice?"

"You know I'm gay. Morales knows. B.J. and my girlfriend,"

Danai responded. "It's not like I can share my dilemma with the class."

Chaffetz was silent for a few moments. "Me ... I'd rather share the good days and those that suck with someone else than come home to an empty house," she said.

"*That's why* I'm considering coming out," Danai said. "Not to make a statement, but to have someone I love to come home to."

"And munch on some carpet," Chaffetz added.

"You're too much, Chafe," Danai said. "I could get to like you ... as a friend."

They finished their cheesesteaks in silence.

"What can you tell me about DeMarius Hawkins?" Chaffetz asked after she had eaten her last fry and licked ketchup from her fingers.

"The husband was abusive to both DeMarius and his mother," Danai began. She had finished moments earlier. "Neither seemed all that broken up that he was killed. *But,* I did some digging after you stabbed me in the back yesterday," she added, but smiled to show she understood that Chaffetz had to come after her as she did. "After Shawn Hawkins was killed, his wife had a stroke. Not all that serious, I was told, but she suffered another the night after I questioned her and her son for Morales. She died the next morning. If she blamed Nita, you have motive."

"DeMarius might not be too fond of you either, for bringing up the subject months after Shawn Hawkins was murdered. He could have come after you," she added.

Danai scrunched up her nose. "I didn't come hard at either of them," she said, "unlike someone I know. Nita harassed the family after her rape. She was the one DeMarius would blame."

"Still, watch your back. Why the hell do you stay in the towers, anyway?" Chaffetz asked.

"I've been on the force for all of six months," Danai replied. "I *am* saving my money, not that we get paid all that much. I don't have any great fondness for the projects. In another year I'm sure I'll move. Just have to save my pennies."

"Maybe move in with your girlfriend, if you make the big

decision," Chaffetz said. "She wouldn't be living in Southwark, would she?"

"You're obsessed with my sex life, aren't you?" Danai asked. "And, no, if she transfers it would be to Temple, and there's student housing nearby. *If* I come out, it could be I'd spend most of my nights at her apartment ... carpet munching," she added. "I do want a place of my own away from Southwark but spending nights with her, as long as I didn't become burdensome for her, would lessen the danger of the projects until I can move."

"Another reason to come out," Chaffetz said, then held up her hand. "I apologize. It's none of my business what you do."

"You've made your opinion known," Danai countered. "I-I appreciate the advice and support. If I do come out, I'll need friends to counter the hostility directed at me. I'm not confrontational by nature. With you and Morales, at least I won't be an island unto myself."

"There are others who will have your back," Chaffetz said.

"Precious few," Danai responded. "Any woman who supports me will be considered a closeted lesbian herself. I have no idea how Kyle—my partner—will respond."

"Few are better than none at all," Chaffetz said. "No more on the subject."

Chaffetz had called DeMarius Hawkins earlier. He initially refused to be interviewed. Chaffetz played hardball with him: grant an interview in his apartment at the towers, or she'd get a warrant and haul his ass down to the Roundhouse. He chose the former.

He didn't look too happy when he let Chaffetz and Danai in. "You upset my mother when you spoke to her," he said, looking at Danai. "It brought back memories she'd rather forget. She went on and on about by my father using us as punching bags and watching Nita Jackson's rape as if it was a carnival sideshow. I blame her stroke ... her *death* on you," he said, pointing to Danai.

"I'm really sorry about your mother, DeMarius," Danai said. "It was never my intention to upset her."

"Go to the cemetery and apologize," he snapped. "What do you want now?" he asked, then added, "You better be quick. I ain't got money to pay for this dump. I'll be moving in with one of my boys. His parents take in foster kids. They have room for me as long as they don't have to pay for my food and shit."

"Before we start, can I use your bathroom?" Chaffetz asked. "Something I had for lunch must not have agreed with me."

DeMarius shrugged. "Better the bathroom than having you puke on my couch."

Chaffetz returned in five minutes. Both Danai and DeMarius had remained silent.

"We're here in relation to Nita Jackson's murder," Chaffetz began. "You already told Officer Townes that Nita accused your father of cowardice. Just how bad did it get?"

"My mom wanted to call the police," DeMarius said. "Nita was ragging on us almost every day. My dad told my mom to shut up. Said the police would do nothing more than take a report. He didn't want to be seen talking to no police."

"What specifically did Nita do?" Chaffetz persisted.

"After that one time we let her in, we hoped ignoring her would get her off of our backs," DeMarius said. "But she hounded us day after day. She screamed at us through the door. She confronted both my mom and dad when they were outside. Shit, my mom stopped going outside to be with her friends."

"But she let you be," Chaffetz said. "Right?"

"Screamed at me, too, but just once," DeMarius said. "Got in my face and walked with me stride for stride. Asked me, what if I had been attacked by a gang at night in front of the towers? Would my dad have turned his back on me? I finally told her to leave me alone or—" he suddenly stopped.

"Or?" Chaffetz asked.

"Or she'd be sorry," he finished.

"Sorry how?" Chaffetz again.

"I was just talking trash," DeMarius said. "I mean she was kinda right … about my dad. He acted all tough to me and my mom. But he was a fucking coward deep down."

"After your mom died you wanted to get back at her, though," Chaffetz said.

"Yeah, I was angry with her, but I didn't do nothing to her.

Was mad at you, too," he said looking at Danai, "but I didn't come after you, did I?"

"You weren't just angry at Nita. You respected her, didn't you?" Danai said. Chaffetz gave her a glance, but she went on. "She stood up to your father. No one else would. She knew your father was abusive to your mother. A bully. And if you stand up to a bully he skulks away."

"How would Nita know my dad hurt my mom?" DeMarius asked.

"Rumors ... gossip spreads in the towers like the flu," Danai said. "I didn't know you, but I'd heard your father was sadistic. He yelled at your mother. Hit her. She cried. The walls here are paper thin. Your neighbors knew what was going on. They told their friends and on and on. You *admired* Nita for standing up to the man. And he cowered in front of you when Nita confronted him outside."

"Why would I kill her, then?" he asked.

Chaffetz intervened. She didn't like the turn the interview had taken. If Danai was accurate in her assessment he could very well demand an answer to the question he'd asked. She quickly looked at Danai to make sure she didn't respond to his comment. "You didn't admire her. You were *jealous* of her," Chaffetz said. "She had the balls to stand up to your father. You didn't. Must have made you furious. Emasculated. This little bitch did what you wouldn't." She decided to get the interview on track before DeMarius could respond. "Where were you from midnight until 4 a.m. the night Nita was attacked?"

"At my girlfriend's house," DeMarius said. "She lives on the third floor of the east tower. Look, with my mom gone I had trouble sleeping here alone. I-I sometimes thought I saw my mom, mostly, but also my dad sometimes. Chevelle's father works at night. Her mother passed a few years ago. I spend nights at her place and leave at 6 a.m. Her father doesn't come home until seven or eight."

"And what do you and Chevelle do?" Chaffetz again pressed. She could see the young man's discomfort.

"What the fuck difference does it make what we do?" DeMarius asked. "I'm with her. I mostly sleep. I don't feel anxious with her next to me."

"*Mostly* sleep," Chaffetz said. "We're going to speak to her. She has to corroborate your story. *So, what ... else ... do ... you ... do?*" she asked, emphasizing each word.

"We have sex, okay?" DeMarius said. "Only her pops don't know. He'd kick my sorry ass down the street if he knew. Chevelle be nineteen but he thinks she's still a virgin. Go speak to Chevelle, but not when her dad is there. He leaves the house at six. Goes to a bar for a few drinks before going to work."

Chaffetz looked at Danai. She shook her head almost imperceptibly. Danai had no further questions, Chaffetz saw. She thanked DeMarius after telling him not to call Chevelle.

Their work done other than speaking to Chevelle, Danai invited Chaffetz to her apartment. She brought two beers from the fridge.

"What do you think of his alibi?" Chaffetz asked.

"Similar to mine, aside from the sex," Danai said. "If Chevelle corroborates."

"Which leaves us without a viable suspect," Chaffetz replied. "B.J. is the one with the weakest alibi. And before you remind me, I'm aware there's no way I'm going to break B.J. or catch her in a lie even if I question her nonstop for nine or ten hours. She's a seasoned professional. So, right now I won't even try."

"It could have been a gang initiation," Danai said. "A random attack," she added. "The Kings have the real power here. A lookout saw Nita in the laundry room alone and a new recruit was sent to kill her."

"And the eight blows to her head?"

"A young kid gets carried away," Danai said. "He wants to make sure he fulfilled his task. If he hadn't killed her *he* might have been lying dead that night."

"Something to consider, though personally I feel the brutality is a bit much for a gang wannabe," Chaffetz said. "I'm going to do some digging into B.J.'s background. See if any of the fugitives she recovered turned out the worse for wear. See if there's any violent acts in her past. Depending on what I find, I *may* take another pass at her. And I'll want to speak to DeMarius again. Even if his girlfriend backs up his alibi, I got a vibe from him that he was more than a little angry at Nita. At first, I was pissed that you interceded—his admiration for Nita for standing up to her father. I put a different spin on it. He felt showed up. The man was abusive, but Nita didn't give a shit. Confronted him. Taunted him. Maybe he got ragged on by some of his boys and wanted Nita out of the picture."

"At this point, you lead. I'll follow. I'm out of suspects," Danai said.

They were silent as they drank their beers.

"I don't want to seem out of line—"

"You're going to say something anyway that might irritate me, so go ahead," Danai interrupted.

"Well, I don't fully believe your line about not leaving the towers because you can't afford to. Even as a rookie you make enough money to rent an inexpensive apartment away from here," Chaffetz said. "Somewhere safer."

"Somewhere I could bring a girl for a hookup without her crapping in her pants from fear," Danai replied.

"Seems everything revolves around your sexual identity, Danai," Chaffetz said. "It was an innocent statement. And, if you're in the closet you wouldn't bring a girl to the towers. Look, from what I know people fight to get *out* of the projects. Yet you remain. Still, this apartment doesn't seem like a home. No photos, no artwork—prints or posters, at least, on a cop's salary. Mismatched furniture which I don't think you give a damn about." She waved a hand. "It's none of my business why—"

"Inertia," Danai interrupted. "And maybe a bit of fear," she added. "I've only been on the job for six months. The towers *do* give me the creeps. Always did when I was growing up. I just haven't had … no, make that haven't *made* the time to move. A move would be a big step for me. I've spent my entire life here. I don't have good friends here but I know just about everyone. During the day there's a certain comfort level I wouldn't have if I moved. But a move, regardless of whether I come out or not, is inevitable. I haven't personalized this place because I know I won't be here much longer." She paused. "Now a question for you. Did you find anything incriminating in DeMarius's bathroom? It's a typical cop ploy, plus you didn't get sick from food at Pat's."

"Perceptive, aren't you?" Chaffetz said. "I got a peek at his room. No bloody shirt or jeans. There was a locked closet. That seemed odd to me. Who living alone locks their closet? He doesn't have to worry about hiding his porn stash."

They chatted another twenty minutes. Chaffetz said very little about her personal life, deflecting Danai's questions with ones of her own. Danai looked at her oddly once or twice. Chaffetz looked at her watch. "Time to visit Chevelle."

"You're a very private person," Danai said, still seated after her partner rose. "I probed and prodded but learned nothing about you. Me, on the other hand, I'm an open book. You know far more about my sex life than I wanted to divulge. You, for all you've said, could very well be a nun in your spare time."

"Your carpet munching," Chaffetz said, again turning the conversation back on Danai.

"There's more to making love or just having sex with a woman than—" she began, then stopped. "See, there you go again. Getting me to talk about … well, *me*."

"I live an incredibly boring life," Chaffetz said. "No man currently in the picture. My mother passed years ago. I never knew my father. The job is my life. I get to poke into the lives of others—ones far more interesting than my own."

"You want to be friends, you'll have to do better than that," Danai said. "You're in your thirties and you've summed up your life in a paragraph—a short one at that." She held up her hand. "Not now, though."

"Danai, I don't have any close friends … never have," Chaffetz said. "I'm more of an observer than a participant. I like you. I really do, but I've never revealed myself to anyone. I'm finding it difficult to do so with you."

"I welcome your friendship, Chafe, but it can't be a one-way street. I'm not asking you to bare—"

"You want a morsel?" Chaffetz asked, then went on before Danai could reply. "I'm intrigued by Morales. I've had lunch with him in the park twice. We spar with one another—"

"He's married with a boat-load of kids," Danai interrupted.

"There's that," Chaffetz said. "Maybe that's why we can flirt with one another. We both know it will lead nowhere."

"I don't see Morales having an affair, but—"

"If he opened the door, would I step in?" Chaffetz finished for Danai.

Danai nodded.

"I honestly don't know. I'm just attracted to him. Like I said, we flirt with one another. As you know I like to have the last word, but he often surprises me with a witty ... and provocative comeback. I think about him at night when I'm in bed ... more than I should," she said, then blushed. "That must sound terrible."

"Sounds human to me," Danai said.

"Not a word—" Chaffetz began.

"I don't kiss and tell," Danai said. "And you keep my carpet munching to yourself until I decide whether to go public."

Chaffetz nodded.

"See that wasn't so hard—telling me something personal about yourself," Danai said. "It humanizes you."

"Makes me feel all warm and fuzzy," Chaffetz replied.

"Having the last word," Danai said. They both laughed.

Chaffetz had called Chevelle before lunch. She wasn't thrilled to be questioned by the police but told them to come by at 6:30 that evening.

The woman who opened the door surprised Chaffetz. Danai had said she knew Chevelle but hadn't described her. Chaffetz gave Danai a quick glance. She could see Danai stifling a smile.

Chevelle was almost as tall as Chaffetz. She had coal-black skin and long dreadlocks. She was big-boned, a few pounds overweight, but not fat, with large breasts accentuated by the clingy top she wore. When she greeted them she spoke with a Caribbean lilt.

Unlike a number of apartments Chaffetz had seen in the towers, this one was immaculate with furniture that matched—seemed to all been purchased at the same time. Prints of black authors, poets, singers, and political figures lined the walls. A muted Bob Marley song played on a CD player.

Chevelle invited them to have a seat on her couch. She picked up a shirt that had been lying there and hung it in the closet. Chaffetz wondered if she had worn the shirt for her father's benefit before he left for work. Her tight top was for DeMarius, who would probably be by later. She offered them a drink. They declined, but she insisted.

"You offend me, not having a drink," Chevelle said.

They both agreed to a glass of iced tea.

"How long have you been in this country?" Chaffetz asked.

"We be legal," Chevelle responded.

"We're not here to hassle you, Chevelle," Chaffetz said. "I was just curious."

"Me family moved here when I was ten. I turned nineteen last week," she said. "It's just me and me father now. Me mother had a bad heart. She died when I was twelve. Me older brother was killed in a drive-by shooting three years ago."

"Do you have a job?" Chaffetz asked.

"I work at a restaurant—a waitress, but me be going to school so I can work in a beauty salon," Chevelle said. "In high school I would give all the girls … what they call … make-overs, yes, makeovers. I do their hair and nails." She held out her nails. Nail polish had been elaborately applied in beautiful designs.

"You're very talented," Chaffetz said. "How long have you known DeMarius?" she asked.

"Close to three months," Chevelle replied. "Most of the boys here, they be crass. They scare me. I had me three bags of groceries one day. I was trying to open the door to get into the towers. I almost dropped one. DeMarius caught it and gave me this big smile." She paused. "He no smile often anymore." She shrugged then went on. "So I let him help me upstairs with the bags. I offer him a drink—iced tea," she said and smiled. "We talked for two hours. He was a gentleman. He no hit on me. Most boys in the towers stare at my breasts. DeMarius looked me in me eyes. Kissed me on the cheek when he leave. We became friends."

"And then lovers," Chaffetz said. She intentionally used the word so Chevelle wouldn't be offended.

"If me father finds out—" she began.

"We're not here to cause problems for you, Chevelle," Chaffetz said. "Be honest with us and your father won't know about our conversation," she added. She hoped she could keep Chevelle's secret. "Did DeMarius talk about Nita Jackson, the girl who was killed three nights ago?" she asked.

Chevelle nodded. "He was really ... pissed. Me father thinks the word vulgar. He very strict with me. Tell me to talk like an educated young woman, not like most of the girls in the projects." She took a deep breath. "DeMarius, he didn't like his father, but he wanted to protect his mother."

"Did he think Nita had something to do with his father's death?"

"He did and he didn't," Chevelle said. "I know how that sounds. He said no one messed with his father. But Nita, she called him out in front of others. Called him a coward. DeMarius said Nita wasn't scared of him. Then he would smack hisself on the side of his head," she said and demonstrated, hitting herself gently on her temple. "And he say how could this little girl hurt his father. Then when you asked his mother about Nita," she said, looking at Danai, "DeMarius he went off again. Nita this and Nita that. When his mom died he was quiet most of the time. We—we had sex, but he hardly spoke. He was ... what do they say ... really into hisself."

"That night Nita died, DeMarius said he spent the entire night with you," Chaffetz said. "Is that the truth?"

Chevelle nodded. "He didn't like to sleep in his apartment alone after his mother passed. He came over when me father went to work. We had sex and then he fell asleep."

"He didn't get up at all?" Chaffetz persisted.

Chevelle looked down. She said nothing.

"I was telling the truth when I said I wouldn't involve your father if you were honest with us," Chaffetz said. "If you hold something back from us, I'll have to have another talk with you, with your father present. I know you're holding something back from us. Tell me so I don't have to involve your father."

"I-I wake up around four that morning," she began. "A noise woke me. I wanted to snuggle with DeMarius. Only he wasn't there. He came back around 4:30. Said he had gone out for a walk. He did that sometimes in the middle of the night. That night he was fidgety and anxious."

"Did he have blood on his clothes?" Chaffetz asked.

Chevelle shook her head. "He had changed his clothes. Said his clothes stank so much they could kill roaches, so he went to his apartment to change. He couldn't keep anything of his here, you know. Me father … ," she said and shrugged. "We went back to bed but neither of us fell asleep. He had to be out by six so me father wouldn't know he slept over."

"Did he say anything about Nita when he returned from his walk?" Chaffetz asked.

Chevelle shook her head. "After he told me why he changed his clothes he didn't say nothing more. He be like that sometimes. Silent and moody. I knew better than to ask him if anything was wrong."

"Are you saying he had a temper?" Chaffetz asked.

"Sometimes he do," Chevelle said. "Mostly he talked about Nita or your partner bugging his mom," she said, and glanced at Danai. "Sometimes when we be outside and someone said something about me breasts or me … behind, DeMarius would go off on them, you know. Just words, though. He never got physical. And he never hit me. He be good to me. But, he be hurting with his mom dying."

Chaffetz looked at Danai, who shook her head.

"We won't bother you anymore," Chaffetz said. "We appreciate your being honest with us."

Chaffetz and Danai went back to Danai's apartment. Neither said a word until they had closed the door behind them. Danai had taken a seat. Chaffetz was pacing.

"Did you notice anything … odd about Chevelle?" Chaffetz finally asked.

"You mean the ways she talks?" Danai asked then went on. "She can talk perfect English but she often slips into the grammar of the country where she was born. Like I said, I don't know her, but I've heard her with friends outside. With them her accent is even thicker. The few times I've seen her with her father, there's hardly any accent and her English is as good as mine. She was nervous with us. She dumbed herself down.

Seemed to be searching for words. I don't think she was lying, though."

"You're observant for a rookie cop," Chaffetz said, offering a smile.

"DeMarius's alibi is shaky, at best," Danai said when Chaffetz went silent. "Should we question him again?"

"Not yet," Chaffetz replied. She continued to pace. "I'm interested about what's in that locked closet in his bedroom. I'll brief Morales, but I think we have enough to get a search warrant. We check that closet and then we take a second stab at DeMarius."

"And B.J.?" Danai asked.

"Priorities, Danai," Chaffetz cautioned. "I want to rule DeMarius out before I approach B.J. again." She took a deep breath. "I'm going to see Morales now. We should have a warrant by mid-morning tomorrow, if he agrees. Want to tag along?"

"If my sarge agrees," Danai said.

"Something else I'll mention to Morales," Chaffetz said. "I want you on this full-time."

"You falling for me?" Danai asked.

"What the fuck—"

"Kidding," Danai said. "Look, I'm new at this. Since Rain left, I've had no one to kid around with. I'll watch my mouth … promise," she added.

"Or I'll *wash* your mouth with soap, young lady," Chaffetz countered.

Danai smiled. "Deal," she said.

CHAPTER FIFTY-EIGHT

Morales looked at his watch. It was 8:50. Another dinner his wife would have to reheat in the microwave. Chaffetz had called him a little before seven. They might have a break in the case. Could she debrief him tonight? Morales had reluctantly agreed. One of the few perks of being a sergeant was getting home at a reasonable hour. For a detective, there were cases that demanded odd hours. His wife had been thrilled that as a sergeant he was usually home for dinner. He could also share responsibility with his younger kids. He would supervise homework or play board games with his kids while his wife bathed their nine-month-old daughter. Now, two days in a row, his carefully worked-out routine had been altered.

He was thrilled that Chaffetz had a legitimate suspect. He had been despondent the day before. He was relieved that Chaffetz had cleared Danai, and like his detective, he didn't think B.J. had killed Nita, even without an airtight alibi.

DeMarius Hawkins's alibi hadn't completely panned out, and Morales agreed that the locked closet could hold evidence that might crack the case. He had immediately approved her request to secure a search warrant.

He had wondered if the case could be solved. Around one-third of murders went unsolved. Most homicides were committed by friends or relatives of the victim. Most of those cases were quickly solved. Nita's murder differed in a number of ways. Aiyana was Nita's only relative, and she had been exonerated. Nita was a loner without any close friends. She didn't have any enemies either, other than strangers she harassed for having literally stood by and watched her be gang-raped. And, there was the jaguar-within-her angle that Morales knew couldn't be pursued. He hoped the search warrant would bear fruit. If the trail went cold and he went to Aiyana empty-handed, he didn't know what she was prepared to do. He didn't think she would indiscriminately kill *all* the various suspects Chaffetz had questioned. But he didn't think Aiyana's last words in the matter would be "Thanks for the effort. It's appreciated." For this reason, he hoped Hawkins was the perpetrator.

He stood up to leave when McGowan walked in. Morales cursed under his breath. As usual, McGowan didn't knock. He wanted Morales to chastise him for not knocking. Baiting him again. The man loved fucking with the minds of others, Morales thought. What a petty man ... but also someone he didn't want to make his enemy. McGowan held grudges he would take to his grave. Morales would challenge McGowan if necessary, but not on something as inconsequential as this.

And, Morales knew it was no coincidence that McGowan was at his door just minutes after Chaffetz had left. McGowan seemed to have eyes and ears everywhere ... possibly from someone within his own squad. The thought saddened him. He had thought those in his squad were loyal to him.

"Don't you ever go home, Russ?" Morales asked.

"The path towards advancement is hard work and long hours," McGowan answered. "I'm at a severe disadvantage when it comes to promotion, as I've told you before. Quotas have to be filled. So I have to work doubly hard."

"I was just leaving," Morales said, hoping whatever McGowan had to say or ask could wait until the next morning. "Got kids to put to bed."

McGowan ignored his comment. "Making any headway with the case I handed over to you?" he asked.

"We've eliminated most of our suspects," Morales said. He decided to withhold information about the search warrant Chaffetz would ask a judge for the next morning.

"You should learn from your mistakes, Estefan," McGowan said. "Our job is to close cases, not add failures to our boards. And it's never prudent to personally get involved with a case. This history you have with the Jackson girl from way back has come back to bite you in the ass. Some pussy isn't worth a case that's dead on arrival," he added.

"So didn't *I* do you a favor taking it off of your hands?" Morales asked. "Maybe I repaid that earlier favor I owed you."

"That's the way it may turn out—a blemish on your record," McGowan responded. "But *you* sought *me* out, so you still owe me one. You will let me know if you catch a break. Professional courtesy."

"You'll be the first to know," Morales said, though he had no intention of telling McGowan *if* an arrest was made. The man would find out regardless. "Now I must get home." He smiled as he left. If McGowan only knew he had actually solved ten open homicides Aiyana and Nita were responsible for, he'd be far more interested. While he couldn't prosecute Aiyana or Nita and officially the cases would remain unsolved, he felt vindicated.

CHAPTER FIFTY-NINE

(DAY THREE OF THE INVESTIGATION)

Armed with a search warrant, Chaffetz, Danai, and two additional officers knocked on the apartment door of DeMarius Hawkins at ten the next morning. Chaffetz handed DeMarius the warrant. "Want to unlock your closet or do we have to break it down?" she asked.

"Why—" DeMarius began

Chaffetz put a finger to her mouth. "Which will it be?"

DeMarius gave Chaffetz a set of keys, pointing out one for the locked closet door. Chaffetz handed the key to Danai. "Do the honors."

Chaffetz told one of the officers to remain with DeMarius and told the other to search for anything suspicious in the living room. "Only items in plain sight," she told him. "The warrant gives us limited access."

Danai called for her to come to DeMarius's bedroom. She held a baseball bat covered with blood.

Chaffetz produced a long plastic evidence bag. Danai dropped the bat into the bag. "Any bloody clothing?" Chaffetz asked.

"Just one other item of interest," Danai said. "He must have wrapped the bat in a blanket." She picked up a blanket with her gloved hand and showed it to Chaffetz. "Note the blood on the blanket. We'll need a second bag for this."

"I'll call for a crime scene unit to thoroughly search the closet," Chaffetz said. "We'll then get an amended warrant so we can toss the entire apartment."

"Then what?" Danai asked.

"I'll have the two officers secure the scene," Chaffetz said. "We'll take DeMarius to the Roundhouse and let him sweat until we see if we come up with anything else. You can come with me."

Chaffetz brought the bag with the bat over to DeMarius. "Want to explain this?" she asked.

"Ain't never seen it before," he said.

"You're under arrest for the murder of Nita Jackson," Chaffetz said. She read DeMarius his rights, handcuffed him, then talked to the two officers. She and Danai escorted DeMarius to a squad car Chaffetz had called for.

It was three hours before Chaffetz began her interrogation of DeMarius. Four officers armed with the amended warrant had been searching the Hawkins apartment. Nothing incriminating was found, Chaffetz was told. The crime scene unit brought everything in DeMarius's closet to the Roundhouse. Zeke Foley, the officer in charge, met briefly with Chaffetz.

"We have a lot to go through," Foley began. "There are traces of blood on clothing that was next to the bat, but no blood splatter on those clothes. My guys tell me there's a bloody print on the bat. We'll match the prints with those of Hawkins. We'll compare the blood to that of Nita Jackson." He paused a moment. "Odd that he got rid of the clothes but kept the bat. Could be a trophy," he added.

"Or he could have a baseball game coming up and it's his lucky bat," Chaffetz offered.

Foley smiled. "I'm told he's been processed so we have his prints. Give me twenty minutes and I can tell you if they're a match and if the blood is that of the victim."

Chaffetz nodded. "Then DeMarius and I have a chat."

Chaffetz received a call fifteen minutes later. Yes, the blood matched that of Nita Jackson. And the prints on the bat were those of DeMarius Hawkins.

Chaffetz walked into the interrogation room. Danai watched through a two-way mirror outside. She found it hard to believe that DeMarius had killed Nita. Then again, he had lost his father six months earlier and his mother just a few days before. And his feelings towards his father were ambivalent.

Danai had been too young to be enraged when her father was killed. And her mother hadn't been snatched from her soon after. As she got older her anger festered, but she had never considered killing Aiyana.

DeMarius never had a chance to cool down. She watched as Chaffetz went in for the kill.

Chaffetz sat across from a frightened looking DeMarius Hawkins. He had been read his rights but hadn't asked for a lawyer. "You lied to my partner and me yesterday, DeMarius. You didn't spend the *entire* night with your girlfriend."

"What are you talking about?" he asked. "Chevelle will tell—"

"The walk Chevelle said you took prior to 4 a.m.," Chaffetz went on. "You also changed your clothes."

"I-I'm a light sleeper," DeMarius said. "I got up and couldn't fall back to sleep, so, yes, I went for a walk."

"Which you didn't mention yesterday," Chaffetz repeated. "You lied, DeMarius."

"It was a fifteen minute walk," he said and shrugged.

"Chevelle says it was longer … far longer," Chaffetz lied.

"I went to change my clothes after my walk," DeMarius said.

"Or you went to the laundry room, maybe thinking of washing your clothes," Chaffetz went on. "You saw Nita, went back to your apartment, and brought back a baseball bat. Your anger against Nita intensified. She badgered your family after her rape. After Officer Townes spoke to you and your mother about Nita, your mother suffered a fatal stroke. An eye for an eye, right, DeMarius?" Chaffetz asked.

"I never went to no laundry room," he said.

"What about the bloody bat found in your *locked* closet?" Chaffetz asked.

"I never seen the bat before."

"It has Nita Jackson's blood on it … and *your* fingerprints," Chaffetz said, raising her voice.

DeMarius shook his head again and again without speaking.

"This is how I see it, DeMarius," Chaffetz said, more calmly. "Nita harassed your family. Your father was then murdered. Your mother died after Officer Townes asked her about Nita. You didn't plan on killing Nita—no premeditation. You wanted to scare her. You saw her. You were enraged. You killed her in the heat of passion."

DeMarius kept shaking his head.

"Before you deny it DeMarius, I want you to keep in mind that if you killed Nita in the heat of the moment, you might only be charged with manslaughter," she lied. "Fifteen years in prison—maybe just ten or twelve with good behavior. Even less with the mitigating circumstances—your mother's death weighing on you. *But* ... ," she began, then paused. "Listen to me carefully, DeMarius. Continue to deny your guilt and you'll be charged with premeditated murder. Twenty-five years to life at best. Life with no possibility of parole."

"But I didn't kill Nita," DeMarius said. It was more a plea than a statement.

"Let's look at the case against you, DeMarius," Chaffetz went on. "Then put yourself in the place of someone on the jury and consider what you would decide. You had motive. Nita was like a curse on your family. Officer Townes suggested to me you might even be jealous of her. *She* stood up to your abusive father when you wouldn't. The prosecuting attorney will use that, too. Neighbors heard Nita yelling at your father outside your apartment. Others saw Nita confront your father when he was outside. Let that sink in for a moment," she said and paused. "Then we found the bat used to kill Nita in your *locked* closet with her blood on it and your prints on the weapon," Chaffetz continued. "Pretty damning. And your alibi works against you. Even *you* admit you didn't spend the entire night with Chevelle. You said you were gone fifteen minutes. Chevelle says otherwise. Who will the jury believe?"

Chaffetz stood. "I'll give you some time to consider your options. Admit you killed Nita and the district attorney pleads you down to manslaughter. Or, go to trial and spend the rest of your life in prison."

Chaffetz came out and stood next to Danai, who had been watching through a mirror.

"And I thought you were rough on me," Danai said.

Chaffetz smiled. "All I had on you was motive. You had an airtight alibi. Yes, I came at you hard, but I had little ammunition. With DeMarius I have all I need."

"Will he go for the deal?" Danai asked.

"Not right away, but I'll keep at it all night if necessary. At some point he'll confess. He has no wiggle room."

"What if he asks for a lawyer?" Danai asked.

"I laid out my case against him and he didn't ask for an attorney. Unlike gang members at the towers, who are in and out of prison like a revolving door, DeMarius is a novice. If he was going to ask for a lawyer, he would have done so before I left the room."

"And the district attorney's office will cut him a deal?" Danai asked.

"Not likely. We get his confession and at best he'll be offered second degree murder—twenty-five to life with the possibility of parole."

"You lied to him," Danai said.

"Girl, you should pay me for the education you are getting," Chaffetz said with a smile. "I forget you're a wet-behind-the-ears rookie just out of the academy. In time you'll learn we often lie to suspects. They lie to us. DeMarius didn't tell us the truth. He went out for his so-called walk. He conveniently forgot to mention that when we spoke to him yesterday. So, yes, I lied to him. All I want is a confession. Then we let the lawyers decide what he's charged with and what he'll plead to."

"I was told Chevelle has been brought in for questioning," Danai said. "She'll be pissed that we didn't keep her secret." She paused. "Did you ever intend to honor your word to her?"

"*If* we hadn't found the bat. *If* we didn't have the evidence we needed to make an arrest, yes. I wouldn't have dragged her in without what we found. But once we had the bat we needed an official statement from Chevelle which contradicts his alibi. DeMarius claims he was out for fifteen minutes. I want you to question Chevelle. She woke up and he was gone. So he *could* have left well before 4 a.m. Get her to admit he could have been gone as early as three or three-thirty and it's more ammunition I can use against DeMarius."

"She won't be cooperative now that her father knows the two of them were sleeping together," Danai said.

"Such is life, Danai," Chaffetz replied. "Look, Danai, tell her we had no intention of bringing her in—which is true. *But,* we found the bloody baseball bat. *That* changes everything. We have proof DeMarius murdered Nita, but we need her testimony to counter his alibi. Her father will be pissed, yes, but he'll get over himself. She'll be grounded, but her father sounds like a decent man who doesn't want his daughter sleeping around. He'll forgive her. She'll come out of this unscarred. Tell her that. Be persuasive. You have it in you."

Danai left, and Chaffetz let DeMarius stew for another twenty minutes. She entered with a bologna sandwich and a can of soda.

"Thought you might be hungry. Thirsty, too," she said and slid the sandwich and drink across the table. DeMarius took a few bites of the sandwich and drained the entire can of soda.

Chaffetz repeated what she had said before. Motive, weapon, and opportunity. Twenty minutes later there was a knock on the door. Danai gave her a file folder. Chaffetz returned to DeMarius.

"My partner is questioning Chevelle," Chaffetz began. She opened the folder read its contents then closed it. "Your girl-friend says the two of you engaged in sex until around eleven. The two of you then went to sleep. She had *no* idea when you got up and left for your walk. She's a sound sleeper. You could have left as early as one, she now says. There goes your alibi."

"I don't believe you," DeMarius said. "Chevelle—"

"See for yourself, DeMarius." She slid Chevelle's statement across to DeMarius. "In her own handwriting. And she signed it."

Chaffetz repeated her offer and then left again.

Six hours later, DeMarius confessed. He wanted the man-slaughter deal Chaffetz had offered. Chaffetz had him write his confession.

"Do I get my deal now?" he asked.

"It's out of my hands," Chaffetz said. "I'll take this to an assistant district attorney. I'll recommend they offer you man-slaughter," she lied. "But the decision is theirs."

Chaffetz left and brought the confession to Morales. She would let him go to the ADA—let him claim credit for the con-fession. She had shown him her worth. And knowing Morales, he wouldn't hog the limelight. She had pulled it off. She walked to Morales's office content.

CHAPTER SIXTY

It was 8:30 p.m. Chaffetz decided to go back to the towers to confront Aiyana. She wondered what approach would be best. Aiyana wasn't at her apartment when Chaffetz knocked. Just as well, she decided. She picked the flimsy lock on the door and entered. She would wait. When she heard Aiyana's key in the door, she retreated into the bathroom. She heard Aiyana enter.

Chaffetz came out of the bathroom as a jaguar, her inner self. She saw Aiyana carrying a laundry basket. Aiyana dropped it and transformed into a jaguar as well. She emanated a low growl.

Chaffetz morphed back into her human form. Standing, she raised her hands in surrender. Aiyana, still in jaguar form, peered at her guardedly. She transformed back into human form.

"If I was into women … ," Aiyana began.

Embarrassed, Chaffetz picked up clothes she had discarded before shape-shifting and got dressed.

Aiyana, still naked, watched. "Ripped my damn clothes. You don't know how many times that happened to me when I was first able to change." She went into her bedroom and returned wearing a cotton bathrobe. "What the fuck was that all about? I thought I was the only—"

"I'm your half-sister," Chaffetz interrupted. "I could have tried explaining it to you, but showing beats telling. I can't believe you're so … composed, I guess is the word."

"I have no half-sister," Aiyana replied as if she didn't hear Chaffetz's last sentence. "My mother died after giving birth to me. I haven't seen anything different in my dreams."

"You saw Bly leave … mortally wounded," Chaffetz said. "Don't ask me why you didn't see what happened next. Bly went to Fairmount Park to die in the woods. She passed out in the park. A couple found her as a jaguar. They saw her transform into human form. They weren't horrified. They took Bly to their home and nursed her back to health."

"Why didn't she come to see me? Take me out of the foster system before I was adopted?" Aiyana asked, finding it difficult to comprehend what she was told.

"It took months for Bly to heal," Chaffetz explained. "She never fully recovered. She couldn't be taken to a hospital. A blood test—"

"I'm fully aware why she couldn't be taken to the hospital. You can skip ahead," Aiyana said.

"Henry, my … grandfather—at least that's what I considered him—was an ER doctor. He did the best he could. Both as a human and a jaguar, Bly walked with a pronounced limp when she had recovered. Later, her health further deteriorated."

"So she abandoned me when she recovered. Had you … as a replacement," Aiyana said. Chaffetz could hear the bitterness in her voice. "I needed guidance. I had *no one.* I was cheated. Left to my own devices. I made mistakes," she began, but didn't finish. She sat down on the floor.

Chaffetz joined her, sitting across from her. "Not out of choice," she said. "Like I said, it took her months to recover. She had no idea where you were placed. If she had gone to the Department of Human Services and said she was your mother—"

"A blood test would have been required," Aiyana finished for her. She paused. "So she had you."

"Not to replace you," Chaffetz said. "She got pregnant again shortly before she turned seventeen. It wasn't intentional. She met a stranger at a bar … had sex and was impregnated. She thought it was the jaguar's biological imperative. She didn't find out about you for another seventeen years, though she never gave up trying. There was a short article about Danai's father. The way he was killed suggested to her an animal attack—a jaguar. She came by the towers and recognized you—your long black hair was a dead giveaway."

"Yet she never came forward," Aiyana said. "For me ... for her granddaughter, Nita."

"I'm not defending her, but she felt too much time had passed," Chaffetz replied. "And as I said, her health continued to deteriorate."

"Is she alive?" Aiyana asked.

"A few months after I turned sixteen, she left ... went to die."

"After you became pregnant?" Aiyana asked. "Before she could see ... hold her granddaughter?" She shook her head. "That makes no sense."

"I never got pregnant," Chaffetz said. "Bly stayed those extra months to see if the jaguar within me would force me to procreate. Until I turned seventeen, there was this internal conflict between me and my other self. It was physically debilitating. It was as if each generation before me demanded I have a child. Twice I succumbed to their demands, but each time the boy wore a condom. After I turned seventeen, the power of my other self diminished. I haven't had sex since."

"You had an obligation," Aiyana said.

"We've outlived our purpose for existence, as so many animals have that are now extinct," Chaffetz explained. "We were always an aberration. It's one thing to live in the wilderness, where we did little harm, and quite another in the Southwark Towers where hundreds of people are packed in like sardines. Look what you've done. Forget the rapist you killed. That could be considered justifiable, though from what I know about us, you wanted to be raped. Nita, too. But Danai's father and the others—those you killed because of their cowardice. It was totally uncalled for."

"Because I had no mother to provide guidance," Aiyana snapped.

"Bullshit. You didn't need Bly to tell you what you did was wrong," Chaffetz shot back. "And Nita learned from you. Became a killer like you. What the two of you did goes against our heritage. Nita would have passed it on to her child. Our line must end with you and me."

"What if Nita hadn't been killed?" Aiyana asked.

"I framed DeMarius Hawkins," Chaffetz said.

"Meaning what?"

"Do I have to spell it out for you?" Chaffetz asked, but didn't wait for a response. "*I* killed Nita. She couldn't give birth. Our line became perverted with you. Blame it on Bly if you must, but our line ends with you and me."

"What are you suggesting?" Aiyana asked.

"We're sisters. We both have the jaguar within," Chaffetz began. "We can leave this city where we don't belong, go to the wilderness and be our true selves. When we die, our kind ceases to exist."

"Maybe you're too domesticated to survive in the wilderness," Aiyana said after a few moments of silence. "I raised one child. I have no desire to be your mother."

"I go to the park and release my true self," Chaffetz countered. "I'm no more … domesticated than you are."

"Prove it," Aiyana challenged. "Let go to the park now and see if you can keep up with me."

They walked to the park. Aiyana had a bag for her clothes. She gave Chaffetz one Nita had used. At the park they both undressed, put their clothes in their bags, and hid the bags by a tree, covering them with twigs and leaves.

"You're no better than me," Aiyana told Chaffetz before they transformed. "Far worse, I'd say. I killed strangers. A rapist, a cop who harassed me, and cowards who watched me as I was raped." She spat on the ground. "You killed my daughter and her unborn child. Killed *our* own. I can never forgive you for killing Nita and my granddaughter. I've learned to control my rage within the towers. It's you who are barbaric. One of us will die tonight."

"What—" Chaffetz began, taken aback.

"We fight for supremacy," Aiyana said. "We fight for the right to determine the fate of our kind. Kill me and you can slink into the wilderness to die alone. If I prevail, I'll have another child and our line will continue."

"You can't have another child," Chaffetz said. "We can only procreate when we're sixteen."

"That's not my interpretation of the dreams I've had," Aiyana said.

Before Chaffetz could respond, Aiyana transformed into a jaguar. She lunged at Chaffetz, knocking her down. With her powerful jaws, she clamped down on her adversary's shoulder. Chaffetz changed into a jaguar and pushed Aiyana off of her. A chunk of skin and muscle hung from Aiyana's mouth.

The pain in her shoulder was excruciating. Chaffetz knew she was vulnerable. With her claws she slashed at Aiyana again and again, opening up wounds in Aiyana's flesh.

She could see from the other's yellow-red eyes that Aiyana had been surprised by her aggression. Rather than retreat or run when she had been wounded, she had gone on the offensive. Aiyana quickly recovered after Chaffetz's initial attack. The two circled one another. Aiyana lunged at Chaffetz in an attempt to rip her throat. Chaffetz again lashed out with her claws, aiming for Aiyana's eyes. She hit Aiyana's forehead. Blood dripped into Aiyana's eyes and she stepped back, shaking her head to clear her vision. Aiyana bounded for the forest. Chaffetz followed her.

This was no fight to the death as Aiyana had vowed. Aiyana was trying to escape. She had underestimated her opponent and fled. Chaffetz knew she had to kill Aiyana now or she would forever be looking over her shoulder. That, or Aiyana would leave the city and, if she was correct, have another child. Their line would continue, which was unacceptable to Chaffetz. It *must* end now.

Chaffetz chased Aiyana for twenty minutes. Her shoulder ached. With her injury, she couldn't keep up with her sister. She began to fall behind her adversary. Aiyana leaped out of view. Chaffetz followed. She approached a small brook. Had Aiyana crossed? Suddenly Aiyana jumped from a tree onto Chaffetz's back. Her teeth clamped onto the back of her head. Chaffetz tried to roll over to free herself. Aiyana refused to let go. Her teeth sunk in deeper. Chaffetz was no longer able to fight back, unable to free herself and flee. She no longer felt pain from Aiyana's teeth. Her legs gave way when she tried to rise. She was unable to move. She felt Aiyana's loosen her grip and bite her a second time. She tried to let out a growl or resignation. Even that took more strength than she possessed.

CHAPTER SIXTY-ONE

(FOURTH DAY OF THE INVESTIGATION)

Morales had decided to postpone his press conference announcing the arrest of DeMarius Hawkins until nine the next morning. He wanted both Chaffetz and Danai by his side. Both had been integral to the investigation. Danai, a rookie beat officer, would benefit the most. Her path to detective would be far smoother even if she did come out as a lesbian. And Chafe might be promoted to homicide now rather than in two or three years. With sergeants like McGowan wanting nothing to do with a female homicide detective, Morales might get her assigned to his squad.

He had attempted to call Chaffetz at 7 a.m. His messages all went to voicemail. She hadn't reported for duty at eight that morning. Morales called Sykes, her sarge, and was told she had never been late before. Had never taken a sick day. Had left accrued vacation days lapse. A few times Sykes told her to take vacation days even if she only stayed in bed. In Sex Crimes in particular, one had to get away from the daily horrors one faced or be driven mad. If Sykes suggested Chaffetz take three days off, she invariably returned after two days, saying she was going stir crazy.

Morales was clearly worried. He sent Danai to Chaffetz's home in South Philly. Danai returned alone and met with Morales.

"She didn't return home last night," Danai told him. "Didn't call. She lives with her grandparents. Nothing was out of place. Henry, her grandfather, was concerned. Chaffetz had never stayed out a full night without first telling them. The times she stayed out all night were few and far between. She *always* alerted them. She has no boyfriend. No girlfriend." Danai shrugged. "I wanted to cover all bases. No close friends. No other relatives."

Morales reluctantly held his press conference at 9 a.m. He praised Chaffetz, saying that she couldn't be with them because she was under the weather. He lauded Danai for leading them to DeMarius Hawkins.

"We have a rookie police officer acting like a seasoned professional," Morales said, glancing and smiling at Danai. "A beat cop doing the work of a detective. Without Officer Townes we would have been rudderless. The department needs more officers with the dedication, intellect, and perseverance of Officer Townes."

Danai was asked to step up and say a few words to the press and answer questions from the gathered media. Most questions she answered without going into specifics. "While we have made an arrest and have a confession, the investigation is still ongoing," she repeated more than once. Morales had told her to be discreet and give out no details as to what evidence there was to charge DeMarius. She did answer one question, though. She recognized Valeria Martinez of the *Philadelphia Inquirer*. The woman had written a number of stories about discrimination in the department against women. If—no, *when*—Danai came out, she knew gossip and rumors would abound. She would face hostility from fellow officers. The media would soon find out. If approached, she had decided she would grant just one interview—to Valeria Martinez. Her question called for more than her vague responses.

"Sergeant Morales has implied you had insight that helped propel the case. As one with so little experience on the job, can you tell us what that insight was? I imagine it's not female intuition," she added to laughter from the gathered press corps.

"I'm from the Southwark Projects. I *still* live there. I know the people—some better than others, obviously. Gangs and drug dealers plague Southwark, to be sure, but there are legitimately good people who live there. And I have never been shunned because I'm a police officer. Sergeant Morales has already

stated that Nita Jackson was a victim of a gang rape outside
what we call the towers. Because of my intimate knowledge of
Southwark, I was able to point Detective Chaffetz to possible
suspects. She did the hard work of interviewing those suspects,
all but one of whom we exonerated."

"Why do you remain in Southwark?" Martinez followed up.
"As a police officer you can certainly afford—"

"Money has nothing … well, little to do with where I live.
I've been out of the academy all of six months. If I move, it will be
when I've saved a bit more money. But there is a certain comfort
for me living in Southwark. I know just about everyone and they
know me. It's been my home my *entire* life. When I move it will be
on my terms and I'll have many fond memories I'll take with me."

After the press conference she went up to Morales. "Sarge,
I—I helped Chaffetz. You made it sound—"

Morales cut her off. "You did more than just help. If I embellished a bit, it was only because Chaffetz wasn't present. I didn't
investigate Nita's murder. I wasn't about to take credit for what
I didn't do." He lowered his voice. "If you do come out, the accolades you received today will help with the brass, if not your fellow officers." He paused. "I'm going over to see Aiyana. I didn't
want her to hear about the arrest from a press conference, but
I've been unable to reach her."

"Both her *and* Chafe," Danai said. "More than a coincidence," she added.

"You *are* a quick study," Morales said, with a smile. "I'm
more worried about Chafe. She's a creature of habit. I don't
know a hell of a lot about Aiyana. I do want to fill her in on
some of the details I withheld from the media."

After Morales left, Valeria Martinez came up to her. "An interesting response to my question," she told Danai.

"It's the truth," Danai responded.

"Not the whole truth, though, I imagine. You sort of glori-
fied living in Southwark. From what I hear, most tenants are
clamoring to get out."

"What can I do for you?" Danai asked, not allowing herself
to be baited.

"At some future time I'd like to interview you ... both as a young female police officer and a resident of Southwark. Would that be of any interest?" Martinez asked.

"At some future time," Danai said. "This has all been a bit ... overwhelming for me. Chaffetz deserved most of the credit. But call me in a month and we can talk about the parameters of an interview."

"You do sound like a seasoned pro," Martinez said. "*Parameters* of an interview."

Danai gave Martinez her card and smiled.

When Morales knocked on Aiyana's door, there was silence for several moments. Morales identified himself and continued to knock.

"Not now," Aiyana said. Morales thought her voice sounded weak.

"We made an arrest. We have Nita's killer in custody," Morales said. "I'll only be a few minutes."

Aiyana opened the door and stepped back. She was wearing a bathrobe. She had scratches on her forehead and cheeks. Blood was seeping through the white robe.

"Where is Chaffetz?" Morales asked. He had a premonition Aiyana's wounds had something to do with Chaffetz's disappearance.

"I killed her. It was self-defense," she said. "And you have the wrong person in custody."

"I'm to believe your killing Chaffetz was self-defense with *your* history?" Morales asked. He had no interest, at the moment, in her other assertion about DeMarius Hawkins. *Priorities.*

Aiyana removed her robe. She stood naked before Morales. He saw lacerations all over her body, arms, and legs. She turned around. More scratches—some quite deep—crisscrossed her back, buttocks, and legs. An animal attack was Morales's first thought, which he quickly tossed aside. It was impossible. "Put your robe back on," he said. "You need to go to the hospital."

"I've already begun to heal," Aiyana said. "I lost a lot of blood. I'm weak, but I'll recover."

"How could Chaffetz have done this to you?" he asked.

"She's a shapeshifter like me. My half-sister," Aiyana said without emotion.

"Your—"

"I thought my mother died after giving birth to me," Aiyana interrupted. "She left to die but was found by a couple who nursed her back to health. I had no idea until last night that she hadn't died. Had no idea she had given birth to another child— Chaffetz. And Chaffetz killed Nita and her unborn child."

"That makes no sense," Morales said. "Why—"

` "To put an end to our existence," Aiyana replied. "Chaffetz had no child. She didn't want one. I can't bear another child. Killing Nita meant our extinction with our deaths."

"Why would she attack you?" Morales asked. "You said it was self-defense."

"We went to Fairmount Park to be our true selves," Aiyana began. "I was furious at her, but I'm no longer a killer. At the park, before we transformed, she admitted she could never trust me. She had killed Nita. She felt I would seek revenge at some point."

"Would you have?"

"I honestly don't know," Aiyana said. "I didn't want to be alone. Chaffetz was my half-sister. It was a lot to take in. My half-sister, just a year younger than me. There was so much we could share. I wouldn't have had to be alone." She paused. "She talked about leaving the city and living out our lives in the wilderness. It had its allure. This city ... these projects have brought only pain. Still, whenever I looked at her I knew I would see Nita's murderer. I'm leveling with you, Estefan. She didn't give me a choice. I *was* a killer. I stopped killing long ago. But it was a part of me. She shapeshifted and began clawing at me. I shifted too. We fought ... and I prevailed."

"Where is Chaffetz now?"

"She'll never be found," Aiyana said.

"What am I to do with you?" Morales asked, talking as much to himself as to Aiyana.

"Arrest me," Aiyana said.

"You know I can't. You're a shapeshifter. Chaffetz was a shapeshifter. *I'd* end up in a psychiatric ward."

"End me, then," Aiyana said.

"You know I'm no vigilante," Morales responded. "Danai has more of a motive, but she's a cop and no threat to you."

"Then let me be," Aiyana said. "I'm no threat to anyone. I'm childless, can't have another child, and have no desire to harm anyone. I don't even know if I want to remain here. The towers never felt like home to me. I may do as Chaffetz suggested—leave, go to the wilderness and live out my days as a jaguar."

"Do I have another option?" Morales asked. "If Chaffetz is found—"

"She won't be found," Aiyana repeated.

"If her *remains* are found, there will be an investigation and it will be out of my hands. If she's not found, Missing Persons will investigate. I'll be out of the loop," Morales said.

"I'm not asking you to protect me, Estefan," Aiyana said.

"Chaffetz was good people," Morales said. "I don't want to believe that she framed an innocent man for Nita's murder."

"My face … my body are proof she attacked me," Aiyana said. "And now that you know she killed Nita, you'll find her case against the man she pinned it on won't hold up to close scrutiny. You'll believe the evidence, won't you, Estefan?"

"I won't see you again," Morales said, "*unless* you turn to violence."

"Then it's goodbye," Aiyana said. "Tell Danai not to visit, whether you tell her what occurred or not. I'm done with humans."

Morales saw a tear course down Aiyana's cheek. He let himself out.

CHAPTER SIXTY-TWO

When Morales got back to the Roundhouse, he called Danai's sergeant and told him he needed to speak to her. He would tell Danai the truth. With what he had to do, he couldn't leave Danai in the dark. Much as he enjoyed investigating like the detective he used to be, he recalled the frustration of cases that went sideways. All that was left for him to do now was damage control.

Danai arrived at noon. Morales told her they should go to the park for lunch. He needed complete privacy, and the thin walls of his office wouldn't suffice.

"I was at Aiyana's this morning," he began after they'd both purchased two hot dogs and a soda apiece. "She told me Chafe was her half-sister. A shapeshifter, like Aiyana. Aiyana hadn't been aware until after the Hawkins arrest when Chafe visited her."

"How could Chaffetz be Aiyana's half-sister?" Danai asked.

Morales explained what Aiyana had told him. "Like Aiyana, Chafe was a shapeshifter—a jaguar like her sister."

"I'm speechless," Danai said.

"Sadly, there's more," Morales said. "Chafe killed Nita."

"That's impossible," Danai replied. "DeMarius Hawkins confessed. The bat with his prints was found in his *locked* closet."

"Chafe interrogated Hawkins for over six hours," Morales said. "She offered him a deal for manslaughter which we know was bogus. Cops lie to suspects. DeMarius had served a short stint in prison, but he didn't seem to have learned how to game the legal system. Chafe could manipulate him as long as he didn't lawyer up. The alternative to pleading out, she told him, was a premeditated first degree murder charge." He hesitated. "It's irrelevant. Chafe told Aiyana she killed Nita and framed Hawkins."

"Why would Chafe kill Nita? It makes no sense. You're being played … again."

"I know how much you respected Chafe—"

"And liked her," Danai added. "She never treated me like a newbie."

"I was fond of her too," Morales replied. "Look, Chafe didn't have a child when she turned sixteen. She wanted her line of shapeshifters to end. Aiyana couldn't have any more children. But Nita was pregnant. Both she and her child would carry on their line. Chafe had but one solution. She killed Nita."

"Chafe isn't missing, is she?" Danai asked. "Aiyana murdered her for revenge," she said, angrily.

"That's not Aiyana's version—"

"And you believe her? The woman who killed my father?" Danai interrupted.

"Hear me out and decide for yourself, Danai," Morales said. "Chafe confronted Aiyana. Her solution was for her and Aiyana to leave Philly and live out their lives in the wilderness. Aiyana said Chafe attacked her in Fairmount Park, as a jaguar."

"Again, why?" Danai pressed.

"Aiyana killed your father sixteen years ago. It's why you became a cop," Morales began. "His death in many ways defined your life. Your anger festered. You wanted to take Aiyana down *legally*. We had proof Aiyana was guilty but we were stymied— her being a shapeshifter. You considered going rogue—vigilante justice." He held up his hand when Danai was about to respond. "Don't deny you didn't consider the option. But it's not in your nature. Chafe must have felt it would be no different with Aiyana. Chafe murdered her daughter and unborn grandchild. She would never have felt completely safe from Aiyana's wrath. They fought. Aiyana prevailed. Chafe is dead."

"And you have Aiyana's word—"

"Aiyana didn't get off unscathed," Morales interrupted. "She showed me her wounds. Unmistakable claw marks all over her body. She didn't murder Chafe. Chafe put up one hell of a fight.

Two equals. Maybe it was Aiyana's anger at losing Nita and her granddaughter that allowed her to prevail—"

"Or maybe it was the fact she had more practice killing," Danai shot back.

"Does it really matter?" Morales said. "Go and visit Aiyana if you don't believe me, though she doesn't want anything more to do with 'humans', she told me—which includes you and me. You'd see Aiyana's wounds firsthand."

"And Chafe's body?" Danai asked.

"Aiyana says it will never be found," Morales asked. "I told her if Chafe's remains are discovered, she's on her own."

"So she gets away with another murder," Danai said bitterly.

"She insists it was self-defense," Morales said.

"And you believe her," Danai snapped.

"It really doesn't matter," Morales said, then went on before Danai could respond. "Chafe killed Nita and framed Hawkins. Is she any better than Aiyana? Unlike your father, what went down between Chafe and Aiyana was a battle. Aiyana has the wounds to prove it. There is no doubt in my mind that the two fought to the death. As with your father, Aiyana can't be prosecuted. What's worse, Chafe framed DeMarius Hawkins, someone totally innocent. Aiyana and Chafe were cut from the same cloth."

"And what of DeMarius Hawkins? He's to rot in prison?" Danai asked.

"His situation is one reason I've told you all of this," Morales said. "If not for him, I could have left you in the dark. Chafe will never be found. But I'm not going to be responsible for ruining the life of an innocent young man. I hate to do it, but with Chafe gone I'll throw her under the bus ... and take a beating myself for allowing her to manipulate a coerced confession. I'll interview Hawkins myself and have him tell me he asked for a lawyer. You were outside listening when Chafe interviewed him, so you can corroborate his claim. Chafe had to have planted the bloody bat in Hawkins's closet. I'll have the lab do a more thorough analysis."

"Are you going to say Chafe murdered Nita?" Danai asked.

"That would raise too many red flags," Morales responded.

"I'll just say Chafe was blinded. She was certain she had Nita's killer and manipulated the evidence to prove so. I'll tell the brass and the press I'm personally taking over the investigation. I'll come up blank, of course."

"Won't that harm your career?" Danai asked.

"A setback for sure, but I've told you I have no desire to move further away from the action. I don't want to supervise sergeants. I may eventually have to for financial reasons, but I can take a hit now. And I'll toss you a bone. After Chafe went missing, you recalled Hawkins asked for a lawyer. Chafe suggested you were mistaken. Told you all the evidence pointed to his guilt. You reluctantly remained silent since he confessed. You couldn't get it out of your head that Hawkins had lawyered up, and with Chafe missing, you decided to pursue the matter on your own—with my approval. *You* suggested the lab do a more complete analysis of the bat. Again, you recalled how quickly Chafe wanted results, which isn't a lie."

"You don't have to do that," Danai said. "Like you said, you're taking a hit as it is."

"Might as well be a good one," Morales said, with a weak smile. "I won't have your career tarnished by Chafe. You're coming out, aren't you?" he asked.

"That came out of left field," she responded.

"You're deflecting."

"How do you know?"

"With the case over ... before what I just told you, I imagine your mind was focused on your decision. When we were eating you looked relaxed ... or content. You're very intense, with good reason. Not so much while you were eating your hot dogs." He paused. "I'm known for being able to read my detectives. I know when partners are having a falling-out. I intervene before it becomes irreparable. Or decide the breach is hopeless and splitting up the pair is in the best interests of all, including me. You're a bit of an open book, Danai. Remember I told you that you were holding something back. Your body language as well as the questions you asked told me so. I saw a different side of you today. So, out with it," he said.

"I've decided to come out when Rain arrives," Danai said.

"No big announcement, but we'll go out in public, and if asked, I'll say Rain is my girlfriend. Some cops who know me will see the two of us together holding hands—maybe even kissing. Like the flu, word will spread quickly."

"Then you helping DeMarius Hawkins get justice will counteract any negative response—at least as far as the brass is concerned—to your coming out. Yes, you're gay, but you saved an innocent man from going to prison."

"I don't know what to say," Danai replied.

"Tell me you and Rain will come over for dinner once you feel comfortable," Morales said. "I've told my wife a lot about you. She'd love to meet you and your girlfriend. And if you get hassled when you come out or just need advice—career or otherwise—my door's always open."

"Yes to the dinner and yes to your offer. I-I do—" she began and hesitated. "Valeria Martinez from the Inquirer wants to interview me. She's unaware I'm a lesbian and will be coming out. She's interested in obstacles faced by women in the department. Should I take the interview?"

"You have to tread lightly, especially after you've outed yourself," Morales said. "The brass will scrutinize the story she writes." He paused, in thought. "This is what I'd suggest. Let's get Hawkins exonerated. You come out whenever you feel the time is right. Then give it a few weeks. You'll undoubtedly face some hostility, *but* there will be others who will support, even respect your decision; many who won't condemn your lifestyle. When you are interviewed, openly discuss the hostility but also mention the support you've received. Tell the world the department is not unlike other jobs. Regardless of where you work, there will be those who condemn you. And let Martinez know this was a personal decision and—if accurate—you are not a political activist interested in self-promotion or causing problems for the department. Be genuine, of course. If the hostility you face is more than I expect, you have to face that head-on in the interview. But try to throw the department a bone. You can even mention you confided in Chaffetz, who accepted you as a cop, not a lesbian cop. And toss my name in as well. As regards hostility towards women in the department, be honest. There are roadblocks for women in general in the department, as in most occupations. You want to be treated on your merits, not your gender. I'm sure you'll handle yourself well."

"I was going to go with spontaneity if you agreed an interview was acceptable, but from what you've said, I'll have to research and plan before I agree to speak with Martinez."

"Don't over-prepare," Morales cautioned. "Think out your positions on a variety of questions. You can even have Rain interview you. But don't have answers scripted out in your mind. Just bullet points. You want to sound genuine, not rehearsed. Make her your only interview, is my last word of advice."

"That was my intention," Danai said. "I don't want to be the poster child for either women's rights or gay rights."

"I'll be looking forward to reading it," Morales said.

CHAPTER SIXTY-THREE

(THREE DAYS LATER)

McGowan came into Morales's office, once again without knocking. "I have to admit I was a bit envious when you held your press conference announcing the arrest of the man who killed …" he began, then stopped.

"Nita Jackson," Morales finished for him.

"Right. I doubted you would make an arrest. Nobody talks in the projects. We both learned that firsthand when we canvassed for witnesses when your girl … Aiyana Jackson was raped," McGowan said. "Then the shit hit the fan," he went on. "What happened to your case? What the fuck happened to Chaffetz?"

"I put too much faith in Chaffetz," Morales said. "She was ambitious and took a few unfortunate shortcuts," he added. He had given his *mea culpa* press conference the day before. Further analysis of the baseball bat proved the single set of DeMarius Hawkins' prints had been applied to the bloody handle. Officer Townes had informed him, he told the press, that Hawkins had asked for a lawyer and Chaffetz had ignored him. When Townes broached the subject to Chaffetz, she had been told it had been her imagination. Morales had re-interviewed Hawkins. With the new evidence and tainted confession, all charges against Hawkins had been dropped. Morales himself would investigate Nita's murder. An official missing persons report had been filed on Chaffetz's behalf. He would not speculate what might have happened to her.

"Damn women cops—always taking the easy way out," McGowan said.

"Yet a woman cop brought Chaffetz's culpability to my attention," Morales countered.

"You banging her?" McGowan asked. "At every press conference you give her props for solving the case."

Morales remained silent. He wondered how McGowan would respond when Danai came out.

"And the lead detective on your case goes missing. What's up with that?" Morales asked.

"I haven't the foggiest," Morales responded.

"You know your career took a hit with this one," McGowan said.

"I'll recover ... with time," Morales responded. He didn't tell his adversary he was glad no one would be asking him to be a lieutenant for a good while.

McGowan smiled. "Case in the crapper and you still owe me a favor."

"Which I see you're not letting me forget," Morales said.

"Damn right," McGowan responded, smiled again, then left.

Morales recalled the two of them as beat cops talking about the future. McGowan hadn't changed a bit. Morales, on the other hand, hoped he had grown a bit wiser.

CHAPTER SIXTY-FOUR

McGowan walked back to his office content with himself. The walls were crumbling around Morales. If Morales were Caucasian, he would never have made sergeant before McGowan. But the pressure to advance minorities and women had conspired to work against him. He had heard rumors that even with less than a year under his belt as sergeant, the brass wanted to promote Morales to lieutenant. And not too long after, make him captain. It didn't matter that Morales was competent at best, while McGowan was exceptional. His olive skin and last name were his ticket to meteoric advancement.

Morales, though, had been arrogant. Reports on his first press conference prefaced his name with "the fastest Hispanic to rise to the rank of sergeant in the history of the Philadelphia Police Department." And sprinkled in media reports were references to "a rising star in the department." All because Morales had solved the murder of a no-name project dweller. Morales was milking his success for all it was worth. The man was just as ambitious as he was.

But his house of cards had collapsed. A coerced confession. Planted evidence. And his star detective, rather than face the heat, had fled. It was further proof to McGowan that women just couldn't cut it as police. Not for a moment did McGowan feel Chaffetz had gone "missing." She had fled of her own volition. Now, while lauding Morales for owning up to a botched investigation, the media were asking the question, "Has Morales been promoted to sergeant too quickly?" A Channel 6 reporter wondered aloud if the unraveling of the Nita Jackson murder would have occurred with a more seasoned professional at the helm. It was music to McGowan's ears.

It could take years for Morales to recover. By then, McGowan would be lieutenant and Morales would be answering to him. And, it was all because Morales had gotten too close to the victim of his first rape case. McGowan had warned the rookie. Had suggested to Morales seventeen years later that it was foolhardy to tackle the Nita Jackson murder. One of McGowan's prime directives to his detectives was to never overly sympathize with the victim. Doing so could come back to bite you in the ass when lies were uncovered, when the victim might have been the perp or at least partially responsible for being victimized. *Keep your distance* had always been his mantra. Solve the crime and run, don't walk, away from the victim.

If he had an ounce of compassion, he would have felt sorry for Morales. But McGowan lacked empathy. He only felt contempt for the man.

CHAPTER SIXTY-FIVE

The evening after Morales's second press conference, Danai went to see B.J. Chaffetz's notes, which Danai had seen, had the name and room number of the motel where she was staying. Danai knocked on the door and announced herself. She was told to come in.

"You don't lock your door?" Danai asked. B.J. was lying on her bed, wearing the same jeans and denim shirt that she had worn when she had picked up Danai.

B.J. lifted her hand. It held a gun. "I'm prepared if someone doesn't knock."

"Why are you still here?" Danai asked. "I know you were told you could go."

"Nita's death turned into a real shitstorm," B.J. said. "A man arrested and then let go. The lead detective goes missing. And this Morales parades himself in front of the press *twice* singing your praises. If I didn't know you, I'd think you were sleeping with the man."

"He's kinda my mentor," Danai said. "You didn't answer my question."

"Aiyana's still here," B.J. said. "Maybe in all the chaos—"

"I have information that may change your plans," Danai interrupted.

"I'm listening," B.J. said. "I assume you want something in return."

"You already gave me what I wanted," Danai said.

"A lesbian sex tutorial?"

"I-I enjoyed our ... night together, but that's not what I'm referring to," Danai began. "I spoke with Rain. She'd come back ... for me if I come out."

"And?"

"There is no better time," Danai said. "I told Morales I was gay. Asked him how much it would retard my advancement."

"So that's why he's taking the heat and giving you the glory," B.J. said. "A stand-up guy. Who would have thunk it?"

"I'm coming out when Rain returns," Danai said. "Any backlash I get for being a lesbian will be offset by how I handled the investigation. I guess I owe you."

"I could argue with you but I'm going a bit stir crazy here. I'm not a big city gal. I'd like to take care of Aiyana, then—"

"Aiyana is no threat. She can't bear any more children. She told Morales," Danai interrupted.

"She's still—"

"Bly didn't die after giving birth to Aiyana," Danai cut her off again. She explained how a couple had helped Bly. "She never fully recovered. Her health actually deteriorated. She went off to die sixteen years ago."

"So, it's back to Aiyana," B.J. said.

"I should have led off with the headline," Danai said. "Bly had another daughter before she turned seventeen."

B.J. sat up straight in her bed. "You're shitting me."

"Chaffetz," Danai said. "A shapeshifter. Aiyana's half-sister. She killed Nita and framed DeMarius Hawkins."

"Why? And more importantly, who is her daughter?"

"She had no child," Danai said. "Bly was dying, but she stayed around until Chaffetz turned sixteen and didn't leave until she was certain that the jaguar within her couldn't force Chaffetz to procreate. *That's* when she left. Chaffetz wanted to end her line. That's why she killed Nita. Now neither she nor Aiyana can have children. The line ends with their deaths. You don't have to kill Aiyana. Don't have to risk going to prison. And it's Chaffetz who was raised by Bly, not Aiyana."

"So I can leave this piss-poor city and hunt for Chaffetz," B.J. said. "Kill her without the repercussions associated with killing Aiyana."

"That's the way I see it," Danai said. "Unable to bear a child, your killing Aiyana would be simple revenge. Vigilante justice that's not required."

"Why did Chaffetz flee?" B.J. asked, ignoring Danai's last remark.

"I have no idea," Danai replied. "Maybe she felt the case against Hawkins would unravel. Nita was dead. She had accomplished what she set out to do."

"Any leads on where she might be?"

Danai shook her head. "I reached out to a friend of a friend in Missing Persons. They're totally in the dark. They may turn the case over to the FBI."

"Guess I'll be packing my bags." B.J. gave Danai a card. There was just a phone number on it. "If you hear anything—"

"I'll call," Danai said.

"You know I didn't show you my entire bag of tricks the last time we—"

"Fucked," Danai finished for her.

"If you wanted," B.J. began but didn't finish.

"Now that I'm committed to Rain, I would be cheating on her," Danai said.

"Your loss," B.J. answered. "Seriously, I hope it works out for the two of you. You're far stronger than I envisioned after … well, after meeting Rain. You can handle the shit that will come your way when you come out. You'll have Rain and your Rabbi Morales." She paused. "It's been real. Don't let the door hit you in the ass on your way out."

EPILOGUE

(FOUR MONTHS LATER)

It took Aiyana almost four months to heal. Her jaguar within aided her in the healing process. Her half-sister had been a worthy adversary. The pain she felt was a daily reminder. She was unable to go to Fairmount Park for the first three months of her recovery. Her true self remained quiet, as if aware healing was required.

Fully healed—bearing only scars from the deepest lacerations—Aiyana went to a local bar. She had three scars on her forehead, just above her eye, but none on her face. Someone who tried to pick her up at the bar told her the scars gave her character.

At the bar she checked out potential partners. She saw a tall, dark-skinned man in his early-twenties—the youngest man in the bar. He wore a tight shirt that showed off his muscles. She walked over to him.

"Wanna fuck?" she asked.

"Aren't I a bit young for you?" he asked in return.

"Are you into rough sex?" Aiyana asked, not answering his question.

"I'm into anything with a pussy," he responded.

"So, wanna fuck?"

"Don't see why not," he answered.

He took her to his apartment. She let him have his way with her. He commented on the many scars on her body. She had asked for rough sex and that was what she got. Consensual sex, so when she left later that night she kissed him on his forehead rather than scratch him on his wrist.

The next day, she knew she was pregnant. Her line would continue. That night, she shapeshifted into a jaguar and left a city she had never called her home behind.

ABOUT THE AUTHOR

Barry Hoffman is the author of ten thriller/dark suspense novels; HUNGRY EYES, EYES OF PREY, BORN BAD, JUDAS EYES, BLINDSIDED, BLIND VENGEANCE, and BLIND RAGE. All but BORN BAD are part of Hoffman's SHARA FARRIS/ RENEE LESHAY series. HUNGRY EYES was nominated for both a Stoker and International Horror Guild Award for Best First Novel. Hoffman was also nominated for the 2001 PEN/ Newman's Own First Amendment Award, for his fight against censorship of BORN BAD. He's also published two short story collections FIREFLY BURNING BRIGHT and LOVE HURTS. He is editor/publisher of Gauntlet magazine, the only mass market magazine dealing with censorship and exploring the limits of free expression and publisher of Gauntlet Press through which he has published signed limited books by Ray Bradbury, Richard Matheson, Poppy Z. Brite, F. Paul Wilson and numerous others. Gauntlet won the 1999 HWA Award for Best Small Press. Hoffman is also author of the YA dark fantasy Shamra Chronicles which consists of CURSE OF THE SHAMRA, SHAMRA DIVIDED and CHAOS UNLEASHED. His most recent (2020) adult thriller is TRACKS OF MY TEARS, a fictional account of sexual assaults on a college campus.

Curious about other Crossroad Press books?
Stop by our site:
http://www.crossroadpress.com
We offer quality writing
in digital, audio, and print formats.